A distant rumble, like the sound of a gentle thunder grew louder as the band rounded the canyon wall. Kate's breath caught at the sight below. Filing in one at a time down the narrow path, several horses slowed to a trot and gathered at the stream to drink. Kate had been waiting for this moment ever since her young student Nate Springfield walked into her office two days earlier pleading for her help. It didn't take much to convince Kate to cancel her upcoming lectures and arrange for a leave from her new assignment.

Kate watched as a young colt kicked up its hind legs and butted its mother. Suddenly, Kate's feeling of wonderment dissolved into anger. She knew the ultimate fate of these rare animals if she failed in her efforts. Then, as if sensing her ire, one of the stallions let out a high-pitched whinny that echoed through the canyon with a furor that sent shock waves deep into Kate's spine.

"They're jittery tonight," Ida said. "Those ponies can sense when an intruder is around. Nate's the only person who can get close to them."

Though anxious to hear the details, Kate decided to enjoy the moment and leave her questions for later. Through the stillness of the night, she heard the splash as the horses waded into the stream, their flanks fluttering, shaking off the night's swarming insects.

"See that ornery roan bringing up the rear?" Ida pointed. "He's the dominant stallion. He keeps the herd together for protection. And that stout dapple, standing at the water's edge is the alpha mare. She leads her band to the best grazing fields and watering holes."

Fed by the Pryor River, the stream below glistened in the moonlight and caught Kate's eye. Like a silver ribbon flowing through the canyon, it eventually spilled into a basin forming Ida's lake. With a perpetual water supply and the absence of natural predators, the herd had managed to survive in this austere region of the state. But that was about to change.

"I can only imagine what this land was like two hundred years ago," Kate said. "Horses roaming over millions of untamed acres."

"Now Montana's fenced, grazed, and regulated," Ida spat. "And if you can't help me, then these mustangs will be slaughtered as sure as I'm sitting here."

Praise for Kathleen Kaska

"If you're looking for action and adventure, you're definitely in the right place."—Samantha DeWright, Readers' Favorite

A Two Horse Town: A Kate Caraway Animal Rights Mystery is a fast-paced and exciting story set in the Pryor Mountains of Montana. I was fascinated by those Montana mountain ranges and loved learning about the Pryor Mountain Wild Horses. Kaska's characters are marvelous! Kate is strong, smart and willing to put herself out there to protect Ida and the horses. I also enjoyed getting to know Kaska's feisty senior, Ida, her twin sister, Veda, and Karen, the diminutive Park Service worker who helps Kate. The plot gives the armchair sleuth plenty of puzzles to mull over as well. *A Two Horse Town*: A Kate Caraway Animal Rights Mystery is most highly recommended. —Jack Magnus for Readers' Favorite

Intriguing, poignant, and intense, A Two Horse Town will keep you guessing all the way through. I couldn't put it down."—Regan Murphy, Reviewer

A Two Horse Town

by

Kathleen Kaska

A Kate Caraway Animal-Rights Mystery, Book 2

A Two Horse Town

Contact Information: info@thewildrosepress.com

Cover Art by *Kristian Norris*

The Wild Rose Press, Inc.
PO Box 708
Adams Basin, NY 14410-0708
Visit us at www.thewildrosepress.com

Publishing History
First Edition, 2022
Trade Paperback ISBN 978-1-5092-4140-8
Digital ISBN 978-1-5092-4141-5

A Kate Caraway Animal-Rights Mystery, Book 2
Published in the United States of America

Dedication

To Clayton, whose smile warms my heart

Acknowledgments

A huge thanks to all the folks who read these pages as I created the story: Karla Locke, Denise Morrow, Mary Ann Berkbigler, Mary Kalbert, Pam Herber, and Mike Herber.

Chapter One

Fumbling her way in the dark, Kate Caraway climbed hand-over-hand, scaling boulders that seemed to trail off into oblivion. One wrong step meant a fast return to the bottom of the canyon. Too late to turn back, she had no choice but to trust her guide, and follow the sound of her boots crunching gravel. To make matters worse, clouds that had blocked out the glow of a full moon were now starting to dissipate, creating beams of unwelcome light.

Kate pressed her body against the steep rock and, keeping her head down, reached for the ledge above. Scree crumbled in her grasp and pelted the brim of her cap. She heaved herself up onto the next boulder. A sudden gust of wind threatened to send her over the edge. Her head spun. She slowly inhaled, visualizing oxygen flowing deep into her abdomen, the way her yoga teacher had taught.

It was late spring in Montana, but winter had not yet released its hold. Snow whitened the highest peaks of the Pryor Mountains, and unpredictable cold fronts dropped temperatures to deadly lows. Despite the cold, Kate's skin grew clammy, dampening her innermost layer of clothing.

"Here we are," Ida said, sounding less winded than Kate. "Watch your footing, honey. Scooch up next to me."

Kate looked up to see Ida already seated, her skinny little legs dangling over the precipice. She resembled one of the spindly scrub oaks that grew tenaciously from the mountain. Not willing to show her fear to this eighty-two-year-old woman, Kate crawled to the edge of the cliff and reluctantly joined her guide. A vast, empty space opened up before her and Kate took another deep breath of the cold night air. The dizziness subsided.

"Take a look at what nature gave me. What'd I tell you? The best time to see the horses is during a full moon." Ida motioned for Kate to move closer. "I never thought you, of all people, would be afraid of heights."

"It's that obvious?" Kate said.

"I heard your teeth chattering all the way up. You sounded like a hungry woodpecker going at a sweet gum. We're only about a hundred feet up."

"The height I can handle," Kate said. "It's the sheer drop-off that scares the piss out of me."

Kate tried to relax, but sitting here on the edge of the cliff caused her phobia to obliterate all reason. She wished she could ignore the scant inches of rock that separated her from the abyss that ended with the canyon floor. The wind kicked up and the clouds separated again. Light from the moon reflected brightly on the canyon below. In the distance, the outline of the Pryor Mountains rose into the sky, creating a jagged silhouette on the horizon, adding an ominous feeling to the evening. Kate gripped the rock on which she sat and questioned her sanity.

"The only time I've ever been to Montana was when my husband, Jack, and I drove the Hi-Line across the northern part of the state where it's flat and wide," Kate said. "Nothing like this."

"This is the real Montana. We have steep cliffs and bottomless canyons. And we like it that way," Ida chuckled.

"Let's change the subject before I melt into a puddle of fear."

Ida gave Kate's knee a reassuring pat and, for the next several minutes, they sat on the edge of the world, each silent in her own thoughts. Then just as Kate's pulse began to slow, Ida grabbed Kate's arm. The sudden movement almost sent Kate over the edge.

"Listen, they're coming," Ida whispered and pointed to the west side of the canyon. "Watching the herd from up here is magical."

A distant rumble, like the sound of a gentle thunder grew louder as the band rounded the canyon wall. Kate's breath caught at the sight below. Filing in one at a time down the narrow path, several horses slowed to a trot and gathered at the stream to drink. Kate had been waiting for this moment ever since her young student Nate Springfield walked into her office two days earlier pleading for her help. It didn't take much to convince Kate to cancel her upcoming lectures and arrange for a leave from her new assignment.

Kate watched as a young colt kicked up its hind legs and butted its mother. Suddenly, Kate's feeling of wonderment dissolved into anger. She knew the ultimate fate of these rare animals if she failed in her efforts. Then, as if sensing her ire, one of the stallions let out a high-pitched whinny that echoed through the canyon with a furor that sent shock waves deep into Kate's spine.

"They're jittery tonight," Ida said. "Those ponies can sense when an intruder is around. Nate's the only person who can get close to them."

Though anxious to hear the details, Kate decided to enjoy the moment and leave her questions for later. Through the stillness of the night, she heard the splash as the horses waded into the stream, their flanks fluttering, shaking off the night's swarming insects.

"See that ornery roan bringing up the rear?" Ida pointed. "He's the dominant stallion. He keeps the herd together for protection. And that stout dapple, standing at the water's edge is the alpha mare. She leads her band to the best grazing fields and watering holes."

Fed by the Pryor River, the stream below glistened in the moonlight and caught Kate's eye. Like a silver ribbon flowing through the canyon, it eventually spilled into a basin forming Ida's lake. With a perpetual water supply and the absence of natural predators, the herd had managed to survive in this austere region of the state. But that was about to change.

"I can only imagine what this land was like two hundred years ago," Kate said. "Horses roaming over millions of untamed acres."

"Now Montana's fenced, grazed, and regulated," Ida spat. "And if you can't help me, then these mustangs will be slaughtered as sure as I'm sitting here."

Kate reflected on the conversation she had had with Nate. He recounted the conflict brewing among the citizens of Two Horse over the proposed construction of a new dam on the Pryor River, a tributary of the Big Horn River. The reservoir would provide benefits for ranchers experiencing the worst drought in decades. The dam would also cause smaller streams like the one that fed Ida's ranch to dry up, and in Ida's case, cause the horses to lose their water source.

"We've always had water problems," Ida told Kate

earlier that afternoon on the way from the airport. "Whoever said ranching in Montana was easy? But the town's planning commission done lost their citified minds with this dam idea. I went to the federal Bureau of Land Management for help. They laughed in my face. Those idiots think the town's proposal is a good idea. They're siding with the ranchers."

"But BLM is responsible for protecting those wild horses," Kate said.

"Like hell! They claim their jurisdiction doesn't cover private land like mine. They told me the horses were my problem. The National Parks Service said they'd help. Those bastards offered to remove the horses and auction them off. That herd's lived on my land longer than I have. The only folks who'd buy wild mustangs on the auction block are looking for a quick profit. They'd sell them to a slaughterhouse, and then they'd be shipped overseas where people eat horsemeat. If those NPS idiots try to move them, it'll be over my cold, dead body."

Kate had no doubt that Ida meant that literally. Nate had shown Kate a newspaper article with a picture of his great-grandmother addressing the town council with a shotgun cradled in her arm. Someone needed to leash Ida Springfield before she landed in jail. After a few phone calls, Kate had decided that the someone would be her.

"Veda named all of them," Ida said. "This was her favorite spot. It's been years since my little sister's been able to climb up here. That dominant stallion she named Randy. I've always wondered if Veda knows how appropriate that name is. When a mare goes into heat, his testosterone level shoots up, and he goes wild."

"I'd like to see the records you've kept on this herd."

"Is tomorrow soon enough? I have a big day planned for you. Hope you're ready."

"I'll do whatever it takes."

Ida glanced at Kate, and for a moment, Kate's confidence waned. As if reading Kate's mind, Ida said, "Nate speaks highly of you. My great-grandson don't often ask for help and neither do I, but we both got to swallow our pride. These horses ain't gonna survive without that water. Hell, this is their land and I plan to see that it stays that way."

"But it's also your ranch. Don't you have rights to the water here?" Kate said.

"My land is mostly undeveloped. I don't do no serious ranching any more. I just keep a few cattle to keep my agricultural tax exemption. Besides, I know those goofballs down at town hall are thinking that I won't be around long enough to keep them from getting what they want. Besides you, I got a card up my sleeve."

Suddenly, the band became fidgety. Randy reared up on his hind legs, agitating the herd.

"What is it?" Kate said.

"Probably a coyote. He won't do no harm, just makes the horses nervous."

The stallion raised his head and curled back his lips. Then giving an invisible signal, he sent the horses bolting across the stream out of sight. Dust rose and the sound of hoofbeats thundered through the canyon.

"That's it for the night." Ida said. "Show's over. Besides, those clouds are rolling in faster than buckshot from a gun barrel. I want to get home before that storm scares the hell out of my dogs and makes my little sister jittery."

Kate turned to see black clouds boiling in the sky

just above the horizon where moments ago the stark outline of the Pryor Mountains was visible. Just as she backed away from the edge, a flash of streak lightning danced across the sky.

Kate smelled ozone and felt the hair on her arms stand straight up. Getting off this peak was a good idea. She had no desire to turn into a human lightning rod. Ida began climbing down the boulders like a surefooted mountain goat. Kate scrambled after her as the wind picked up. A crack of thunder sounded and lightning struck near where they had just perched.

"Get the lead out!" Ida shouted.

Kate, despite being in good shape, had trouble keeping up with the old woman. The tall, steep rocks made the climb down much harder than the ascent. The moon was now completely hidden behind the thunderheads. More than once Kate had lost sight of Ida. She was moving farther and farther away, and Kate suspected that Ida's sister, Veda, became more than just a little jittery during a thunderstorm.

Suddenly, raindrops pelted down, stinging Kate's skin. Something hard smacked her on the shoulder and then again on the side of her head. Kate feared a rockslide until she saw the crystal-like nodules falling on the ground around her. The storm had brought with it hail the size of walnuts. At that moment, her fear of heights was replaced by a more realistic danger. Kate no longer heard Ida and wondered if she had taken cover.

"Ida, slow up." Kate called.

No answer.

Another hailstone struck, smacking Kate behind her ear so hard that she felt a warm trickle run down the side of her neck. Catching up with Ida was no longer a priority. Kate rushed to a low overhanging rock to take cover. As she ducked under, her foot slipped and pain shot up her leg. She crawled farther back and wedged herself between the rocks. Then as abruptly as it had started, the hail stopped, only to be replaced by heavy sheets of rain. Kate circled her foot, and although her ankle was painful, she knew it was not broken. She thought about shouting for Ida again, but the deafening sound of roaring rain and crashing thunder would make it impossible for Ida to hear.

Kate was not sure how long she sat crouched between the rocks. She was soaked to the bone, and her ankle swelled inside her boot. Although she was safe for now, behind that wall of black clouds, a cold front had set its sights on the mountain. She couldn't stop herself from recalling a near-disastrous college hiking trip in Maine. She and a friend were dressed for a day hike when a cold front blew in, dropping the temperature forty degrees in less than an hour. If it had not been for the hospitality of a Boy Scout troop camped near a shelter, Kate and her friend would have succumbed to hypothermia before they reached the parking lot at the visitors' center.

Kate began to shiver, more from the memory than her immediate predicament. Thunder echoed in the distance. Lightning flashed, then another crack of thunder, slightly fainter than the last. The storm was moving away quickly, and the hard downpour slowed to a steady rain. The stars began to sparkle in the western sky.

Kate crawled out and stood up, gingerly putting weight on her throbbing ankle. She stepped out to the edge of the rock and looked around. No matter which way she turned, she saw no way down. In the short time since she had lost sight of Ida, Kate had wandered off the path. She retraced her steps—no good. Stuck on this slab of rock, the next outcropping loomed at least ten feet below. The only way to go was up. Kate climbed onto the outcropping that had just given her shelter and looked for a different route. Turning, she stepped down too hard and sent streaks of pain up to her pelvis. Kate gritted her teeth and hoisted herself upward, trying as best she could to keep weight off of her foot. After a short while, she noticed a less steep path to the right. As far as she could tell, it was her only choice. The thought of Ida finding her battered body the next morning was enough incentive to get moving.

Kate shuffled her way down the escarpment, but the going was slow. Her biceps protested and her shoulders burned with exhaustion. The thought of a warm fire in Ida's cabin kept her going. A coyote howled in the distance. The eerie sound caused Kate to ignore her painful ankle, and as Ida had said, "get the lead out."

After what seemed like forever, Kate spotted a soft glow in the distance—Ida's cabin at the base of the mountain. Knowing that she was only moments away from kissing flat ground, Kate allowed herself a short rest. The rain had eased to a light sprinkle. She sat down and was surprised to find the rock still warm from the day's sun.

Kate got her bearings and realized she had accidentally wandered around to the wrong side of the mountain. When they started out, she and Ida had walked right out the front door across a field, less than a hundred yards, and then straight up. From here, Kate saw the back of Ida's cabin clearly. She would be on the doorstep before too long.

Below the next rock, the narrow trail began to slope gently. The rock's surface, no longer bare and steep, was dotted with wheatgrass and sage. The ground turned soft and muddy, and suddenly Kate slipped. She reached out to grab hold of a bush, only to discover at the last moment that it was spiked with thorns long enough to pierce a kidney. Losing her footing, she fell to her hands and knees—mud squishing between her fingers. Kate pulled herself up and decided she needed something to help her maneuver the slippery path. She reached for a limb protruding from beneath the bush, but it resisted. Determined to dig out her quarry, she tightened her grip and tugged harder. The limb refused to budge. She slid her fingers under for a better grip and grabbed a hand clutching the other end.

Chapter Two

Shocked by the gruesome discovery and hobbling in pain, Kate finally reached the cabin as her watch pinged two o'clock am. Ida greeted Kate on the porch with a flashlight and an apology for leaving her behind. "I was coming to look for you. You're bleeding."

"I took a tumble and twisted my ankle."

"Come in and sit down. Let me take a look."

"I'm okay."

"You might need stitches. I'll get a cloth."

Kate plopped down on the sofa, causing two dogs to scatter.

"Here, hold this over that cut." Ida handed Kate a wet cloth. "I was afraid the storm would wake Veda, and I figured you were smart enough to climb down on your own. I didn't think it would take you that long."

"I ran into someone on the way down."

"Damn poacher! I'm getting my shotgun."

"That won't be necessary. The guy's dead."

"I saw buzzards over that side of my mountain yesterday, but I thought they were probably picking at a dead deer or skunk or something." Ida did not sound the least bit surprised at Kate's gruesome discovery.

Kate reached down to tug off her wet boots. "Help me with this one. My ankle's swollen."

Ida picked up Kate's foot. "It's a good thing these fancy boots have zippers."

Before Kate could respond, Ida had the empty boot in her hand. Kate squelched a scream and swallowed before she found her voice. "He wasn't only dead."

"What do you mean?" Ida said.

"He was naked from the waist down."

"This I gotta see. But first you need to get out of those wet clothes. I'll get you a cup of something hot. Your lips are turning blue."

After reviving herself with a cup of hot tea, Kate wrapped her ankle and donned a pair of sneakers. Then Kate and Ida ventured back into the night. Ida turned on a floodlight perched high upon a utility pole in the back of her cabin, and, with each of them toting a flashlight, they headed back up the mountain. Kate's muddy trail made retracing her steps easy, and before long they were standing over the body.

"Do you know him?" Kate said.

"Afraid so. It's Frank Colter Springfield. My number one enemy.

"Springfield? A relative?"

Ida nudged the corpse with the toe of her boot. "You could say that. He's my son. I guess I'd better call the sheriff."

Guess? thought Kate, too dumbstruck to speak.

And with Ida's last comment, spoken as casually as if she were discussing the demise of one of her scrawny old cows, she turned and marched back down.

****

Kate sat on the porch with an ice pack on her ankle. As she watched the coroner's van drive away, she wondered if her stay in Two Horse would be as menacing as last night's storm. The rising sun illuminated the rock she had climbed last night. It loomed over Ida's property and seemed to rise up from the depths of the earth like the hull of a ship. She couldn't believe she'd let Ida talk her into climbing a mountain in the middle of the night, full moon or not.

Despite the dire circumstances, Kate had to smile at the scene unfolding in front of Ida's cabin. Circling the sheriff's patrol car, the Springfield dog pack growled and sniffed their disapproval. The largest male, a brown short-haired mutt, sprayed all four tires and, for good measure, attempted to raise his leg on the sheriff's pants. The sheriff removed his cowboy hat and swatted at the dogs, which seemed to agitate them even more.

Ida stood with her foot propped on the bumper of the patrol car, arms folded over her knee. She looked like a rodeo clown who'd just rolled out of a barrel. The pant legs of her jeans were tucked into the tops of a pair of scruffy purple cowboy boots. An old, orange knit sweater, which stretched loosely over her thin frame, hung down to just above her knees. The left sleeve, minus its elbow, revealed a plaid shirt underneath. Mashed tightly on her head, Ida wore a Doc Holliday-style hat with a rattlesnake band. Stuck in the band was a large turkey feather.

What struck Kate as odd was that Ida and the sheriff seemed to be having a neighborly chat. Finally, Ida slapped him on the back and cackled some parting words. She walked back into the cabin and joined Kate on the porch.

"I'm surprised it took so long." Ida removed her hat and scratched her head.

"This was a murder, Ida. They have to be thorough," Kate said. She lifted the dripping ice bag from the towel draped over her ankle and managed draw a full circle

13

with her foot with much less pain than a few hours before.

"I'm not talking about that," Ida said. "I'm talking about killing that bastard. I'm surprised it took someone so long to bump him off."

Stunned, Kate turned to look up at Ida, who seemed focused on something in the distance. With Ida's hat now removed, Kate studied her host's profile. Pulled tight from her face, her hair was plaited in a long, thick braid. A few gray strands had come loose around her temples and with firm, birdlike hands, Ida brushed back the errant hair. Everything about her was petite. Her near-perfectly shaped nose and slightly pointed chin gave a rather simple face dimension. Her tiny wrinkles looked as if they had been drawn on with a fine-tipped pencil. From a distance she could easily have passed for a woman several decades younger. One had to get close to tell Ida's age. Kate wondered how close she would have to get to understand what Ida was really feeling.

"Luke figures Frank's been dead at least thirty-six hours. There was no question as to how he died—a fancy knife was still lodged in his back."

The thought made Kate shudder.

"Frank was too much like his daddy," Ida finally spoke. "Except that good-for-nothing husband of mine did me a favor. Colter got in his brand new Ford roadster with its whitewalls and shiny red wheels, drove away, and stayed away. Frank came back about six months ago and quickly became a pain in everyone's ass, especially mine." She rubbed the chill from her arms. "Let's go inside."

Kate shooed two dogs off the red and green tweed sofa that looked as old as the cabin and sat down.

"You're staying here with us," Ida said. "That sofa might not look like much, but it's comfy. After what you've been through, I ain't taking you to that motel." Ida began tidying up the room. She pulled pillows and blankets out of the hall closet and tossed them onto the sofa next to Kate, then took a broom and swept up ashes from last night's fire.

"I can't let you do that, Ida." Kate glanced around and wondered how another body could possibly squeeze into the tiny room. At last count, there were five dogs wandering around the place. The entire cabin smelled like wood-smoke and dog.

"Nonsense. Just let the dogs out if you need more room. But, I have to warn you, they'll be back. Those mutts have the run of the place. They don't like to sleep outside when it's cold, especially that Luisa Miller." Ida stopped and looked around. "My father-in-law built the cabin back in the twenties. It's old, but it's solid. After my drunken husband drove away for good back in 'fifty-two, I added electricity and plumbing, and it's suited us just fine ever since."

After a couple of hours of fitful sleep, Kate rose and listened to the cold May wind whistled through the cracks in the walls—the place was old for sure, but solid was questionable. Ida threw a hefty log on the fire and, in minutes, the ancient cabin warmed to a feeling of home. A stack of tattered albums stood next to an old stereo cabinet. Kate was surprised to see the only music in the house was opera.

"Luisa Miller?" Kate nodded at the records.

"Yep. All our dogs have opera names. Tosca, Carmen, Rigoletto, and Don G, short for Don Giovanni. Luisa Miller usually sleeps on the sofa, but she can be coaxed off her bed with a good ear-scratch."

"Luisa Miller wants her bed!"

A gravelly voice spoke from the hallway, and Kate turned to see an identical Ida shuffling out of a back bedroom. Faded, olive-green corduroy jeans hung on her as if she had recently lost weight. A plaid sweater, pulled low over her hips, seemed stifling in this warm room. She wore a pair of droopy socks that sagged over the tops of red sneakers.

"Now, you be nice, Veda. Come on out here and put the kettle on," Ida said. Then, turning to Kate, "Coffee or tea? Veda's real good at heating water. Ain't ya? Come meet our guest." Ida turned to Kate. "We don't get too many visitors. My little sister's sort of shy. She's also been under the weather lately. Got a cold a couple of weeks ago and can't seem to shake it."

"You were born first, then?" Kate said.

"By a whole hour. By the time Veda came, well— the doctors just said that too much time had passed."

Nate Springfield had mentioned to Kate that his great-aunt was mentally challenged, but he had not gone into detail.

Stealing quick glances at Kate, Veda walked over to an old cabinet that sat behind the dining-room table. She pulled out a kettle, sat it on a hotplate, and turned the knob. She removed three mugs from the shelf and started spooning instant coffee into each one. Veda's movements at the cabinet were well-rehearsed. The coil hissed as the hotplate turned a bright orange, and in a few moments the kettle whistled. Keeping a suspicious eye on Kate, Veda poured hot water into the cups.

"We had a fire in the kitchen right after she moved in," Ida explained to Kate. "Veda got burned on her legs pretty bad—left some nasty scars. She doesn't go in there. I set up this little cooking area because she likes to make her own hot chocolate. This way she doesn't have to wait for me to do it for her."

Ida walked over to help her sister. She placed the mugs, a jar of creamer, and a half-empty bag of sugar on a cutting board and set the makeshift tray down on a tree-stump that served as a coffee table. Then Ida walked over, took her sister's hand, guided her to the sofa, and sat her down. Ida perched on the arm.

"This is Kate Caraway, Veda. She'll be bunking here for a couple of days."

Veda stared at Kate with a look of horror. For the second time since she walked in, Kate felt that accepting Ida's invitation to stay in the cabin was a mistake. Then Kate watched as Ida gently took hold of Veda's chin, turned her face, and looked directly into her eyes. "Kate will help us save the horses." Ida spoke slowly as if to ward off any deeper uncertainty Veda might have had about sharing their small home.

"Hello, Veda. I promise I won't be any trouble," Kate said. "And Luisa Miller can sleep on the sofa with me. I like dogs. I have a greyhound named Kenya."

Veda shot Kate a doubtful glare and rubbed her hands across the fabric of her jeans as if to wipe away her discomfort.

"Just give her a little time, Kate. It's been me, her, and Nate over the years. Once she gets used to you, you won't be able to move an inch without her being right by your side."

Kate was struck by the strong bond that existed between the two sisters.

They sipped their coffee while Ida related her

version of the trouble in Two Horse, and although not as frantic, a much more colorful soliloquy than her great-grandson's.

"The situation has become so hot that Mayor Clyde Winford, the skunk, drew a line in the dust of the meeting-hall floor and challenged anyone who was for the dam to step over and join him in the fight to save Two Horse. Us loony liberals, as the mayor likes to call us, stormed out of the room and formed a grassroots anti-dam committee. We're a small group, but we have clout."

"An age-old battle," Kate said. "Ranchers against the environmentalists. Cattle and grazing land against wild mustangs and their habitat."

"It's worse. It's neighbor against neighbor. The controversy went and got too hot. Compromise turned into a dirty word. I like it when things get fiery. Hate mail comes daily, so I know I'm getting folks' attention."

"I'd like to meet the people who have joined your cause."

"You will this afternoon. I guess I gotta take care of Frank first. When Nate gets here, I'll get him to make the funeral arrangements." Ida took the poker and rearranged the guts of the fire. Flames shot up, spreading more warmth into the room. "Frank's wife died several years ago. His son, Nate's father, was killed in the Middle East. Springfield men don't hang around too long. Except for Nate. He's spent a lot of time on the ranch with me and Veda. I know what you're thinking," Ida said.

What Kate was thinking was that too many questions were assaulting her brain. But she had the feeling that Ida needed to say more, so Kate listened.

"How could a mother feel this way about her son?"

Ida said. "Hell, I knew nothing about raising kids, and Frank was a handful. He grew up resenting me. Blamed me for never knowing his dad. Colter was somewhat of a favored son around these parts. I was sixteen when I married. He was almost twice my age. It was a marriage of convenience. He was the only child and if he didn't sire a son, the Springfield name would go the way of the buffalo. My dad struggled for years but couldn't recover from the depression and marrying his daughter into the well-to-do Springfield family seemed like a good idea."

"Not the win-win situation your parents hoped for?"

"That's an understatement. I got pregnant two months later. Colter drank and beat me, just because he could. But I was way too ornery to go home to my parents."

"That must have been horrible for a young girl," Kate said.

"It toughened me," Ida said. "When I was about three months along with Frank, my parents died in a house fire and Veda came to live with us. That was it for Colter. He hated taking care of a pregnant wife and now he was saddled with her retarded sister. He was gone a week later."

"And your son?"

"Frank got uncontrollable. Colter had a sister living in Billings and Frank moved in with her family when he graduated high school—then he went off to college."

"Why did Frank return to Two Horse?"

"Frank lived in Alaska and worked on the pipeline. He made a shit load of money and came back here after an early retirement. He told everyone he returned because of the healthy Montana air. But I knew the truth."

"Which was?"

"He came back to make my life miserable any way he could. I guess he wanted to remind me what a terrible mother I was." Ida looked at Kate as if to make no apologies. "And I was. I wasn't cut out to be a mom. I'm not…what's that word? Nurturing."

"You're great with Veda."

A big, longhaired Ol' Yeller-type dog suddenly jumped up from his place on the floor. He slapped Kate's sore foot with his tail on his mad rush outside.

"Damn!" Kate grabbed her ankle.

"Crazy dog," Ida said as she walked out onto the porch. "Rigoletto oughta give up. He never learns. Those squirrels are smarter than he is. Come out here and take a look."

Kate limped over and joined Ida on the front porch. They stood there for a moment, watching the dog work himself into a lather as two squirrels fussed at him from a high branch in a spruce tree.

"Take those stupid squirrels," Ida said. "They don't ask for nothing. They live in that tree and take their chances. Sort of like my sister. She don't ask for nothing, either. It's easy to love someone who don't expect much in return. I guess that makes me cold and hard."

"Unconditional love is difficult at times," Kate said. "But I understand what you're saying, and I don't think that makes you cold and hard."

"I didn't love my husband and my son was a stranger to me. What does that make me?"

Kate watched the determined Rigoletto as he tried over and over to climb the tree. She could sympathize. Getting information from Ida was just as frustrating. But Kate needed answers to her questions concerning the controversy that brought her here, especially one that could not wait. "Ida, was Frank in favor of the dam?"

"Yep." Ida turned and went back inside.

Kate stared at some faraway point while her mind whirled with the ramification of Frank's murder on Ida's land.

The door slammed and the twins stepped out wearing their jackets. Veda wore a red wool cap pulled down over her ears. Ida had her hat in one hand and her keys in the other.

"Ready?" she asked Kate.

"Where are we going?"

"We're taking you into town. That cut by your ear looks bad. You need to have it looked at. Besides, it's Saturday. Veda and I always go to Ruby's for breakfast on Saturday morning."

"Hang on." Kate went back inside to grab her backpack and sunglasses, but her sunglasses were not where she had left them. She searched under the pillows and blanket and between the sofa cushions.

"Let's go," Ida called.

"Hang on. I've misplaced my sunglasses." Kate stepped back outside. She dug around in her backpack but came up empty-handed.

"Don G's a mean dog," Veda whispered to her sister.

"Goddamn! Wait here." Ida walked into the barn, and quickly came out wiping the sunglasses on her shirttail. "Stupid pack rat of a dog. If he doesn't have time to bury something, he hides it in the barn. I'm really sorry. The left lens has a small scratch on it." She handed them to Kate.

"No harm done," Kate said, although she was

beginning to think she might not survive her visit with the Springfields. "I'm hungry. You said something about breakfast."

To Kate's surprise, Veda grabbed Kate's hand.

****

Two Horse, Montana sat five miles north of the Wyoming border tucked between the Pryor Mountain Range and the Big Horn River. To the north, the Crow Indian Reservation spread out and claimed much of the eastern section of Carbon County. Public access to the reservation was restricted primarily by the topography, giving the wilderness a respite from human interference. Just forty miles to the northwest, however, Red Lodge, the county seat of Carbon County, drew thousands of skiers every year. Because Two Horse was on the way to nowhere, tourism had not made it down that far.

Kate noticed a flashing yellow light up ahead, and seconds later they were in downtown Two Horse. State Highway 310 ran down the middle of town. Businesses offering residents the bare necessities clustered along the eastern side of the half-mile stretch. The post office and Big Sky Bank shared a small brick building that appeared to have been built not long after Lewis and Clark blazed their trail west. Molin's, a combination dry goods, grocery, and feed store, housed in the largest structure in town, sold whatever Two Horse needed to keep going. A farm-equipment repair shop was located in back. An old gas pump—a real antique collector's prize—still pumped fuel from a tank in front of the store. Hanging above the pump was a hand-printed sign made of peeling cardboard, inviting customers to come in for a free cup of coffee on cold days, ten-cents a cup on hot days. The Dead Coyote Bar and Grill stood a short walk from Molin's, advertising free tequila shots for women on Tuesday nights. Johnny Ramos and the Pryor Mountain Boys were scheduled to crank it up every Friday night at nine o'clock.

"Ain't much of a town, Two Horse, but we don't need much," Ida said. "Garden Committee's been sprucing it up a bit." Ida pointed to a quaint town square across the street. Framed by a cracked sidewalk and shaded by silver birch trees, Kate noticed the new gazebo with recently planted Virginia creepers climbing the latticework and red geraniums blooming from the flower boxes. Ida drove around the square.

Located on the southwest corner was Two Horse Antiques and All Stuff Western with an out-of-business sign in the window. St. Vincent de Paul's used clothing store sat on the opposite end of the street, and sandwiched in the middle was Ruby's Cafe. Ida turned left. Sitting in a convenient row were the town hall and the jail, the law offices of Jackson and Jackson, and Tough Times Pawn and Loan.

A new dirt road continued where the pavement ended and there stood the newest building in town, a doublewide portable that housed the office of Sheriff Luke Phillips and a county emergency medical unit.

"The doctor's only here on Monday, Wednesday, and Friday. The rest of the time a nurse holds down the clinic."

"What happens if you have an emergency?" Kate said.

"We either drive to Red Lodge or go without."

The gash below Kate's ear required only a butterfly bandage, and Kate, Ida, and Veda were in and out in less than twenty minutes. As they walked across the square,

Kate noticed the sheriff's car and the same EMS vehicle that had taken Frank's body away that morning. They had not yet left for the county seat in Red Lodge. That meant only one thing—Frank Springfield's body lay just a few feet away.

Surely Ida was aware of this fact, but she chatted to Veda as if this were an ordinary morning, as if Frank's body had not been removed from her mountain just hours ago. Struck by the bizarreness of the situation, Kate watched as the twins walked hand-in-hand toward the restaurant. Kate suspected that, for all her tough-talking and hard exterior, Ida was not as cold-hearted as she claimed.

Kate was curious to know what the authorities had found, if anything. Did other people in town hate Ida's son as much as she did? Maybe those who were on Ida's side, and others concerned with preventing the dam's construction and saving the integrity of the land.

One look around town, and Kate knew that the environmentalists were few and far between, which made the list of murder suspects short if the murder was indeed connected to the building of the dam. To Kate's way of thinking, Ida must be on that list. After all, Frank was murdered less than a hundred and fifty yards from her back door.

While Ida and Veda strolled to Ruby's to get a table, Kate walked across the street to the pay phone to check in with Jack. In keeping with her simple ways, Ida did not have a phone, and there was no cell service in this remote part of the state.

The team was at home this week, but Kate did not expect Jack to answer the phone. When she was invited to join the staff of the University of Illinois at Chicago as a guest lecturer for the spring semester, Kate jumped at the chance to have a new project to keep her busy. Once Jack started spring training in February, Kate saw very little of him.

"Hello," Jack said, sounding winded.

"Did I catch you on the way in or out?"

"My prayers have been answered. I was just coming in from walking Kenya when the phone ring. I knew it was you. But first let me tell you that I love you, I miss you, save those damn horses, and get home."

Kate laughed. "Same here, sweetheart, and I'll do my best. How's our newly adopted daughter?"

"She misses you as much as I do. Last night she went back and forth from her basket to your side of the bed. After about two o'clock, I gave up on sleep and went in the kitchen to make her a BLT."

"Jack, you didn't!"

"Actually, I made myself a BLT and Kenya sampled the crumbs. She likes my meat-loving diet much better than your veggie food."

"Do you think her leg was giving her trouble?"

"Maybe. I gave her a pain pill. She favored the leg when we started out on our walk, but soon she forgot she was an invalid and took off after a raft of ducks."

A semi blew its horn at some kids crossing the highway on their bikes.

"Where the hell are you, at a truck stop?"

"Ida Springfield doesn't have a phone and unless I'm perched high on a mountain, and you know how I feel about that, my cell phone is useless. I'm standing outside at a pay phone. How are things with the team?"

"Overall, fine. The lineup for the series with Atlanta is set. I think we have a dynamite rookie first-baseman that's just about ripe."

"But?"

"But that high-school lefty we drafted for our minor-league system last year is having some head problems."

"The young pitcher from Tulsa?"

"Mike Chambers. I'm going to Des Moines tomorrow to find out what's going on. We were planning on bringing him up for a start in the double header with St. Louis next month. But lately his performance has gone from bad to worse. We're barely six weeks into the season and he's asking for time off. The staff down there doesn't know what the hell's going on."

"Maybe he's homesick."

"Or the one-point-three million dollars we gave him was too much, too soon. I'm driving there so I thought I'd take Kenya with me."

"Great idea. I'd hate to leave her with strangers after what she's been through. So does she really miss me?"

"She pulled your robe out of the closet and used it for another layer in her basket. See any wild mustangs lately?"

"Actually, Ida took me up to the top of her mountain last night. I watched the west canyon band gather at their favorite watering hole under a full moon."

"Nice."

"It was. Then nice turned nasty. On the way down, I got caught in a hailstorm, and took a tumble. I busted my head and twisted my ankle."

"I don't want to hear this. Did you end up with stitches again? I should invest in catgut. I'd make a fortune."

"I'm walking slowly and have a Band-Aid behind my ear. Nothing serious." Kate paused, deciding what more she should tell her husband. Too late.

"What else? You're leaving something out. If you want me to sleep tonight, spit it out."

"If I tell you, you might not sleep until I get home."

"Oh, Lord."

"I tripped over a body on the way down the mountain."

"As in dead?"

"As in murdered. It was Ida's son."

"That's not funny."

"No, but it's true."

"Why I had to fall in love with a woman who draws trouble by osmosis is beyond me."

"You needed someone to think about while you squatted behind home plate all those years."

"Any idea who killed him?"

"No, but the situation is pretty bizarre. Except for his hiking boots, he was nude from the waist down."

"Come home right now."

Kate laughed. "Not when things are getting interesting. Give Kenya a kiss and explain to her that ducks have the right to live in this world. I love you both."

They talked for a while longer, and Kate promised Jack she would call him daily. After that incident involving the greyhounds last summer in Wimberley, Texas, she could not deny his request.

Just as she started back across the street, a Toyota pickup pulled to a stop in front of her. The man behind the wheel tipped his hat.

"Ma'am. You're that lady scientist here on Ida Springfield's behalf. I saw you leave the clinic. Sheriff Phillips told me who you are."

Kate held out her hand. "Kate Caraway."

The man kept his on the steering wheel momentarily before he completed the handshake. "Clyde Winford."

"Nice to meet you, Mayor. Ida mentioned you."

"I'll bet she did. Listen, ma'am, I'll come right to the point. Ida Springfield's been stirring up a big bunch of shit again. That little earthen dam ain't gonna hurt nobody, and it will help out a lot of ranchers who've been hurting for water. Those mustangs on her ranch are a bloody nuisance. They're good for nothing."

Kate knew she'd meet with resistance from some Two Horse citizens, but she didn't expect it to happen so quickly.

"Besides, we can handle our own problems. But since you're here, you need to hear both sides of the story. I want to talk to you before the town council meeting on Tuesday. Maybe you can talk some sense into Ida. With Frank being found dead on her ranch, who knows what she'll do. I don't mean to be disrespectful, but that ol' gal's as loony as a noodle."

He tipped his hat again and sped away, leaving a cloud of dust in his wake.

Kate spit out dust and wiped her sunglasses. Ida was a bit odd, but the gutsy old woman and her innocent sister had captured Kate's heart. True, Kate needed to hear both sides of the story, but when it came to animal rights, Kate could make loony-as-a-noodle seem normal.

Chapter Three

Kate opened the door to Ruby's. A heavy smell of fried bacon and cigarette smoke greeted her before she stepped inside. There wasn't an empty seat in the joint. Every eye in the restaurant followed Kate as she walked over and slid into the booth next to Veda. A mountain of empty butter packets lay next to Veda's glass of milk. The syrup that swamped her pancakes spilled over the lip of the plate. Ida took the syrup pitcher and set it on the other side of the table.

Oblivious to stares, or used to them, Ida said, "We went ahead and ordered. Hope you don't mind."

"Not at all. Just met your mayor," Kate said. "Is that a Spanish omelet you're eating?"

"Sure is, and a damn good one," Ida said, smearing butter on her flour tortilla, adding to her own pile of discarded butter packets.

"Pancakes are good," Veda said.

Except for Veda voicing her concern over Luisa Miller having to give up the sofa, this was the first time Veda had spoken directly to Kate. Her voice, clear and full of joy, sounded like a child's. The waitress arrived and Ida asked for more butter.

"I'll take your word for it, Veda," Kate said. "It's pancakes for me, too. And coffee."

The waitress left in a huff.

"Did I say something wrong?" Kate said.

"Na. Just that you're sitting with two old birds. I cause quite a stir in this town, about one thing or another."

No shit, Kate thought. The hair on the back of her neck bristled. Without turning around, Kate knew they were the cafe's main attraction. She had been here less than twenty-four hours, and she could come up with several reasons why they deserved the attention—a newcomer in town with a wound on the back of her head, sitting with an eccentric woman whose son's murdered body was just discovered this morning.

"That lamebrain waitress ain't worth a damn." Ida left the booth and stomped over to the service table. She grabbed a ceramic cup and a coffee pot. Seconds later, Kate was enjoying her first cup of fresh-brewed coffee. The instant coffee Ida had served earlier had tasted like battery acid. Then the idea took hold that Veda was the only woman at the table who had gotten any sleep last night. Surprisingly, Kate did not feel the least bit tired.

"What did that little banty rooster mayor have to say?" Ida asked.

"Evidently he heard I was coming," Kate said.

"That's cause I got a big mouth."

"He also wants to talk to me before the meeting."

"Go ahead and hear him out. But you remember you're here to help me. Nate recommended you. He said you got this big operation in Africa, and that you were responsible for saving a bunch of elephants from some poachers."

Was it still her operation? Kate was doubtful. The memory of that night still smarted. The last time she saw her staff, fellow researchers, and the volunteers who had become her family, they had waved her and Jack

30

goodbye as they rushed off into the night. This was one topic that was not up for friendly discussion.

"I'll do all I can, but I need more information," Kate assured Ida.

"You'll get all the information you want. I don't leave stones unturned."

"Turn over one of those stones now and reveal your secret," Kate prodded.

"I ain't got no secrets," Ida said with a slight defensiveness in her voice.

"I'm talking about the card you have up your sleeve."

"Oh, right. I keep forgetting what I've told you and what I haven't. I don't know what the deal is with me. I didn't expect my memory to fade until I became an old woman." Ida threw her head back and hooted at her own joke.

"Ida's funny," Veda said without looking up from her plate.

"Karen Gregory, she's a national park ranger at Big Horn Canyon and works mainly on the Pryor Mountain Wild Mustang Range. She wants to help any way possible. I told her I'd donate my entire herd to the preserve, but the BLM boys don't want the horses. Their herd's too large already. She's trying to get her own private wild-horse foundation going. In fact, she and Nate came up with The Nature Conservancy idea for my ranch. If there's an endangered animal or even a plant on some land, they might take the property as a preserve."

"I'm familiar with TNC. It's an excellent organization," Kate said.

"This way the Springfield family, what's left of us, can steward the land while the Conservancy takes the responsibility for its preservation. There's a lot to do before this can happen. We need to check the health of my herd. This is where Karen comes in. She and several volunteers spent the last few weeks building a temporary corral near my lake to hold the horses for blood samples and vaccinations. We're going to round them up on Wednesday. You can help."

"Sounds like a fine idea," Kate said.

"It's a damn good idea." Ida's voice rose. "But if the dam is built, there'll be no water, no horses, and the deal's off."

The waitress walked by pretending their table didn't exist, and Ida cupped her hands around her mouth and shouted that their coffee cups were empty.

"Ida, let's talk about Frank. Any idea of who and why?" Kate wasn't sure if Ida was willing to discuss Frank's demise in front of Veda. Ida's answer to her question cleared things up.

"There's not one person in my group that didn't want him dead, and let me tell you they're all brave enough to put a knife in his back." Ida emphasized her point by jabbing her fork in the air.

"Cut the crap, Ida. Stabbing someone in the back is not an act of bravery. If Frank's murder was connected to the dam, you need to fill me in. Tell me about the people in your coalition."

"I know. I get riled up. We're all good Christians. There's not one of the four of us who'd harm a fly."

"Four? You mean your coalition of environmentalists has only four members?" Kate began to wonder what she had gotten herself into. Fighting a county of cattle ranchers whose claim to the land dated back to the late 1800s, with a handful of wild-horse

32

lovers and ecology-minded people seemed a daunting task.

Veda reached across the table and surreptitiously picked up the syrup container.

"Five, if you count Nate," Ida said. "Veda, put the syrup down."

Kate took two ibuprofens from the bottle in her backpack and washed them down with her coffee. "Tell me about them."

After Ida finished painting a colorful profile of her fellow advocates, Kate's skepticism eased. The coalition consisted of a well-known and respected member of the Crow tribe, the Nelsons, who owned an organic farm north of Two Horse and whose irrigation would be reduced to a trickle if the dam was built, and Karen Gregory, the park ranger. All were opposed to the dam project for various legitimate reasons. According to Ida, their opinions held some weight in Two Horse and in Carbon County. Then Kate's hopefulness turned to doubt again. Why, with knowledgeable people in the coalition, did Nate feel so strongly about Kate joining the group? Maybe it was the lump on her head or the discovery of a body with a knife wedged between two thoracic vertebrae that caused Kate to feel uncertain about her involvement. Lately she'd been plagued with self-doubt, emotions that reached deep down, entangled their tendrils around her gut, and refused to let go.

Kate was jarred from her thoughts when Ida asked, "Why don't you tell me why you're really here?"

"What kind of question is that?" Kate said, feeling annoyed. "I'm here to help you."

"No, Ding Dong. I mean, why are you in Chicago and not in Africa?"

"Long story."

"Give me the short version."

"You're nosy."

"Right. Go ahead."

Kate took a sip of her coffee. "In a nutshell—my husband had an opportunity to work with the Cubs again, this time as a pitching coach. And I needed to come back and do some fundraising."

"Oh, right." Ida rolled her eyes. "That makes a hell of a lot of sense."

"Hell," Veda said.

"You don't let up, do you, Ida?"

"Nope. Just seems odd to me that you'd leave Africa and go teach in a big city. Kinda like me leaving the ranch and setting up house in town."

Ida's assessment of Kate's situation was right on the money. Living in Chicago again was harder than she had anticipated. Working at her research camp in Kenya had left her with no idle time. After two months in the big city without much to do, Kate was starting to lose her mind. Then a phone call from a colleague, asking Kate to join the university's community-outreach program, was like a lifeline, or so she thought. Giving lectures to the general public and student body would keep her busy. Quickly, however, the work became paltry compared to life in the bush. Difficult as it was, Kate preferred to be where life hung in the balance. It was her justification for living, for being part of a world that was destroying itself species by species. Upon her return to a punctilious life in the United States, Kate faced the truth that she had become addicted to her own adrenaline. Giving lectures in a climate-controlled auditorium failed to tap into those adrenal glands.

"Let's just say I needed a break and leave it at that," Kate said.

"Okay," Ida said. "But I don't give up easily."

"I noticed."

"Noticed," Veda said.

Ida reached over and picked up Veda's plate, which was again floating in syrup. The older sister poured a good amount of the liquid onto her own plate and then handed it back. Veda's lower lip protruded like a pouting child, but she voiced no objection.

"Since I am here, let's get back to your situation. What would Frank be doing on your ranch? Did he go there often?" Kate said.

"Who the hell knows why he was there? But let me tell you this—" Ida pointed her fork again at Kate. "—whatever the reason, he was up to no good. I've seen him out there a couple of times recently, just wandering around. I think he comes out to spook the horses and piss me off. He pissed a lot of people off. Maybe he wasn't even killed on my ranch. Maybe someone dumped his body there. Ever think of that?"

"But why?" Kate said. "That's quite a task, dragging a dead body up the side of that mountain."

Before Ida could comment, Veda stopped scraping the remaining smears of syrup off her plate. "Dead body," Veda said, with a look on her face that Kate couldn't figure.

"It's okay, Veda. Let's head to Molin's." Ida threw her napkin on the table. "I need to pick up supplies. Then we can go back to the ranch and talk."

The conversation for the moment was over. They had been sitting at the breakfast table in Ruby's for well over an hour, and their waitress had turned from irritated to down-right hateful.

As they slid out of the booth, Veda said, "Waitress like tips."

"That snooty little bitch is stupider than she looks if she thinks I'm gonna put a cent down on this table," Ida said as she grabbed the bill.

"Waitress don't want a cent, sister. She wants a dollar."

Ida winked at Kate. "What'd I tell you? Veda gets warmed up, and it's Katy bar the door."

"Let me take care of the bill, Ida."

"Nothin' doing. You're our guest and we haven't been too nice to you, seeing as how I left you out in the storm, and you found Frank deader than roadkill."

"She hurt her head, too," Veda added.

"Right," Ida said.

As they walked to the register, Kate threw a five-dollar bill on the table.

"I saw that," Ida cackled. "You'll ruin my image."

****

As soon as they returned to the ranch, Ida said she needed a rest, and rather than discussing Frank's murder, she handed Kate a stack of files to read. Ida had done her homework in preparation for Kate's visit. There were copies of the dam proposal, a history of the mustang herd living on the sanctuary, a study of the effects of the dam on the river's tributaries and streams, and the minutes of every council meeting discussing the proposal.

For the moment, Kate had the small living room to herself. Veda was out back tending to the dogs. By mid-afternoon, Kate's vision began to blur. She leaned her head back on the sofa to rest her eyes. Sleep was a dear friend she'd lost a long time ago. Since she and Jack had moved back to Chicago, Kate's boredom had quickly evolved into depression. Too many nights had passed tossing and turning—her mind on overdrive—until she'd finally drift off to sleep just around the time the alarm rang. Kate was surprised when she opened her eyes and found two hours had passed. But what was more surprising was the throbbing pain in her left thigh.

In Kate's drowsy state, panic swelled in her chest. She couldn't move her leg. Then a loud attention-getting yawn, followed by a squeak brought Kate to full attention. Luisa Miller had curled up on Kate's legs and the dog's knee was wedged deep into Kate's thigh.

"Sorry, girl. You and I are going to have to work out a better sleeping arrangement." With a gentle shove, the dog lumbered off the sofa. Kate massaged the blood back into her limbs. As soon as she was able to focus, she looked over and saw five pairs of eyes watching her. Veda and the rest of the canine entourage were waiting patiently for their guest to wake up and relinquish some of the sofa.

"Luisa Miller's a mean dog," Veda offered as an apology for her pet's intrusion.

"She's not mean, Veda. She's just not used to a stranger sleeping in her spot."

"Nate's comin' tomorrow."

Kate sat up, brushing her hair from her face. "Do you like Nate to come for visits?"

"Nate brings me things."

"Veda," Ida called from the bedroom. "Time to feed those mangy mutts."

Veda left the house with the pack following close behind.

Ida walked out of the bedroom, braiding her hair as

37

she glanced out the window. "Good nap?"

"Yes, how about you?"

"Don't usually sleep in the middle of the afternoon."

"Last night wasn't a typical night." With Veda outside, Kate wasted no time. "You weren't very surprised by Frank's death."

"At eighty-two, nothing surprises me much anymore."

"You're a tough woman, Ida. There's no doubting that. However, it's not every day you find a murdered man on your property, let alone one that was your son."

For the first time Kate noticed a genuine concern in Ida's wise old face. "You're right. This is a bad situation. I often talk to Veda about death. She brings up the subject a lot. I guess it's hard to figure, and she needs to ask questions."

"That's true for anyone."

"I'd do anything to protect her, Kate. And up until lately, I never really thought about myself. My concern has always been for Veda. But what if I go before her? That thought is enough to give me nightmares. I'm concerned about Frank's murder. I mean—him dying suddenly. It could happen to me."

"Do you think the killer is after you too?"

"I've been laying in my room thinking. It's like this—one day Frank's alive and being a pain in the butt, and the next day he's dead. I go around pissing off a lot of people. What if someone did me in? What would happen to Veda?"

Kate understood Ida's concern. The only Springfield left was Nate. Would it be fair to expect a young man who had just begun his college career to come back home and take care of his great, great aunt?

Nevertheless, Kate was perplexed by Ida's lack of concern about the murder of her son.

As if reading Kate's thoughts, Ida said, "But that's not your problem. You didn't come here to get tangled up in Springfield family troubles."

"It's time you leveled with me. Would someone opposed to the dam kill Frank?"

"Some good folks have a lot to lose if that dam goes in. No matter what I said earlier, I sure couldn't imagine killing over this matter." Ida's words sounded more sincere than when she had been holding court in Ruby's Cafe this morning.

"Well, someone killed him and took the trouble to remove his pants." Kate dreaded the next question but had to ask. "Does the sheriff suspect you?"

"What's my motive? The goddamn dam?" Ida paused. "You may be right. I've threatened to kill people for less. The sheriff told me not to leave town, as if I had any place else to go. But I'm too old to kill a man. Besides, I lack the third thing, what's it called? Means, right? I had the motive and opportunity, but not the means."

"I'm not following you."

"Look around. I don't own any fancy new things like that knife with the yellow handle that was in Frank's back. The sheriff needs to look for an angry husband, one who caught Frank entertaining the wife. Caught him with his pants down, like we found him. Frank had a reputation for screwing any woman who'd stand still. And he's had a couple of close calls."

Kate thought Ida's explanation of not having the means was weak but kept her thoughts to herself. "Frank was a ladies' man?"

Ida slapped her knee. "I know what you mean. Who'd want to cotton-up to an old man? I had Frank when I was seventeen. That makes him…let's see…sixty-three. But he was a charmer, believe you me. He had the women, before and after his wife died."

"If Frank was caught with another man's wife, why was he murdered here?"

Ida pulled at her lower lip and squinted her eyes into narrow slits. "Maybe someone killed him and brought his body here, like I said before."

"But why?"

Ida squinted her eyes completely shut this time as if to enhance her thinking. "If someone wanted to hide the body, this mountain would be a good place with all the fissures and crevices. Dump it over a boulder and into a crack between the rocks, and even the buzzards couldn't get to it. Or maybe it was someone who wanted to pin the murder on me." Her eyes popped open. "It's a well-known fact that there was no love lost between me and Frank."

"Maybe," Kate said, although the idea of taking Frank's body up the mountain seemed absurd. "You said that Frank returned to Two Horse six months ago. Had he stayed away all these years?"

"Na. He'd blow into town every now and then. He lived here years back before he moved to Alaska. He was here for a while after Nate's father died. But Frank and I just stayed out of each other's way."

They heard Veda fussing at the dogs. "Get down. Get down."

"I'd better get out there. Those mongrels weren't fed this morning, and it sounds like they're not cooperating with the cook."

The sun had little more than an hour left to heat up the afternoon before its descent behind the mountains, leaving what was left of the day to fend for itself. Winter in Montana reluctantly let go of its claim—a constant tug of war with spring, that continued throughout most of the budding season. The doors and windows were opened, giving Kate's body a chance to absorb some remaining warmth while she tried to figure out this odd puzzle. If Ida was right and an angry husband killed Frank, then there was a distraught wife somewhere in Two Horse. What happened to her? Had her body not yet been found, or did the husband let her live? If she was alive, then she'd know about the murder, unless the husband followed Frank and killed him on some isolated road.

Kate's nap seemed to make matters worse. Zapped of energy, she was too tired to think about murder. She closed her eyes. The sun, coming in through the window, spread over her like a liquid salve, loosening muscles that were still stiff and sore from last night's tackle with the mountain, the storm, and the cold. For the moment, Kate was content to let her mind wander as the sun worked its magic. She was not a cold-weather person. When she had moved to Kenya, she thought she had died and gone to heaven. Kate woke every morning with a prayer of thanks. Every day was beautiful, even when it rained, as if life and weather had declared an everlasting peace. Even her intermittent sleep did not bother her. She'd often awaken in the middle of the night to the piercing cries of non-releasable elephants, sounding an alarm when a lion pride strolled by. On these occasions, returning to sleep was impossible, and she'd often sit up, watching life unfold on the African plain. But things had changed instantly. She had committed the number one scientific sin—losing objectivity. And because of her screw-up, she and Jack were back in the US.

Suddenly a dark shadow drifted across the sun, and Kate silently cursed the cloud for ruining her natural solar therapy. Then the cloud spoke.

"Ida, you in there?"

A deep, strong voice barreled through the screen door, jolting Kate from her reflections on nature's wonder. Before she could get to her feet, he walked in, ducking his head under the doorway. He filled the entire doorframe. She had not heard his steps creak the old, wooden planks that made up Ida's front porch. Kate wondered how such a big man could move so silently. A red and blue striped vest with brown leather fringe dangling from the breast pockets hung open over a denim shirt. The fabric of his black jeans stretched taunt across his thighs, displaying muscles that looked like they belonged to the legs of a Brahma bull.

Kate recognized the visitor immediately. Pete Bear Walks Slowly, a member of the Crow Executive Tribal Council, had made a name for himself as one of the most influential Native American advocates in the country. He could trace his lineage back to a time when the only people living here were the Crow. He was one of the largest men Kate had ever seen, and he moved his hefty frame with grace and ease, with a confidence devoid of conceit, almost an indifference to his own presence. His blue-black hair, braided and long, hung down the middle of his back. His smooth skin stretched tight over a chiseled face, leaving no doubt as to his heritage. Kate guessed his age to be near her own.

Looking into his dark eyes, Kate had the feeling of being sucked into a vortex. She couldn't help but stare.

After a few uncomfortable moments, she said, "Hi, I'm Kate Caraway. The girls are out back."

"Pete Bear Walks Slowly. Ida said you were coming and that you're addressing the council at the next meeting." He slowly looked around, peering over every inch of the cabin as if he expected something evil lurking in the shadows. "Heard about Frank."

"Ida and I have been trying to figure out what happened. She thinks it was a jealous husband."

"Maybe."

"What do you think?"

"Not sure."

"Did you know Frank well?"

"No."

Kate waited, but got no further response. "Ida's grateful for your help in trying to keep water on her ranch."

"I'm not concerned about Ida's ranch."

"No?"

"No."

"Then why are you here?"

"Teepees."

Kate wanted to shake people like Pete Bear Walks Slowly. Either he was uncomfortable with strangers, or he didn't trust her.

"Those horses aren't my problem," Pete said.

"Ida wants to establish a new preserve on her land. Don't you think it's a good idea?"

"Ida's a crazy old woman."

Just then the backdoor slammed. "A crazy old woman who can hear a fly shit across the canyon. Pete Bear Walks Slowly," Ida yelled to Kate from the kitchen, "doesn't agree with me on why the dam should be stopped. He has his own agenda. That's fine. The more reasons we have to stop the project, the more people we can sway in our direction." Ida walked into the living room, leaned against the wall, and folded her arms across her chest. "Besides, who wouldn't notice him. He's a big, scary son of a bitch. I'm surprised you remembered how to get out to my ranch." Ida turned to Kate. "I've been trying to get the SOB to come by and talk over this crazy mess, but he claims he's too goddamned busy."

"I drove out here earlier this morning, but you weren't at home."

"Wow! Two visits in one day. Glad to see you're getting your butt working on this."

"I've other things I'm working on. Visiting you is a waste of time, listening to you bad mouth everyone in the county. I want this dam stopped as much as you, you stubborn old cuss."

Ida laughed and stomped her foot. "Pete talks mean, but he's really got a crush on me, don't you, honey?"

Pete shook his head. "I'm concerned about the teepees," he said to Kate.

"Tell me about the teepees," Kate said.

"One of our families has started a new company, and it's doing very well, bringing in much needed revenue. Teepees are part of our heritage and building them is a honed craft. For centuries they comfortably protected our tribe against the elements. Now they provide an answer to our sixty percent unemployment on the reservation," Pete explained. "There's a market, a substantial one, in collecting Native American arts and crafts, teepees included. The Crow Teepee Company of Two Horse, owned by the Brown Bird family, has taken orders from all over the country, even from Europe. But the structure must be authentic, and that means using traditional woods to build it."

"And these woods are located in the area that will be flooded if the dam is built," Kate said. "I read the meeting's minutes."

"That's part of it. The valley is where the red ash and chokecherry woods grow. These trees are used for the stakes. The pines that are used for the main support grow in the mountains, and will not be affected, but road access will. The frames of the teepees are built in the summer after the snow melts and the roads up to the mountain are opened. If the company cannot get to the mountain, not only will they not fill their orders, they'll risk losing respect. Many orders have been taken and deposits paid. Much of the deposit money has been spent and cannot be returned. If the dam is built, the teepee company will fold immediately and face lawsuits."

"How can that happen so fast? It will take years to build the dam," Kate said.

"This is an earthen dam," Ida said. "It won't take long to build, and the county will claim the land this summer if this blasted project goes through."

"And that's the other problem," Pete said. "The government's been chipping away at our land. Claiming it for whatever reason suits them. The reservation used to cover thirty-nine million acres. Now the tribe owns less than two million and our per capita income is less than ten thousand dollars."

"Not only that," Ida piped up. "My daddy told me about a time after World War One when beef production was low. The government told ranchers who were leasing land on the Crow Reservation to shoot the horses and raise more cattle. Thousands of horses were killed and left to rot."

"Our people's protests fell on deaf ears," Pete said.

"But that wasn't the end of it," Ida continued. "A drought hit in 1929, making grazing grass scarce. More horses had to go. When the smoke cleared, the wild-horse herds were on the brink of extinction. In one case, the carcasses of one hundred thousand ponies were left rotting. The stench spread across the reservation and flies blackened the skies."

"Those reservation ponies were part of our tribal heritage. The sad thing was the Bureau of Indian Affairs supported the butchery. As long as I'm around, that's not going to happen this time."

"If the dam affects the reservation, wouldn't the Crow have an influential voice?" Kate said.

"We do have influence. That's also part of the problem," Pete said. "Many Crow are for the dam. The federal government is the main employer of people living on the reservation, and oil and gas leases keep a lot of families happy. Also, many Crow support using the land for livestock grazing. That's been our problem over the years. We cannot agree on how to sustain ourselves."

"But James Brown Bird, owner of the teepee company, employs a lot of you folks," Ida said.

"It's more than just the loss of a small number of jobs." He turned to Kate. "It's the loss of an ancient art. Our reservation doesn't experience the abject poverty seen on many reservations. But so many of our young people are losing touch with their roots." Now he switched his gaze to Ida, and his voice grew more intense. "They get jobs, they get a paycheck, and they meld into American culture and, before you know it, they disappear. That in itself is poverty."

Ida opened her mouth, closed it, and looked away, but not before Kate noticed the silent exchange between Ida and Pete.

Chapter Four

Kate awoke on Sunday morning to the smell of coffee and the image of a huge slug sliming over her fingers. She looked over to see Luisa Miller diligently licking each finger on her hand. It was still dark outside. A howling wind rattled the windows, but the room was warm.

"I just put a log on the fire," Ida said as she set Kate's coffee cup on the wooden stump. "We had a clear night. It's twenty-seven degrees outside. As soon as the sun comes over the mountains, it'll warm up quickly."

Kate checked her watch—five-thirty. She was naturally an early riser, but the three of them had stayed up past midnight. Pete Bear Walks Slowly had little to say about most things, but when it came to the Crow and their heritage, he was a windbag. Kate had absorbed more about Native American lore than she had learned in college or since.

"I have to fetch Nate at the airport in Billings. Thought you might want to come along."

"You bet." Kate sat up, took two more ibuprofens, and sipped her coffee. At the sound of voices, Tosco and Don G, two medium-sized, tan-colored dogs who looked like they came from the same litter, scampered from Ida's bedroom. Ida went into the kitchen and came back with two saucers full of a chocolate-colored liquid. She placed them in front of Tosco and Don G, and the two mutts lapped up their first breakfast course. Luisa Miller was not interested.

"A special diet?" Kate said.

"You could say that. It's coffee. They have a cup every morning. The three of us get up early. Veda and the rest of the pack sleep in."

"You have one interesting household here, Ida."

"I never was much on commonplace."

"Did you ever read Jenny Joseph's poem, 'Warning'?"

"Nope."

"It's about giving in to eccentricities in old age."

"You mean like doing whatever the hell you want?"

"Exactly."

"I don't know no other way."

Kate laughed. She hadn't known either of her grandmothers. But from what Kate was told, they would not have held a candle to Ida. Kate was not much on commonplace either, but unlike the character in Joseph's poem, Kate's attempts at eccentricity tended to slap her in the face. She had not come across many people like Ida who were thoroughly comfortable in their own skin. At forty-two, Kate had yet to achieve that freedom.

"I'm gonna get Veda up and make some biscuits and eggs. We need to be on our way by seven," Ida said. "Bathroom's yours."

After a quick bath, Kate pulled on her jeans and sweatshirt. She brushed her charcoal-colored hair into a ponytail and covered it with a Cubs baseball cap. Looking in the mirror, she realized that too much time indoors had left her complexion pale.

Kate opened the bathroom door. The aroma of eggs and sausage told her breakfast was ready. Maybe it was the cold Montana morning with its raw ruggedness, but Kate felt ready to eat her weight in biscuits and gravy, a dish she never thought of consuming until now.

Ida and Veda were seated at the small table just outside the kitchen. "I left the sausage out of the gravy for you," Ida said. "I don't know why I bothered. A little meat never hurt anybody."

"Thanks," Kate said and filled her plate. "You're right about that, Ida. It's a moral issue with me. Knowing what animals go through before they are killed…well, let's just say I have no appetite for it."

Veda stopped eating and stared at Kate as if she were speaking in tongues.

"It's just that it takes so much more land to raise cattle than to grow crops." Kate felt an uncomfortable need to explain.

Veda looked down at her plate and frowned.

"Honey, you talk like that here, you'll be run out of the state on a potato truck," Ida said.

"Warning noted," Kate said. "Now tell me about the plans for the morning."

"After we pick up Nate, we'll stop by the Nelsons' farm. You'll feel right at home. Nate worked for them while he was in high school. Ed and Lucy are part of the coalition. They're a bit kooky, but they're on my side."

"Veda doesn't want her sausage," Veda said as she slipped it off her plate and tossed it to Tosco who had sneaked back in the cabin after Ida shooed the dogs out.

"Now look what you've done," Ida said to Kate. "If she becomes a veggie, you're taking her home with you."

By the time they finished the dishes and climbed into Ida's truck, the wind had died down, and the early-morning clouds had blown far to the south. It promised to be a brilliant day. The sky, a robin's egg blue, seemed to reach up to the heavens. Veda sat in the middle, and Kate rode shotgun. As soon as she slammed the door on the old Ford pickup, Ida mashed the accelerator to the floor and took off down the dirt driveway like the proverbial bat out of hell. The yapping dogs, complaining about not receiving an invitation to go along, scampered out of the way of flying gravel. A flock of starlings shot from a nearby Douglas fir. Kate groped for her seatbelt but came up empty-handed.

On the way, they passed the Nelson Organic Produce Farm, now freshly planted. In the middle of the acreage stood a small, two-story white frame house surrounded by several out-buildings. An enormous red barn near the house had a United States flag painted on the side.

At eight-thirty Ida slid the truck into a disabled parking place and hopped out. "Come on. Nate's plane lands in five minutes."

"Don't you need a handicap tag?" Kate asked.

"Anyone wants to tow this piece of shit, they can have it. Besides, the only tag I need is that shotgun. Let's go."

****

The last passengers stepped off the plane, and Nate had not yet made an appearance.

Ida took a sheet of paper from her pocket. "If Nate hadn't faxed me his flight schedule, I'd be sure that goddamned idiot of a deputy sheriff got the time wrong."

"Excuse me?" said Kate.

"Since I don't have a phone or fax-thing, whenever Nate needs to get in touch with me, he calls the sheriff's office and the deputy comes out and gives me the message. Three out of five times, the stupid deputy forgets or gets it wrong."

Ida unfolded the paper and shook her head. "Right day, right flight. I don't understand. It's not like Nate not to let me know when he changes his plans."

"Let's check with an agent," Kate said.

Veda became upset, and Ida tried to calm her with the promise of ice cream while Kate made her inquiry.

"He wasn't on the plane. He canceled his flight," Kate whispered to Ida. "Here's my cell. Why don't you give him a call?"

"You get Veda her ice-cream," Ida told Kate, handing her a five, "and I'll call."

Kate took Veda's hand and they walked to the food court. Kate bought a chocolate donut for Veda and a cup of coffee for herself. The ice cream vendor hadn't opened yet, but Veda was more than willing to accept one sugary treat for another.

"Nate's not coming?" Veda asked between bites.

Kate took a napkin and wiped a smear of chocolate from Veda's mouth. "That's what Ida went to find out. Maybe something came up at school and he had to change his plans."

"Change his plans," Veda echoed.

Ida walked up to the table. Her pasted-on smile told all. Kate wondered if Veda could see her sister's disappointment through the façade.

"I left a message on his voice mail. At least I think I did. Let's drive back to town and see if Nate called the sheriff's office. Like I said, it wouldn't be the first time I didn't get word."

****

When Kate and the twins walked into his office,

Deputy Sheriff Sam Lucas quickly removed his feet from the top of his dirty green metal desk and tossed a magazine into the bottom drawer. He heaved himself out of his chair. Once on his feet, the pudgy deputy tried to tuck an errant shirttail back into his khaki pants, but his overhanging belly made that impossible. Looking slightly guilty, scratching a bald spot on his flaky scalp, he contemplated Ida's inquiry.

"Yeah, Nate called here a couple of days ago—it was Thursday, no wait, Friday. Said he'd changed his plans and you didn't have to pick him up at the airport." Deputy Lucas leaned on the edge of his desk, pulling the remainder of the shirttail free. "At least I think that was what he said. I wrote down the message."

"Friday, Sam? Today is Sunday. I just made a wasted trip to the airport. Did you stick the note on the screen door as usual?" Ida said.

The eighty-two year-old woman brought a twitch to the young deputy's eye. Surely delivering messages was not in his job description, Kate mused, but Sam Lucas cowered as if he had been accused of dereliction of duty. Kate turned aside to hide her smile.

"Well, actually, I gave the note to Niles to deliver. Wait here." Deputy Lucas walked out of his office and down the hall and yelled, "Niles, get in here."

A few seconds later, Deputy Lucas came back followed by a skinny man with hunched shoulders. He clutched a toilet-bowl brush in his hand. At the sight of Ida, his slouch disappeared. He instantly grew two inches taller, which brought him nose-to-nose with her.

"Hi, Miz Springfield," Niles said with a catch in his voice. "I took you the note like Deputy Lucas said to do."

"Well, it wasn't there, Niles."

"I stuck it in the screen door just like you showed me," Niles said as he twisted the brush in his hands as if ringing out a wet rag.

"What time did Nate call?" Ida said to Deputy Lucas.

"Let me see. I remember it was right after lunch. I just came back from eating a chili dog at Ruby's and was about to go to my car for some Rolaids when the phone rang. Nate said something came up. He didn't say what."

Niles scooted back to the doorway. "Uh, Deputy?"

"That's odd. He didn't say any more than that?" Ida's voice rose.

"Deputy, Miz Springfield?" Nile's slouching posture had returned.

"What is it, Niles?" Deputy Lucas barked.

"I didn't think it caused no trouble as long as you got word before Sunday," Niles said, clearly upset, and grasping the brush in front of his body like a shield.

"What didn't cause no trouble?" Ida said.

"Well, I stuck the note in my pocket and was gonna take it to your ranch as soon as I finished with the vacuuming. But then the sheriff come in with a truck of supplies for me to unload and I sort of forgot about the note until later."

"How much later, Niles?" Ida took a step toward the young man.

Kate would not take all the money in Montana to be in Nile's shoes at that moment.

"But you weren't going to the airport until Sunday." Niles was ready to bolt.

"How—much—later?" Ida repeated in a crescendo.

"Well, I always check my pockets before I wash my uniform. If I don't, it comes out all speckled with bits of paper."

"Don't I see you down at the laundromat every Saturday morning," Ida said, "as regular as a rabbit coming into heat?"

"Yes, ma'am, and I delivered that note as soon as I found it in my pocket, even before I started washing." The look on Ida's face sent Niles flying down the hall, and judging by the crashing sound, he must have taken out the trashcan on his way out the door. Deputy Lucas was left to absorb Ida's wrath.

"Well, he does have a point there, Ida," he said. "As long as you got the message before Sunday."

Ida looked at Sam Lucas and flared her nostrils. "I don't care when that good-for-nothing janitor delivered it, I never got it," Ida said. Then she turned and stormed out of the office. Veda followed. Kate took up the rear. Ida stood at the front door.

Veda looked down at an object near the tumbled-over trashcan. "Niles dropped his toilet brush," Veda said.

"Ha!" Ida cried and left the building.

Kate hesitated at the door and then looked back at Deputy Lucas who was standing in the hall. The color began to return to his pallid face.

"How did Nate sound when he called?" Kate said to the deputy. "Was he anxious or upset or what?"

"Sounded okay to me. Just said something came up and to tell Ida that she didn't need to come to Billings to get him."

"He didn't say anything about changing his plane reservations, or when he'd be here?"

"Nope."

"Doesn't that seem odd to you?"

55

"To tell you the truth, ma'am, everything about the Springfields seems odd to me."

Nevertheless, it didn't sound like the Nate she knew. Although she had spoken to him only a handful of times, she was impressed by his commitment to his great-grandmother. The Nate who sat in her office and pleaded his case well enough to get Kate to Two Horse, Montana, would not change his plane reservations without giving any details. Whatever made him alter his plans must have happened the day Frank was murdered. Kate pushed that thought from her mind, but it would not stay away.

Thinking back over her decision to fly to Montana, Kate wondered if had she acted too hastily and allowed her emotions to cloud her judgment. It would not have been the first time. Sure, the consensus among the townsfolk was that Ida was somewhat strange. But then last night's conversation with Pete Bear Walks Slowly lent credibility to Ida's and Nate's cause.

Ida walked over to Kate. "Veda's upset. When she gets this way, it takes forever to deal with her. I can't leave her alone, and I can't get much done here with her. Let's go back to the ranch. You can take the pickup and go on out to the Nelsons'. You saw their place when we drove by on the way to the airport. I want you to visit them before the next council meeting, so you can have as much ammo as possible."

"Ammo?" Kate said. "I don't plan on addressing the council with a shotgun."

Ida grinned, revved the motor, and backed out of the parking lot.

Chapter Five

Ida's pickup was as old as everything else on the ranch. The clutch was loose, and when Kate shifted into second, she had to hold the gear stick up on the column to keep it from falling.

On the way through town, Kate stopped to call Jack. He'd be on his way to Iowa by now with Kenya stretched out on the back seat. They adopted that arrangement on their recent long drive from Texas to Chicago. Kenya had come from Molly Gibson's Greyhound Adoption Kennels in Wimberley, Texas. After a severe racing accident, Kenya's owner wanted to put the dog to sleep. A compassionate vet who had confidence in Molly's remarkable rehabilitation skills with injured, discarded racers spared the life of the three-year-old greyhound. Driving across country with Kenya's leg stiff and sore, and a pin wedged in her hip meant stopping every couple of hours to let her stretch. The trip took nine days, but that was how Kate and Jack liked to travel—taking their time on the back roads, discovering the heart and soul of small-town life.

Once on a trip home from Big Bend, looking for a place to have lunch, they had stopped in Roosevelt, Texas, a speck on the Rand McNally just off Interstate 10. The Roosevelt Post Office housed a hardware store and café in the back. When Kate and Jack walked in, they were informed by the four farmers playing dominos and eating sandwiches that the cook had taken the day off, but to go ahead in the kitchen and make their own lunch—just put some money in the jar on the way out. It was the highlight of their trip, and Roosevelt became a regular stop when traveling through the Trans-Pecos. To their delight, they had yet to visit the cafe when it *wasn't* the cook's day off. A warm feeling welled up inside, and Kate wished more than anything that she were traveling to Iowa with Jack and Kenya instead of eating dust in Montana.

The phone booth was occupied, and someone was waiting. Kate walked around the square. She did not have a good feeling about Nate's no-show and wished she had brought his phone number.

Maybe her worry was unfounded. Ida didn't seem all that concerned about Nate's absence. Her anger was simply directed at the messengers for not delivering the note sooner.

Suddenly the squealing of a squad car as it peeled out of the station and made a sharp right turn down the highway, brought Kate out of her ruminations. She watched the car disappear in a dust cloud.

Finally, the last caller left the booth, and Kate tried Jack's cell.

"Hello." Jack sounded cheerful.

"Are you driving?" Kate said.

"Hey, sweetheart. No, just stopped for coffee. It's a glorious day for traveling and I'd give my favorite fungo bat to have you with us."

"You've been reading my mind," Kate said, feeling that emotional tug even more strongly. "I was just thinking about the Roosevelt Cafe and wondering if the cook has had any time off lately."

At the sound of Jack's laughter, Kate wanted to reach through the phone lines and plant a kiss on his cheek.

"Maybe we can make it back after the season, spend some time in the Texas Hill Country."

"I'll hold you to that. What's your plan of attack with your young pitcher?"

"I'm buying him dinner tonight. See if I can find out what's going on. If I can't, I'm afraid the boy will get a one-way ticket to double-A."

"Sounds serious," Kate said.

"Afraid so. I'll keep you posted. Any idea yet who killed Ida's son?"

"That's the sheriff's job. I'm staying focused on the dam project."

"Uh-huh. Have you forgotten who you're talking to? I know better. Just don't get shot or poisoned, or do anything that takes years off my life."

"I'm on my way to visit an organic farm and then I'm going to prepare my presentation for the town-council meeting. Sound good to you?"

"You have my approval, but you could find trouble in church. Be safe and remember to call. Getting any sleep?"

Kate heard the concern in his voice. Jack did his best to understand Kate's complexities. She imagined him solidly rooted to the earth, having lived eons of past lives. He accepted human frailties as effortlessly as breathing. He passed no judgment and accepted whatever baggage Kate carried.

"Snippets here and there. Keep my place in the car warm. Love you."

"Love you, too."

Less than a mile north of Two Horse, Highway 310 skirted around a mountain slope, bringing into view the vast plains below. To the east, the Big Horn River sliced through Big Horn Canyon, and the Pryor Mountain Range appeared less than forty miles to the north. Along the eastern ridge, the forest that Pete Bear Walks Slowly had spoken of the previous night grew thick and green. It provided the Brown Birds with their livelihood. Their small teepee company suddenly seemed insignificant in the scheme of things. Ranchers needing land for cattle, the Crow leasing the rights to extract what was beneath—Kate doubted that this small company, striving to hang on to a piece of their culture, could have any influence on the election.

Kate felt awkward about arriving at the Nelsons' farm without an invitation. But her trepidation was dispelled when she parked along a fence line with a "Visitor's Parking" sign nailed to a post. Along the side of the house, a string of fruit and vegetable stands sat barren from winter's respite except for one. The sign that hung from the shingled roof of this stand said "Hothouse Vegetables and Herbs." Nestled in wooden boxes below were the healthiest, most succulent produce and fresh herbs that Kate had ever seen. Her stomach began to rumble as she visualized a plate of sliced tomatoes and cucumbers covered in chopped oregano and drizzled with olive oil. The biscuits and gravy she had eaten for breakfast sat in the bottom of her stomach like an anchor. And with her twisted ankle, she hadn't been able to jog off her breakfast. Before she left the Nelsons' farm, she planned to buy something to offset the food on the Springfield's high-cholesterol table.

Kate looked around and noticed a brass cowbell

hanging from an archway where wisteria had woven its way through the latticework. Another sign, this one painted with bluebells, read "Ring for Service." Kate gave the bell cord a tug and then walked under the trestle and into a small garden. Red brick paths wound around plots of rosemary, lavender, and other herbs that didn't need the protection of a greenhouse. Wooden benches and rocking chairs were spaced around the garden, and Kate could picture herself sitting there enjoying a glass of wine in the evening.

Several minutes passed, and Kate considered ringing the bell again. The place looked deserted. She glanced at her watch and decided to give the Nelsons a few more minutes. She reminded herself that people in the country moved slower than city folk, so she took advantage of the wait to study the variety of herbs growing in this luscious garden.

Kate gently rubbed her fingers over a velvety stalk of rosemary and held her hand to her nose. Kate inhaled, allowing the rich, natural aroma to filter deep into her lungs.

"No better smell than fresh rosemary."

A soft tenor-voice floated across the air, and Kate turned to see her host. A sixty-something man dressed in pressed khakis and a starched white shirt greeted her with a handshake. "Ed Nelson. I'm afraid we don't have much to offer yet, just items we grow in our greenhouse. We'll have these stands full in a couple of weeks."

His welcoming smile shone full and natural. His eyes matched the color of the tiny buds on the rosemary bush—a vibrant violet, too striking to be real. Thinning gray-blond hair cut close to the scalp and a well-sculptured goatee gave him a look of an artist rather than a farmer.

"Hello, Mr. Nelson. I was just salivating over your produce. I'm Kate Caraway. Ida may have mentioned me."

Kate detected a slight wane in his smile, which broadened again, but not quick enough to alert her of his misgiving.

"I hope I didn't come at a bad time," Kate said.

"Nonsense. People drop in all the time. That's why we're here. Ida said you'd advise us on our cause."

"I can offer moral support and maybe speak for the mustangs. I'm not sure about advice."

"Oh, I remember now. You're active into animal rights. You have the elephant preserve in Africa."

"Yes, I'm sort of on a sabbatical."

"Oh?"

Kate wasn't sure if the look on Ed's face was confusion or disappointment. "Don't worry," she said. "It's still up and running. I'm just here for the time being."

"Come on in. Can I offer you some coffee?"

"Sounds great."

Ed Nelson led her to a screen door of an enclosed porch. Louver windows were open slightly, letting in fresh air. The room was furnished with hand-painted furniture and hook rugs. Oil paintings of fruits and vegetables hung on the wall. Upon closer inspection, Kate saw that there was indeed an artist in the family, but it wasn't Ed. Lucy Nelson's signature was in the bottom-right corner of each painting.

"I'll be right back with the coffee. I just made a fresh pot. Cream or sugar?"

"Cream only. Thanks."

Kate sat down in a white ladder-back rocker with green and purple grapevines painted from the base of the back frame up to the round knobs at the top. A purple cushion covered the seat. A similarly painted Deacon's bench held a plethora of photos. Younger Nelsons posed on a ski slope.

A woman, whom Kate assumed was Lucy, sat perched on an outcropping of rock above a tidal pool. Ed on horseback, a mountain range in the background. Then Kate noticed a photo of middle-aged woman, probably Lucy, and a young girl standing arm-in-arm, smiling, their heads together.

A couple of minutes later, Ed came out carrying a tray with two cups and a ceramic cream pitcher in the shape of a Holstein.

"I hope you don't mind if we visit out here. It's a beautiful day, and—well, Lucy has a migraine."

"I'm really sorry, Mr. Nelson. I can come back another time."

"Call me Ed. Won't hear of it, and neither would Lucy."

"I get those every now and then. Makes me want to crawl into a cave until the nightmare is over," Kate said. "I can sympathize."

"She'll be all right. This entire thing about the dam has really caused her a lot of stress."

"Ida said that the dam will alter the flow of your creeks as well, providing less water for your crops."

"That's right. We've owned this farm for a little more than ten years and it's been touch-and-go since day one. Every organic farmer knows that one bad year, or some new regulations—and we have a string of them regarding our organic status—can turn the place on its ear."

"The county isn't concerned with keeping your business going? Seems like you have a sizable place that offers jobs for quite a few people."

"Lucy and I have a little over a hundred acres. We do hire a substantial number of folks during harvest and keep a handful on during the rest of the year. But this is ranch country, and ranchers rule, as the saying goes. Our mayor is a rancher. See that land to the left of our spinach field?"

Kate looked to where he pointed over his shoulder. The thin barbed wire that divided the two tracts seemed invisible compared to the color contrast. Lush green fields of the Nelson farm offset the brown land next to it.

"That's Mayor Winford's ranch. He runs about five hundred head of cattle."

"Isn't he concerned with the water issue?"

"Yes, but he has the money to drill wells for his water, and he professes to make that financial sacrifice if needed to help out ranchers in Carbon County."

"A real politician."

"Right, and he makes us look like cutthroats because we won't follow suit. The cost of drilling our own water wells would break us."

"Looks busy over there," Kate said. She did not see any cattle, but several vehicles were parked in front of what looked like a new barn. A crew was replacing old fencing and a surveyor's tripod stood next to a black pickup parked in the middle of the pasture.

Ed reluctantly turned and looked. "Clyde's not known for sitting on his butt, wasting time. He's already making changes fast and furious."

"Maybe with a strong opposition rally you can

convince enough people to vote against the dam, especially if alternatives can be offered. I may be able to help in that regard. I spoke to Pete Bear Walks Slowly yesterday and he plans to be at the meeting on Tuesday. He is concerned about the—"

Before Kate could continue, she was stopped by the look of surprise on Ed's face.

"Pete's here in Two Horse?" he said.

"Yes. Is something wrong?"

Ed sat down his coffee cup. "No, no, nothing's wrong. I thought he was lobbying in Washington this week and wouldn't be able to attend. I'm glad he's back. You're right, we need all the help we can get." Ed looked around as if he had expected to find Pete Bear Walks Slowly creeping up on them from behind a garden hedge.

They sat for several moments without speaking. Finally, he stood up and walked into the kitchen. He came out with the coffee pot and refilled Kate's cup.

"Ms. Caraway—"

"Kate."

"Kate, I need to be frank with you. Lucy and I have been talking a lot about this issue. We've been wondering if it's worth the fight. Maybe it's time to sell and retire. Take things easy for a change."

They had not spoken of Frank Springfield's murder, but Kate wondered if the incident had something to do with the Nelsons' change of heart.

"Ida and Pete will be disappointed. They need as much support as they can get."

Ed looked across his lush fields, and Kate knew for certain that retirement and selling this farm was not a pleasant alternative.

"Lucy and I just want to be prepared. We will do

what we can to help. But the task seems insurmountable."

"I wish you luck with your decision," Kate said for lack of anything else, then added. "I hope you'll be at the meeting."

"Sure, we'll be there." He set his cup on the end table and stood. Kate took the hint and saved Ed Nelson from coming up with a reason to end the visit.

"Thanks for your time. I'm on my way to meet Karen Gregory at the national park's south location. I'm afraid I'm going to be late."

"Take the short cut through the Pryor Mountain Wild Horse Range. You'll see the sign a mile up the road. It'll save you about an hour's drive. And it's a lot more scenic than the highway."

"Thanks, I will."

Kate placed two large grocery sacks full of tomatoes, cucumbers, onions, cilantro, and parsley on the front seat of the pickup. She had to shove a ten-dollar bill into Ed's hand. He did not want the money. Her willingness to come to Montana was payment enough. As Kate walked around to the driver's side, out of the corner of her eye she noticed movement from a second-story window.

When she looked up, a white eyelet curtain quickly dropped back into place, but not before the split-second image solidified in Kate's brain. The face in the window was red and swollen. Migraines had certainly brought Kate to tears on occasion, but something about Lucy Nelson seemed different from the Lucy in the photos. The feeling she had earlier of intruding on the Nelsons suddenly became stronger.

****

The drive through the western entrance of the wild horse range was spectacular.

Tall golden grass danced in the breeze, creating undulating shadows across the valley. Kate was less than a mile into the preserve when a small band of horses, grazing just off the road, raised their heads and watched as she drove by. Even through the tall grass, their telltale zebra-striped legs, genetic markings unique to the species, were visible. Kate slowed, eased the truck onto the shoulder, and parked. Keeping her eyes on the mustangs, she slid her camera from its case, clicked on her telephoto lens, and snapped several shots before her subjects became fidgety and trotted away. Feeling guilty about the intrusion, Kate wrestled the gearshift into first and continued on her way.

Within minutes, she came upon a monstrous yellow sign with black letters, warning drivers to slow as they approached Devil Canyon Overlook. Kate stopped again and pulled a map from her backpack. Damn! Ed had failed to mention her short cut included a steep mountain road. Kate prayed for one long mountainside lane she could hug all the way down. She stepped from the truck and walked to the overlook. This was not her lucky day. An eight-foot high battered chain-link fence with yellow flashing lights separated Kate from the canyon floor a thousand feet below. The one-lane gravel switchback road was carved out of the mountain face. On the way back to the pickup, Kate cursed the engineer who had the gall to blaze this vertigo-inducing trail. Just standing so close to the cliff made her lightheaded. Even if she were not afraid of heights, she did not trust Ida's old rattletrap pickup to maneuver the sharp, steep turns.

Kate walked back to the truck and spread the map

on the hood to look for another route. She'd have to backtrack through the preserve and take the highway south of Two Horse into northern Wyoming and through the town of Lovell, a two-hour delay at the least. Although keeping an appointment was high on Kate's priority list, there was no way in hell she was driving this road.

As she folded the map, she heard the whine of a vehicle approaching from the preserve. A black one-ton Chevy Avalanche with *GS&E, LMT* stenciled on the door slowed and stopped next to her. The dark-tinted window on the passenger side slid down.

"You're a brave woman if you're planning to drive that heap of metal down the mountain." A huge man with sandy-colored hair and skin to match hung his arm out the window. The rest of his body filled the entire passenger side.

"Actually, I'm a coward," Kate admitted. "It's not the condition of the truck. But thanks for giving me a face-saving excuse for turning around."

"I'm Lloyd Stenson." He pressed his huge body back into the seat as far as he could. With his thumb, he pointed to the driver. "This is my partner Alan Miles."

"Kate Caraway."

"Where're you headed?"

"To the Big Horn ranger station."

"We'll take you down, if you like."

Now a true cowardly feeling fluttered in Kate's stomach. She did not want to admit to these strangers that even as a passenger, the trip down would transform her from a mature, intelligent adult into a whimpering child.

Lloyd Stenson opened the door and heaved himself out. Kate took a good look at his oversized pickup and swallowed hard.

"I go through this drill all the time with my daughter. No matter how many times she does it, it never gets easier. I'll drive you down in our truck and Alan will drive yours."

"If you don't mind me saying so, your truck looks wider than that road."

"The bumper hangs over the edge on the turns, but the tires never leave the gravel. I promise."

"What if a car meets us on the way down?"

"Folks from around here know the rules of the road. You have a good look before you take off. If another vehicle approaches from the opposite direction, the drivers signal to one another. The one at the top has the right-of-way and the one at the bottom waits. In case you miss seeing someone, you honk around each turn."

To refuse his offer would be silly. They would be at the bottom of the canyon in ten minutes and Kate would be in Karen's office shortly thereafter.

Alan was already walking back from the overlook. "It's all clear. Just enjoy the view," Alan said. "We'll be down before you know it."

Easy for you to say, Kate thought. Jack had driven her down steeps roads before. Nothing she ever did kept her from panicking. Closing her eyes, taking in the scenery, listening to Jack tell jokes, nothing distracted her from the terror that overtook her mind and body.

"Let's get this over with," Kate said, trying to sound gracious.

"Alan will go first and we'll follow. I don't want the brakes to go out on that wreck while it's behind me."

Kate didn't need to hear that. She buckled herself into the passenger seat and laid her head against the headrest. Her palms started to sweat before they approached the first switchback. Lloyd kept quiet, and Kate tried to keep her whimpers to an audibility that only she could hear. Then Alan hit the horn around the first turn, and Kate let out a mousy squeak. Both vehicles were traveling no more than five miles per hour. Kate could hear the crunch of gravel under the tires as the transmission of this giant hunk of machinery protested in low gear. Kate started counting in her head. In ten minutes, or six hundred seconds, they should be at the bottom. Before the first minute ticked away, Kate gave up the effort. Her rapidly beating heart was out of sync with her counting. Vertigo symptoms assaulted her one after the other—dry mouth, racing heartbeat, ringing ears, clammy skin. She had to remind herself to breathe, but her lungs seemed frozen. She gripped the leather seat and leaned toward the mountain, as if that gesture would keep the pickup on the road. Her feet pressed hard on imaginary brakes—insane behavior, but she was no longer rational.

Alan sounded the horn again at the second turn. Now she'd be on the outside just inches from the edge. Her body instinctively leaned toward the mountain again. Kate heard Lloyd chuckle. *Let him laugh*, she thought. *He's going to think it's funny when he gets to the bottom and has a heart-attack victim on his hands.* Her breathing seemed too shallow to keep her body functioning. She closed her eyes and forced herself to draw in deep breaths. Along with them came sickly groans. Kate was beyond embarrassment, beyond dignity. She was in survival mode. Honk number three came. They were back on the mountainside. As best as she could figure, they were about a quarter of the way down. Counting the honks was something she could do to occupy her mind.

Then about two-thirds of the way down, the sound of the horn changed. It was also out of sequence, and Kate was certain that it did not come from Ida's pickup. Before she could make sense of what was happening, Lloyd Stenson uttered an expletive under his breath.

"Damn fool."

"What?" Kate said.

"Tourist. He should have seen us and waited at the bottom. I hope he realizes he's going to have to back down."

At the announcement, Kate heard Miles shouting. She blinked her eyes open for a split second, and terror took a tighter hold. Peeking out from behind the next turn was the nose of an RV.

"That idiot is not supposed to have that giant contraption on this road," Lloyd said through clenched teeth.

Kate closed her eyes again. She heard Miles climb from Ida's truck. More voices, then the sound of his boots as he walked up to the company pickup.

"He can't back down, and we're not backing up," Alan said. "He's pulling over as close to the mountain as he can, and we're going to inch around him."

"You've got to be kidding!" Kate couldn't believe what she was hearing.

"It's okay," Lloyd said. "The road is a little wider here, sort of a lookout point. You'll be on the outside. Just keep your eyes closed."

Kate's fear turned to anger—at herself for being talked into this, at Lloyd Stenson for seeing the worst side of her, and at the stupid driver of the RV.

"His side mirrors are pushed in. This lady's truck doesn't have any. Stay put, Lloyd. I'll get yours."

"Holy shit," Kate said. She hoped with all her might that she would pass out—heart attack, stroke, shock—anything to render her unconscious. Lloyd gunned the motor and they started moving again. In her unnatural state of mind, Kate felt the right side of her body sliding off into oblivion.

A sudden reflex, born out of curious fear—the same type of fear that sends a person down into a dark basement on a stormy night to investigate a mysterious sound—caused Kate to open her eyes. It was no joke. The right side of the front bumper hung over the edge and the world below her opened into nothingness.

Then Kate heard Lloyd's words somewhere amidst the ringing in her ears. "Not too bad, was it?"

She must have remained conscious but had managed to go somewhere created by a panic-induced memory block. They were parked at the bottom of the cliff. Kate opened her eyes and then the door. She needed cold air. Lloyd handed her a bottle of water.

"You better sit here for a minute. You're as white as a palomino, but you did good. I didn't need to break open my ammonia pill."

The funny thing about vertigo was that when it was over, one's body was pumped with so much adrenaline, it was like experiencing a high. Embarrassment gone, courage and dignity returned, Kate wanted to throw her arms wide open and celebrate.

Alan Miles readjusted the side mirrors while Lloyd Stenson checked the tires on Ida's truck. "You might want to have this left front tire checked. It's too worn to be safe on any road. In fact, I'm surprise it's made it this far.

"The spare is not much better," Miles said. "I can change it for you. You should be good until you get back to town."

At the moment, Kate was not interested in Ida's tires. She just wanted to breathe, taking in precious air, as if she had just popped her head above water after a long swim. She walked to the other side of Ida's truck, happy to feel her feet on the ground. Kate looked at the tire in question. The guy was right. Some of the thread had already separated.

"Are you sure you don't mind?" Kate said. "I'm in no hurry. My ears are still ringing."

"No problem. I'll get right to it."

"Coming from Two Horse," Stenson said. "You're probably not a tourist. Most tourists don't know this short cut."

"I'm here on an assignment I guess you'd say."

"Now you got me curious."

"It has to do with the upcoming election involving the construction of the dam."

"You an engineer?" Stenson said.

"Not quite. I'm here to help a friend who's concerned about what the dam will do to the water supply on her ranch."

"From what I gather the number of those outspoken on each side of the issue is about the same. However, truth be told, many voters in the county aren't affected by the dam. They'll vote for whoever speaks the loudest."

"Yeah, well, I'm trying to keep my friend out of trouble. She often speaks behind the barrel of a shotgun."

"You're here on account of Ida Springfield?"

"You know her?"

"Not personally, but I've heard about some of her exploits. She's part of that grassroots movement to stop the dam?"

"She is, along with a small group of Crow who have a lot to lose, and the Nelsons, who own the organic farm north of Two Horse. They'll lose their main water supply."

"The Nelson place? That's the one next to Clyde Winford's property," said Alan. "That's a great piece of land. I hope everything works out for them. We better get going, Lloyd."

"Thanks again," Kate said. "Sorry you had to see my sniveling, cowardly side."

"Your secret's safe," Stenson said, and after a brief pause added, "Good luck with your cause. Here's my card." He chuckled. "Call if you ever need a driver."

"I'll do that."

Chapter Six

Except for a National Park Service pickup parked next to a shed in back of the ranger station/visitor center, there were no cars in the parking lot. *Too early in the season for tourists*, Kate guessed. Sticking out from behind the building, a rusty silver RV, the type that looked like a potato wrapped in foil ready for baking, was anchored by its hitch to an iron stake protruding at the edge of a concrete slab. A small satellite dish attached to the roof was the only sign of habitation. A gust of brisk wind swirled dry leaves and dirt up into the air. Kate covered her eyes and ducked inside the ranger station. Barely audible, a Nanci Griffith song told of a time that held strong in her memory.

Kate closed the door and looked around. The inside of the building was devoid of people.

The log-cabin style structure housed a gift shop in front and offices in back. Along one wall, stuffed toys filled the shelves: buffalos, wolves, bald eagles, and for sale at half-price, a misplaced orca whale. The opposite wall contained a display of nature books, puzzles, and games. Racks of T-shirts occupied most of the floor space, and a display counter at the register contained key fobs, beaded bracelets, black-stringed necklaces looped through various polished stones, and pocket knives with Big Horn Canyon burned into their wooden casings. Kate picked up a laminated bird identification chart.

"We're near the Central flyway," a perky voice spoke.

Kate heard the squeak of a chair and turned to see a young woman come out of the office. "The whooping cranes should be up from Texas soon," Kate added.

"Yep. We got word from Wood Buffalo last week, sixty-six of them in all. We're lucky to spot them though. For such a large bird they manage to fly through unnoticed—probably at night."

"Smart birds. Hi, I'm Kate Caraway."

"Thought so. Karen Gregory." Packed solidly into her brown NPS uniform, Karen Gregory stood just under five feet. Her hair, as red as a sailor's-delight sunset, cropped her freckled face just under her chin in a swing-style cut. She looked too young to be out of college. The park ranger pulled one stool from behind the register at the counter and brought another stool from her office. "We'll visit out here if you don't mind. This time of the year, we're shorthanded. Our gift-shop volunteer had to make a trip to Lovell to pick up a prescription, so I'm it until she returns. Besides, my office is stacked with paperwork, and my trailer is not exactly warm and cozy. Make yourself comfortable."

"Thanks. I'll stand. I like the idea of my feet touching the floor."

"You look a little pale. The Devil's Canyon road will do that to you. How about something to drink? It froze last night and I'm still waiting for the pipes to thaw. I can't make coffee, but I can offer you freshly canned juice from our vending machine. Let's see—there's strawberry-kiwi, papaya-peach, or plain ol' orange."

"That vending machine doesn't happen to have those little bottles of tequila, does it?"

"Sorry. I always said that an innovative entrepreneur could make a fortune with a bar at the bottom of that cliff road."

"Orange juice will be fine," Kate said.

Karen reached for a key in the register, opened the vending machine, and extracted two cans of juice.

"One of the perks of the job." She handed Kate a can. "How's Nate doing? He's really excited about you coming to help."

"That's an intense young man. He was very convincing," Kate said. "I can see where he got his passion. It runs in the family."

"His great-grandmother is some feisty old gal. It's hard to say no to her."

"Ida wants me at the council meeting on Tuesday. She has me signed up to speak on behalf of her proposed horse preserve with The Nature Conservancy. So that I don't sound like an idiot, maybe you should fill me in on the issues."

"No problem. I have the agenda here. Actually, you're not officially on the list of speakers, but you will speak in Ida's place right after me. That was my idea. We don't need a shoot-out at the old town hall."

"I heard about Ida and her shotgun," Kate said.

Karen laughed. "With Ida Springfield, life in Two Horse is far from dull. I want you to talk about the importance of breeding populations and the benefits of genetic diversity. Regardless of what you hear, folks are interested in the wild horses, at least those on the preserve. The Big Horn Canyon Recreational Area averages two hundred thousand visitors a year, and the Pryor Mountain Wild Horse Range is part of the attraction. Some of that money is starting to trickle into

Two Horse. So, despite what Ida says, there are ranchers around who are interested in conservation."

"That's encouraging," Kate said. "Those are the ones whose attention we have to grab. What about Ida's herd? It seems she and Nate are the only ones interested in their well-being."

"I'm interested, but from a genetic aspect. If something happened to the Pryor Mountain herd, we'd have another gene pool right at our fingertips. I'll introduce the topic at the meeting, and maybe you could give supporting statistics that would hold weight with these people. Nate gave me one of your papers to read, and you have a way of making something technical and complex easy to understand."

"I brought stats from my research. I also did some reading. Equines are not much different from pachyderms. Their mating rules guard against inbreeding."

"Exactly." Karen sat up straight and continued. "There's still so much to learn about these wild horses. They may prove invaluable for improving the stamina of domestic species. The wild ones are able to withstand severe weather conditions. And because of their compact size, they require less food than the domestic variety. I envision a breeding program that will build a better horse, so to speak. The NPS is not into breeding, and there are no funds for this type of research. My boss and I argue a lot about this issue. He thinks my work here is useless."

"Ida mentioned your Wild Horse Society," Kate said. "but she didn't go into detail."

"George Stokes, my boss—he's stationed at the headquarters near the reservoir—is an old-time NPS character and has barely tolerated my extracurricular activity. The time will come when I'll have to make a choice. As for now, I want to be sure that each and every wild horse is protected. By the way, have you spoken to Nate today? That young man was supposed to stop by last night and help me finalize a list of volunteers to work the gathering on Wednesday."

Kate smiled at the twig calling the sprout a seed. Karen seemed close to Nate's age, no more than two or three years older.

"Change of plans. He was supposed to arrive this morning, but something came up. How many volunteers do you need? It's been a while since I've been on a horse, but I can keep my butt in the saddle."

"Ida has eighteen horses, four families. At least half a dozen riders should be enough to corral them. Once they're rounded up, we need experienced cowhands to herd them into the squeeze-chute for vaccinations and blood testing. Two other rangers from the parks service, Daniel and Ted Little Coyote, they're Meg's sons— she's the volunteer who works here—should be able to handle the testing, but I'd like a couple more riders. We haven't gathered horses using this roundup method in a while. It can be tricky. But I need Nate. He has a way with Ida's horses. It's sort of a mixed blessing."

"What do you mean?" Kate asked.

"Ida's horses are used to Nate. He's managed to get the less skittish ones to eat out of his hand. Not exactly tame, but they don't spook as easy as they should. Their being used to people will help at the gathering, but human familiarity is not really good for wild animals, as I'm sure you know."

"Is that why this gathering is different?"

"Most gatherings usually involve a large number of horses spread over several hundred acres. We used to hire wranglers, but that really stressed the horses and it took too long. The animals were worn to a frazzle. Now we use skilled helicopter pilots who can get the job done in a fraction the time and with hardly any stress or injury to the horses."

"Why not use the helicopters now?"

"Ida's herd is small and there are too many narrow canyons for choppers to be effective. Besides, these horses are on private land. Stokes is mad enough that I'm using park horses and employees. The idea of paying for helicopters to gather Ida's horses was out of the question."

"The gathering still sound risky."

"It is, that's why we need Nate here."

"Any thoughts on what might happen to them if the dam's built?"

"They'll have to be moved, no doubt about it. Nate and I have spoken many times about this. He's pleaded for us to take the horses, but the preserve is at maximum capacity. In fact, we have to cull about fifteen horses each year—put them up for adoption. Not long ago, I wrote a proposal to acquire more land. We had a chance to pick up one hundred and fifty acres north of the preserve, but Stokes procrastinated too long and someone else bought it. To tell you the truth, I don't think that proposal ever made it off his desk. If we'd gotten that acreage, we could've taken Ida's horses, no problem."

"How about putting Ida's horses up for adoption? I don't like being pessimistic, but she needs to look at alternatives."

"Easier said than done. Adoption can lead to more problems," Karen said. "Many folks feel sorry for the animals, but they don't know beans about caring for them. We're very careful in our adoption process. But we don't have the resources to follow up on the conditions of the horses after they leave the preserve. Ida doesn't either. We try our best to screen applicants, but occasionally the horses end up in the wrong hands and sold to PMU factories. I'd sooner shoot them than let that happen."

"Pregnant mares' urine—an industry that uses equine urine for the production of estrogen replacement drugs—I've heard of it. The conditions in those factories are atrocious. The mares are repeatedly impregnated and forced for weeks on end to stand in 'pee lines' for urine collection.

"That's not the worst of it. Due to the poor condition of the mothers, the foals are born weak and underdeveloped. When that happens, they're usually clubbed to death." Karen's face flushed and she paused a moment to let the image settle in. "The urine quality is not dependent on the mares being adequately nourished, so when the mares are too emaciated and frail to reproduce, they're sent to slaughter pens. But in their weakened condition, they usually die before they can be humanely destroyed."

"Aren't these horses under the protection of the BLM, even after adoption?"

"Who's going to check? Actually, once they leave the preserve, the government has no claim to them. Private adoption agencies try to place the horses on suitable ranches, but in Ida's case, we're talking about eighteen animals. That's a huge project, and even with the best intentions, follow-up is almost impossible. Nate hates the adoption idea. He's such a bleeding heart. Splitting up Ida's herd, to him, is like separating a group of siblings."

"And if they're not adopted?"

"They'll be shot. I need to be honest with you, Kate. Part of the problem on Ida's ranch is her own fault. Since I came to work here I've been trying to get Ida to consider what would happen to those mustangs if this drought continues. She argued that droughts had always been a factor. She never listened until the dam threatened to cut off her water supply. So we're having to work fast. Had we tested those mustangs months ago, we'd have more time now to consider options. Nate finally got through to her with The Nature Conservancy idea. He's the only person Ida listens to." Karen's expression suddenly changed from frustration to surprise. "I just heard about Frank Springfield's murder."

"Ida thinks he had it coming," Kate said. "His womanizing finally caught up with him."

Karen hesitated. "Frank had quite a reputation."

"Maybe Ida's right, but I couldn't help but think that his murder had something to do with the dam," Kate said. "Was Frank influential enough to cause someone to want him out of the way?"

"The election is a very hot topic. Both sides have lots to lose or lots to gain. I don't think Frank's murder will change anyone's mind about how they would vote."

"Murder's a personal thing. If someone thought Frank's actions were a betrayal, that might be motive enough for wanting him dead."

Just then the door opened and a hefty woman bounced in. "You must be talking about Frank

Springfield. Sorry I'm late, Karen, but I got caught up in the chitchat at the Lovell Drugstore. Seems like everyone in Carbon County has a theory on why that guy was killed. Talk about getting caught with your pants down. Sounds like the scorn of an angry woman to me." The woman took off her coat and made herself at home behind the register. She didn't wait for Karen to introduce her. "I'm Meg Little Coyote. You must be that animal-rights person from Chicago. Everyone's talking about you too."

"This is Kate Caraway, Meg," Karen said.

"Well, Kate Caraway, I, for one, am glad you're here. Some people don't like the idea of a stranger nosing into our business, but, hey, that's been happening since the white men got here, right?" There was no malice, only humor in her voice.

Karen stood up. "I'll walk you to your car, Kate."

On the way out the door, Karen brought the conversation back to the topic of most immediate concern. "Tell Nate to call me as soon as he comes in. I want to be sure everything goes well on Wednesday. We only get one shot at corralling those mustangs. They can't be tricked toward that enclosure a second time unless Nate can lure them with his charm."

"I understand," Kate said. "And I'm looking forward to the gathering. See you at the meeting?"

"I'll be there."

****

Kate arrived back at Ida's around four. Her head spinning with information from her talk with Karen Gregory, she did not notice the sheriff's patrol car leaving Ida's cabin until it pulled up beside her. It slowed to a stop and waited for Kate's vehicle to do the same.

"I just wanted to warn you. That woman's madder than a cornered rattlesnake," Sheriff Phillips allowed.

"Why, what happened?"

"I'll let her tell you. You think you had a bad night here on Friday? Just wait. Remember there's the Days Inn about ten miles out on the way to Red Lodge." He guffawed and drove away.

Veda was sitting in the front-porch rocking chair with Luisa Miller curled up in her lap.

"Sister's mad," Veda announced. Her red sneakers pumped away, rocking the chair back and forth as if the motion could clear the tension in the cabin.

"I heard," Kate said. "Is sister inside?"

"Yep. She's in the kitchen. I don't like the kitchen," Veda said, staring into another world.

Kate heard the clatter and clanging as soon as she opened the cabin door.

"I'm coming in," Kate shouted above the noise and slowly pushed open the kitchen door. "I'm on your side, remember."

Kate set her bag of vegetables and herbs down on the table.

"What's that?" Ida snapped as if Kate had delivered a bag of trouble.

"Veggies from the Nelsons. What happened? I spoke to the sheriff on the way in."

Ida looked inside the bag as if the thought of eating from the bottom of the food chain was a sin against nature. "They found Frank's truck on a back road in my canyon. Seems as if he had been snooping around my ranch the day he was killed." She pulled out a bunch of parsley and sniffed.

"It's great in boiled potatoes," Kate said, wondering

84

how the Springfield twins managed to live so long while surviving on fats and carbs. "So, he was killed here on the ranch?"

"Looks like it. He came in the back way, north of the canyon. That no-good-bastard. And that idiot sheriff's looking for Nate." Then in a quieter voice, Ida added, "Seems Nate was in Frank's truck the day Frank was killed."

"Nate's here in Two Horse?"

"They found his boarding pass under the front seat. He's been here since Thursday."

"Why haven't you heard from him?"

Ida threw the bunch of parsley in the sink. "I don't know what the hell's going on."

"Nate must know about Frank's murder. Is he a suspect?"

"My great-grandson wouldn't hurt a goddamn fly if it landed on his nose." Ida pulled a knife from a drawer and slammed it on the counter. "I don't want to talk about it." She picked some potatoes from a basket under the sink and started scrubbing each one under the faucet.

Kate helped prepare the evening meal. Neither she nor Ida said much. While Ida deep-fried a chicken and put the potatoes to boil, Kate made a salad with the fresh herbs she'd brought from the Nelson farm. By the time they placed the meal on the small dining room table, Ida looked every year her age.

Kate avoided the fried chicken, and Veda avoided the salad, staring at it as if it were something from another world. Ida ate very little. As soon as they finished, she told Veda to go to her room. Veda gave Kate a menacing look on the way out as if her preparation of the salad were the reason Ida was upset.

As soon as they were alone, Ida put an old recording of Madame Butterfly on the phonograph, reached into the bottom drawer of the hutch, and retrieved a bottle of Southern Comfort. The sound of Caruso's voice was barely audible over the scratches on the record. Then Ida set two juice glasses on the table. Without asking Kate if she would like to partake, Ida poured a goodly amount of whiskey into each glass and handed one to Kate.

"Nate tried to give me a newfangled record player with those little records, but I wouldn't have it," Ida said as she slumped back in her chair. "Where could Nate be?"

"Maybe he's with a friend," Kate offered.

"Maybe."

"Ida, did Nate have much to do with Frank?"

Ida sipped her drink and thought for a moment. "Nate and Frank weren't really close, but they did stay in touch. After all, Frank was the boy's grandfather." She tossed down the rest and slammed her glass on the table. Tears formed in her eyes, and Kate was certain they were not due to the sting of the whiskey.

"Nate could be in a lot of trouble. We have to find him. Did Sheriff Phillips sound like he was going to arrest Nate?"

"He said Nate was wanted for questioning. But we know what that means." Ida covered her eyes with the palms of her hands. "Nate would never kill anyone."

Kate heard the conviction in Ida's voice, but sensed the fear her determination could not hide.

"I can go into town and start calling some of Nate's friends," Kate said. "Surely someone has seen him. Can you give me some names?" After a long silence, Kate realized Ida was not up for action at this moment. Kate sipped her drink and respected Ida's need to think. Kate was surprised at the sweet taste. Whiskey was not on her libation list.

"Anytime Nate's in trouble, he always comes to me. I don't mean bad trouble. Nate's never been in bad trouble. Today is Sunday. He's been here for three days, and I ain't seen hide nor hair of him."

Reasons for Nate's absence ran through Kate's mind. Maybe it was something as innocent as finishing midterms early and coming to town to visit friends. But surely Nate knew of Frank's murder by now. If he had seen his grandfather on Thursday, maybe Nate was too frightened to come forward. Or maybe Nate killed Frank.

"The devil's gonna have his day," Ida said. "I've been a mean ol' woman, and God's not going to allow me to escape this world unpunished." Ida had poured herself a second glass.

"I don't think God works that way, Ida," Kate said.

"No matter. When Nate was little, I never held my tongue. I had no qualms about bad-mouthing Colter or Frank. I wanted Nate to be different. After he came to stay with us, I thought I was doing him good by telling him how rotten his grandfather and great-grandfather were."

"Nate's a fine young man, Ida. He has a good head on his shoulders."

"Then why in the hell is he hiding out somewhere with the law on his tail?" She slumped back in her chair and covered her face with her hands.

"Tell me about Nate's parents," Kate said.

"Nate was only seven when Reese died. He wasn't in Iraq one week before he was killed."

"And Nate's mother?"

"Sarah couldn't cope after Reese died. She wasn't all that stable to begin with. Took an overdose of pills. Nate was twelve."

"Damn," Kate said.

"Nate moved in with us. Two crazy old women. What the hell do we know about raising a boy?"

"Whatever trouble Nate's gotten into might not have been his doing," Kate offered. "We need to find him first before we start making rash assumptions." She stood up and put the cork back in the bottle. "Do you have any aspirin, Ida?"

"In the bathroom medicine cabinet. Got a headache, honey?"

"No, but you will in the morning if you don't take some now. Get some rest." Kate helped Ida from the chair. To Kate's surprise the old woman did not argue. Kate washed Ida's glass and refilled it with water. She found the aspirin bottle and handed it to Ida on her way to her bedroom.

With both sisters ensconced in their rooms, Kate went back into the kitchen to clean up. She scraped the plates clean and laughed when she noticed Ida and Veda had both picked the parsley out of their potatoes. *What a family*, Kate thought. The Springfields were straight out of the soaps. At sixteen, Ida marries into a wealthy ranch-family and becomes pregnant. When her parents died, Ida and her abusive, alcoholic husband take custody of Ida's mentally challenged twin. Feeling too burdened, Ida's husband leaves, Ida's son grows up, hating his mother, and for the next fifty years Ida and Veda cocoon themselves on their ranch. Then a great-grandson comes along, loses his parents, and the only other male in the family is found with a knife in his back.

In the midst of all this chaos, a wildlife biologist blows into town and was supposed to help this family keep their wild mustangs. Kate laughed out loud. Though a PhD, she was not the type of doctor this family needed.

****

When Ida stepped into the kitchen the next morning, she looked worse than she had the night before. It was seven-thirty, and Kate had breakfast ready. A pan of migas was warming on the stove, and last night's boiled potatoes spruced up with chopped onions, picked free of the remaining parsley, had been metamorphosed into hash browns.

Ida shuffled over to the stove and poured herself a cup of coffee. "Aspirin came in handy," she said, sounding hoarse.

"Sweet, strong liquor is bound to bring on a hangover," Kate replied.

"Aspirin's not for me. I gave some to Veda. She has a fever. Too much excitement. With her glassy stare, she seems unbothered by things that go on around her. But she takes everything in and, when she's had too much, she takes to her bed."

"I'm sorry, Ida. What can I do to help?"

"Oh, honey. You've done so much, and we keep dishing out more shit. You made a lot of sense last night. I just wanted to drown my sorrows."

Kate walked over and gave Ida a hug. "One and a half glasses of whiskey isn't exactly a drowning."

Ida handed her a slip of paper. "Here are the names of Nate's friends. Don't stand at that ol' phone booth in town. Drive out to the Nelsons' and use their phone. If they haven't heard about Nate yet, they need to know. Hell, if Nate wouldn't come to me, he may have gone to them. Nate's worked for them every summer since his first year in high school. They're still close. I should be shot for not having my own goddamned phone."

Kate looked at Ida. Her anger and frustration from last night had given way to genuine fear.

"I need to stay here with Veda."

"Are you sure Veda shouldn't see a doctor?"

"She'll be okay. I have a pot of soup in the fridge. She likes soup." Ida chuckled. "I told her if she took her aspirin, she could have some soup. She looked scared and wanted to know if you made it. She's gonna have nightmares every time she sees little green specks in her food."

"I've surely lost a friend," Kate said.

"She'll get over it," Ida assured Kate. "But if you really want to get back in her good graces, you can bring her back some root beer and chocolate ice cream."

"Got it," Kate said.

****

Regardless of Ida's insistence that the Nelsons did not mind unannounced visitors, Kate felt more comfortable calling ahead, especially after intruding on Lucy Nelson's migraine yesterday. As she was about to lift the receiver on the telephone in town, Sheriff Phillips walked across the square and waved. Kate put the receiver down and waited for him.

"Survive last night?" he asked.

Kate became annoyed at his cavalier attitude towards Ida's troubles. "I came away unscathed, but Ida's very upset, and Veda's sick." She immediately regretted her accusatorial tone.

He pulled his head slightly back as if Kate had slapped him. "I have my job to do, ma'am. I just came over to tell you that if you hear from Nate, we need to be told right away. We're not messing around here."

"We're anxious to find Nate as well, and we'll let you know if we hear anything." Kate was about to go back to her phone call when she decided to turn the investigative tide and ask a couple of questions herself. "You found Nate's boarding pass in Frank's pickup. What was Nate's arrival time?"

"He came in on United at eight-oh-five Thursday morning."

"I wonder how he got to Two Horse from the airport?" Kate asked, more to herself than to the sheriff.

"We're looking into that as well. Probably a friend picked him up."

"Probably." Kate smiled and turned away.

As soon as the sheriff was out of hearing range, Kate called the airport in Billings and asked for the names and numbers of all rental car agencies there. Ten minutes later, she had her answer. Nate had rented a white Chevy Malibu from National. She looked over at the sheriff's office across the town square, but Sheriff Phillips was nowhere in sight. *Darn*, Kate thought. She'd have to keep the information to herself for now.

Chapter Seven

Kate was about to hang up the phone after the seventh ring when she heard a faint "Hello."

"Ed, I've got it here in the kitchen," a female voice said.

"Mrs. Nelson?" Kate said.

"Yes?"

"This is Kate Caraway. I was at your farm yesterday morning. I'm sorry I missed meeting you. I hope you're feeling better."

From the road noise behind her, Kate had a difficult time hearing. At first she thought that Lucy Nelson had hung up.

"Hello?" Kate said.

"Yes, yes, I'm here, Ms. Caraway. What can I do for you?"

"I hope this is not a bad time, but I need to stop by and visit with you and your husband." Kate wasn't sure how much she should say over the phone. Her conversation with Ed Nelson yesterday was slightly strained, and she had not yet met his wife face-to-face. "Ida has some concerns about Nate, and she feels that you and your husband—"

"Nate? Nate's not here." Lucy Nelson sounded annoyed.

"Do you mind if I stop by, Mrs. Nelson?" Kate asked again, raising her voice over the traffic sounds.

Again, another long pause.

"Where are you now?" she asked.

"I'm sorry. It must be hard for you to hear me. I'm at the phone booth on the town square."

"Okay, we'll be here. Park in front. I'll meet you at the front door."

****

Lucy Nelson was standing on the porch of the farmhouse when Kate drove up. Kate detected a slight curl of Lucy's upper lip at the sight of Ida's rattletrap truck. Lucy waved and pointed for Kate to pull off the brick drive and park on the gravel at the side of the house.

"I hope you don't mind parking off to the side," Lucy called from the porch as Kate walked up. "Ida's truck dripped a bit of oil yesterday when you were here."

"Sorry," Kate said. "That's a pretty old truck she's got."

"That's okay. Ed took care of it. Please come in." Lucy held open the screen door. She wore a simple, calf-length, rose-printed cotton dress under a tastefully matched cardigan. She pulled her sweater tightly around her. The day was bright and sunny, but the frigid gusts coming over the mountains cut deep and cold, whipping her loose auburn hair across her face and blowing her skirt up over her knees. "Hurry up, let's get out of this wind before we're blown off the porch. I'll never get used to it. Where I'm from, the wind is humid and warm with a heavy smell of salt."

Kate shook her hand. "I thought I detected a southern accent. Louisiana, maybe?"

"Close. Mississippi. A little town on the coast—Biloxi. At least it was a little town before Katrina nearly whipped it off the map. We were lucky compared to most people."

They stepped into what could only be described as an Early American parlor, complete with Chippendale furniture, hook rugs covering a shiny hardwood floor, and framed needlework on the walls. A collection of Royal Doulton porcelain figurines were perched neatly on a three-tiered cherry wood table. A fire was burning in the fireplace. Kate was not the collecting type, unless elephant scat preserved in labeled zip-lock bags in her old refrigerator back in Kenya counted.

"Please sit down, Kate. Ed will be in with the coffee in a moment."

This visit was clearly more formal than the chat she had had with Ed on the light, airy back porch yesterday. Kate sat on a brocade Queen-Anne chair while Lucy sat on the sofa.

"I know Biloxi well," Kate said. "My dad and I stopped there often on the way to Florida when I was little. It was a sleepy little town. And about six years ago, my husband and I hugged the Gulf coastline on the way to Atlanta. I couldn't believe the changes when we passed through Biloxi."

"To some, the casinos were a blessing. But the town grew too fast too soon, and Ed and I were ready for a change. I worked as a nurse for twenty years, and when Ed retired from the air force, we moved to Montana. It had always been our dream to run an organic farm."

Kate heard the clinking of china as Ed made his way down the hall into the formal room to join them. On a tray, he carried three blue Wedgwood china coffee cups and saucers with a matching pot, sugar bowl, and creamer. He put the tray on the coffee table, and joined his wife on the sofa, patting her knee when he sat down.

"You wanted to talk to us about Nate?" Lucy asked.

The small talk was clearly over. "Yes," Kate said. "He was supposed to fly in yesterday. Ida and I went to the airport in Billings, but he wasn't on the plane. He left a message at the sheriff's office about changing his plans, but Ida never got it."

"So when will he arrive?" Lucy said.

"Well, actually, it looks like he arrived on Thursday," Kate said.

"Oh?" the Nelsons said in unison.

"I'm afraid Nate might be in some trouble. The sheriff was at Ida's yesterday. Nate's wanted for questioning concerning Frank Springfield's murder."

"Nonsense!" Lucy stood up and walked to the fireplace. "That's ridiculous."

"Evidently Nate was with Frank the morning he was killed, and no one has seen Nate since," Kate continued. "Ida thought Nate might have contacted you."

"We haven't heard from him," Lucy said, massaging her forehead.

"Ida gave me a list of Nate's friends. Since she doesn't have a phone, she thought you wouldn't mind if I made some calls from your house."

Ed spoke first. "Not at all. You can use the phone in the dining room."

Lucy shot Ed a glance of disapproval, but quickly covered it with a smile.

"Ed, just bring the phone in here. The dining room's too cold," Lucy said.

"I'll be right back," he said and disappeared.

"And bring the phone book." Lucy called after him. "We'll help any way we can. Nate is very dear to us. Ed and I never had children, and having Nate here on the

95

farm…well—" She left the statement hanging as her expression hardened slightly and a thin film of anger appeared.

Despite this woman's Southern hospitality, Kate wasn't sure if she wanted to be left alone in the room with Lucy Nelson.

Ed returned with a portable phone, phonebook, notepad, and pen. He moved the coffee service out of the way and set up the table for Kate to work.

"Do you mind if I take a look at Ida's list? I might be able to add a name or two." Lucy pulled out a pair of reading glasses from her sweater pocket as Kate willingly shared the information.

"Matt Trouter—he worked with Nate here on the farm. But Matt's away at college in Southern California. Jim Brown Bird and Clayton Farley. They were Nate's good friends. Jim and Nate went to high school together at St. Francis Xavier Catholic Mission. Clayton went to public school. I don't think Nate kept up with Clayton much after graduation. I would start with Jim. He's your best bet."

"How about the last name of the list?" Kate asked. "A girlfriend perhaps?"

"Rachel Martin? I wouldn't bother with her. When Nate was a senior, he dated Rachel for a while. She's a couple of years younger than Nate." Lucy's forehead wrinkled. "She's still in high school but recently moved to Red Lodge to live with her mother. There was a falling out between Rachel and her father, and Rachel decided that life with Mom was more appealing. That was probably the best. Pete Bear Walks Slowly was out of town most of the time, and Rachel was always left with her older brother."

"Pete? Rachel is Pete Bear Walks Slowly's daughter?" Kate said.

"That's right," Ed said, staring into his coffee cup. "She took her mother's last name after the divorce. I guess it was sort of a rebellion thing. Rachel dated Nate for a while, but Pete didn't approve—"

Ed was cut short by Lucy's glare. "Let's start calling," Lucy said. "We're getting nowhere sitting here talking."

Kate had hoped to make the calls in private, but the Nelsons remained in the room. Twenty minutes later, Kate had no more information than when she started. Lucy was right. Matt had not been home from school since Christmas. Clayton was out, and Kate left a message with a confused younger sister who was sick and home from school. Kate repeated the Nelsons' phone number twice to the young girl but doubted that the message would get to Clayton. There was no answer at the Brown Bird household.

"Pete visited Ida a couple of days ago," Kate said. "At that time, we didn't know Nate was missing. But if Rachel isn't living with Pete, then he probably doesn't know who she's spending time with."

"That's an understatement," Lucy said with enough vehemence that told Kate that Lucy did not approve of the way Pete and his wife handled their family situation.

"Lucy," Ed said. "We don't know—"

"We know enough. Sorry, Ms. Caraway, this is a small town and everybody knows everybody else's business. Like it or not."

If Kate had suddenly reverted to Ms. Caraway, either Lucy was still feeling the effects of yesterday's migraine, or Kate's presence and assistance in these matters was becoming unwelcome. Or, maybe it Lucy was truly worried about Nate Springfield.

"Any other suggestions?" Kate asked.

Lucy and Ed exchanged looks but offered no helpful ideas. The longer Kate sat in this Southern-style parlor, the more she became convinced that things were not right in the Nelson world. Why was Ed so willing to let this place go, and accept defeat now after working so hard? Did Lucy truly share his feelings that this farm was too much for them?

"How often did Nate come home?" Kate said, deciding not to leave without something that might give her a lead.

"Usually just on holidays. He couldn't afford to fly back to Montana very often," Ed said.

"Was Ida the one who usually picked him up at the airport?"

Again more glances. Finally it was Lucy who answered, "Most of the time, but we picked him up once or twice. Why?"

"He rented a car when he arrived on Thursday, but no one has seen him," Kate said.

"Young people, you never know what they'll do." Ed's chuckle seemed feebler than his excuse for Nate's behavior. Kate's suspicions rose, and Lucy's lips tightened into a thin white line. Her nostrils flared.

Kate did not have to tell this couple that Nate was not an irresponsible youngster, or that he would not treat his great-grandmother so casually. She did not have to tell them that Nate's passion for Ida's cause came straight from his heart. It seemed obvious the Nelsons knew this as well.

Ed started to speak, but Lucy interrupted him.

"You're right. Nate knows he can come to us if he's in trouble."

Then why didn't he? Kate thought. She had to bite her lip to keep from telling Ed to grow a spine. Kate was certain as soon as she left the Nelson home, Ed would get a tongue-lashing from his wife.

Discerning that Lucy was about to end their visit, Kate reached for the porcelain coffee pot and refilled her cup. Then she walked over to the cherry wood table. Maybe if she could bring the conversation back to small talk, Ed would let slip whatever he and Lucy were skittish about. She picked up a small elephant figurine. "How long have you been collecting Lladro?"

Lucy flinched. "That's not Lladro. It's Royal Doulton. Porcelain of this quality is too refined to be manufactured by an upstart company like Lladro." She snatched the elephant from Kate's hand and replaced it on the table.

Kate stifled a giggle and sipped her coffee.

If Ida were destined to burn in hell for her ornery behavior, Kate surely would be seated on the pitchfork next to the old lady. Much to Kate's satisfaction, she managed to annoy Lucy Nelson for another half an hour by asking more about her collection. What was its origin? How long had Lucy been collecting? To reciprocate, Kate described in the most graphic detail possible her elephant-scat collection she had back in Kenya. What the different scat shades meant. How a slimy yellow sheen could mean the beginning of dysentery, and if red specs were present, bleeding of the intestine was a sure thing. Kate had just begun to expound on different scat odors, when Ed suddenly remembered an errand he had forgotten to run in town.

Except to confirm her suspicions that the Nelsons were hiding something, Kate's extended stay had produced nothing, unless postponing Lucy's lecture to Ed counted.

****

Instead of stopping at the market and going straight to Ida's, Kate decided to swing through town. She did not really expect to find a white Chevy Malibu cruising around, but it wouldn't hurt to look. There must have been a significant turn of events to bring Nate to Two Horse early, rent a car, visit his grandfather, and keep that entire mission from the person he cared about the most, his great-grandmother. There were two more people Kate wanted to speak to, the mayor, who was Frank's buddy, and Pete Bear Walks Slowly. Regardless of Lucy's insistence that Nate and Pete's daughter no longer kept in touch, Kate decided to have another talk with Pete. After all, Rachel did end up on Ida's list, and that was good enough for Kate.

Kate had been gone for less than two hours. Toting a six-pack of root beer and a half-gallon of ice cream, she stepped onto the cabin porch only to have a white-faced Ida meet her at the door.

"You were right. At our age, I can't mess around." Ida had her jacket on.

"Veda's worse?" Kate asked.

"Her fever is up to a hundred and three," Ida said.

"Oh, God. I should have come right back." *Instant karma*, Kate chided herself as shame washed over her for wasting time just for the pleasure of annoying Lucy Nelson.

"It's not your fault, honey. Veda's fever went down after the aspirin, and she fell asleep. I just checked on her about ten minutes ago, and she was boiling. I hope there's a nurse on duty."

"Let's get her bundled up and ready to go."

Convincing Veda to leave Luisa Miller was difficult, but the promise of root beer and ice cream later finally got her into the truck. Before they reached the clinic, her sweating had turned to shivers. They were in luck. A nurse was on duty, and a quick examination showed numerous white spots on Veda's throat and her blood pressure and pulse rate were alarmingly high. The nurse said that, while strep throat in a younger person was treated with a round of antibiotics and a few days home from school, strep in an eighty-two-year-old was a different matter altogether. The nurse called for the EMS to transport Veda to the hospital in Red Lodge.

Ida rode in the back of the EMS vehicle, and Kate rode shotgun. She was surprised to see Meg Little Coyote driving.

During the forty-minute trip, Meg chatted nonstop, filling Kate's ears with more than she cared to hear. Now Kate understood why Karen Gregory had quickly ushered Kate out of the visitor's center yesterday.

"Strep's been going around. Nurse Michaels was right to send Veda to Red Lodge General. Find Nate yet? Wasn't he supposed to be in town today? Karen is anxious to get that horse gathering nailed down. You think you can help sway some votes around here?" Meg said, without taking a breath.

Kate also learned that Meg liked to refer to herself as the Volunteer Queen. Not only did she pull duty at the Bighorn Canyon Visitor's Center, she was a trained EMT, and a volunteer tutor at the high school. This virtual wellspring of information was right here in the driver's seat. When Meg paused to draw a breath, Kate wasted no time with her questions. Nate's disappearance would soon be public knowledge, and Kate decided to level with Meg.

"Nate was supposed to have come in on Thursday, but Ida hasn't heard from him. I called some of his friends this morning, with no luck. Since you—"

"I know what you're about to say. Since my nose is everywhere, do I know anything?"

Kate laughed. "Something like that. Ida has her hands full right now, and I want to help as much as possible."

"So, Nate's been here since Thursday, and Ida hasn't seen him? Have you talked to Jim Brown Bird?"

"Not yet."

"He and Nate are pretty tight."

"I also wanted to speak to one of Nate's old girlfriends, Rachel Martin."

"Not possible. She's in drug rehab. At least she was."

"What do you mean?"

"Lila, her mom, checked Rachel in about two weeks ago." Meg was silent. When she spoke again, she prefaced her next bit of information with, "I run my mouth, but I don't gossip. So that's why I feel comfortable telling you this because I know for a fact it's true."

"What's true?" Kate said. She wondered how Meg defined gossip.

"First off, Pete and Lila are good people. Rachel's their youngest. Sometimes, no matter how good the parents are, the kids are just trouble. Rachel's one of those ADHD kids. Nothing seemed to work—Ritalin, counseling, nothing. Rachel just couldn't get it together.

Lila tries to keep a pretty tight leash on that girl, but since Lila's always working, it's impossible. I saw Rachel and Jim Brown Bird together—let's see—sometimes early last week."

"Here in Two Horse?"

"Yeah, here in Two Horse. I thought that it was too soon for that girl to be out of rehab. Then I heard that she had run away from the clinic."

"What day did you see them?"

They had just reached the outskirts of Red Lodge and Meg flipped on her siren to cut through the traffic. As they turned off the highway, Meg silenced the siren. "It was Wednesday, no Thursday morning—early. I remember because I was on my way to the medical center. Rachel was with Jim, and they were heading out of town. I thought about calling Lila, but I didn't want to meddle."

A best friend, an ex-girlfriend, and then a missing Nate—connecting these dots seemed too easy, and the picture was forming rapidly.

"Do you think he did it?" Meg said.

Kate knew what Meg meant. The thought of Nate stabbing his grandfather in the back was incomprehensible, but she couldn't find words at the moment. She didn't have to.

"I mean—kill Frank," Meg lowered her voice and glanced over her shoulder to see if Ida had heard. Satisfied she had not, Meg continued, "I don't think he did. Nate's just too sweet. But listen—this is common knowledge too, so I don't mind telling you—Frank and Imagene Porter had been sneaking around. Frank was really living dangerously this time. Sonny Porter, Imagene's husband, is meaner than an ornery badger.

Here we are."

Meg pulled into the emergency drive and two waiting attendants helped Veda out the back of the van. Before going inside to admit her sister, Ida handed Kate the plastic bag of melted ice cream.

Veda was soon resting in a semiprivate room. Ida made a list of things she and Veda would need. There was no telling how long Veda would be there. Kate worried that the events of the past few days had taken a toll on Ida as well. With Frank's murder, Nate's unexplained disappearance, and now Veda's illness, Kate's role of wild-horse consultant had evolved into sole caretaker of two elderly women.

Now, in between deliveries of chicken soup and ice cream, she had to find Nate before Sheriff Phillips and make sure her presentation at the town council meeting would sway enough votes to keep a herd of wild mustangs from ending up in canned dog food or spending the rest of their lives in pee lines. She wanted to ask Ida about Imagene Porter but decided to wait. Ida had too much on her plate at the moment.

"I'll be back as soon as I can," Kate said.

"Veda and I are okay," Ida said. "You don't need to hurry back. I want you to do what you can to find Nate."

Kate hesitated.

"Promise me you'll at least try," Ida said.

"Okay, I promise."

"That's why you came to Two Horse. Now get the lead out."

****

Luckily, life in Two Horse during the last hour or so had been free of emergencies. Meg was able to wait for Kate and give her a ride back to town and to Ida's truck.

Kate returned to the cabin to gather the items on Ida's list. This was the first time Kate had actually been in the sisters' bedrooms. They were not unlike her setup at her camp in Kenya—sparse and simple. What struck Kate as odd was that each room was identical—a twin bed with a once-white, but now slightly yellowed chenille bedspread with a folded olive green thermal blanket at the foot. On the opposite wall stood a pine chest-of-drawers and a matching nightstand with a simple lamp. A braided oval rug covered the hardwood floor. Several photos of Nate stood on each chest. The only difference in the furnishings was the framed picture that hung on the wall above each bed. Ida's was of a Montana landscape, and Veda's was a painting of a guardian angel watching over two little girls as they crossed a crumbling bridge.

Kate stood at the door of Veda's room. A long-forgotten image suddenly made its way into her memory. That same picture had hung in Kate's grandmother's home. Gazing at it, Kate wondered where her grandmother's picture was now. It had taken two weeks for Kate and her father to clear out Georgia Caraway's home when she died. Kate was fifteen at the time, and the task was quite burdensome and disappointing to a teenager who was forced to spend her Christmas vacation sorting, packing, and discarding possessions her grandmother had accumulated during her sixty-three years at the rickety old farmhouse outside of Austin. Kate's father had kept only a few choice pieces from the estate sale. Those treasures were in storage with Kate's own mound of stuff from her and Jack's seventeen years in Chicago. Now she wished she had paid more attention to the distribution of her grandmother's possessions.

Having that guardian angel picture hanging on her wall in Kenya would have been a good thing.

Kate shook those memories from her mind and turned to Ida's list: two changes of clothes for Ida, Veda's nightgown, sundries from the bathroom, Ida's reading glasses, and health insurance papers from a file in the desk. They were all right where Ida said they would be, an advantage to having minimal possessions. When the sisters passed on, it would take Nate hours, not weeks, to sort through his relatives' things.

Kate looked for something to pack the items in. Evidently, the sisters stayed put on the ranch because Kate could not find luggage of any type. She grabbed two large paper bags from the cabinet underneath the kitchen sink. After packing Veda's things, Kate went into Ida's room and started filling the second bag. She pulled open the second drawer of the chest and took a couple of T-shirts and a brown knit sweater that looked as old as its owner. Appearance wasn't a top priority with Ida, but Kate replaced the brown sweater and reached for a newer looking one underneath. As she picked up the gray and white tweed, a heavy object wrapped inside slid out. Kate laid the sweater down and picked up the gun. Old, but well-polished, the .38 caliber revolver must have weighed five pounds. It did not surprise Kate that tiny Ida would own a big gun. She tucked the pistol back under the layer of clothes and closed the drawer.

The last thing on Ida's list was to feed the dogs. When Kate drove up, there was only Carmen, a shy, submissive Dalmatian mix who clearly did not have the same reputation as the character she was named after, and Don G, one of the third-world dogs. But the instant Kate began rustling around in the barn, the three other dogs materialized, acting as if feeding time arrived only once a year. Just as Kate was filling the last of the bowls with dry dog food, all five mutts erupted in an earsplitting ruckus. Kate dropped the scoop and whirled around. The dogs flew out of the barn and around to the front of the cabin.

"Get down, you good-for-nothing hounds!"

A door slammed, and someone laid on the horn.

"I said get down, goddamn it!"

Kate walked out of the barn to see Mayor Winford encircled by five yapping dogs. Tosca was springing up on all fours like a kangaroo, while Luisa Miller and Carmen sniffed at the mayor's boots. Rigoletto and Don G took to the tires to mark the intruder. The mayor swatted at them with his cowboy hat, which excited the dogs even more.

Kate whistled and clapped her hands and was surprised to see the dogs settle down. That was when she noticed the other person riding shotgun.

"You're really good at that." Mayor Winford brushed dusty dog-prints from his khaki pants.

"Afternoon, Mayor." Kate had a good idea what had prompted this visit.

"While you're here, maybe you can talk that stubborn woman into getting herself a phone. A call sure would've been a hell of a lot easier than driving out to this goddamn place." He walked through the swarm of dogs, pushing and kicking as he went. The mayor pointed his thumb over his shoulder. "This is George Stokes. He's with the National Parks Service at Big Horn Canyon." The other man opened the car door and emerged, causing the canine corps to leave the mayor and scamper over for another inspection.

Karen Gregory's boss looked like a man who spent too much time on a horse. His bowed legs put a hitch in his stride, and his lower back swayed from too much pull by a sagging belly. Circling a splotchy bald spot was a crown of curly rust-colored hair that needed shampooing. Across his face, a roadmap of red blood vessels seemed to converge on his bulbous nose. At first Kate thought he was sunburned. Then she realized that he had one of the worst cases of rosacea she had ever seen.

"Hello," Kate said. "You'll be happy to know that Ida may be ready to bring some modern technology into her life. Veda became ill this morning, and Ida admitted how vulnerable they were living out here without a phone. They're at the hospital in Red Lodge."

"I know. I heard. Not much gets by me, being a mayor in a small town, you know." Then as an afterthought, he added, "Hope Veda gets to feeling better."

Yeah, right, Kate thought.

George Stokes then spoke for the first time. "We're here to help out the old woman. We figured—" He was silenced by a menacing glance from the mayor.

"What George means is, I'm willing to do something about Ida's horses. We studied the situation, and George here thinks there's a piece of property where we can relocate them."

Kate held her tongue about the reference to Ida as an old woman, and said simply, "And where's that, Mayor?"

"My ranch," Winford said. "I have a fine spread north of town. Most of it supports my cattle, but there are several acres across the river that are pretty much useless for ranching. George believes it's large enough to accommodate Ida's herd."

Kate wondered why the mayor was so willing to assist. He was going to pay for the drilling of expensive water wells to sustain his ranch after the dam dried up his creek.

And now he was willing to donate several acres to save Ida's horses.

"I thought maybe you could talk to Ida. She's too hotheaded to listen to anything I have to say," Winford said.

"She's too hotheaded to listen to anybody," Stokes added, receiving another dirty look from his cohort.

"Ida hopes The Nature Conservancy will accept her land," Kate said.

"If there ain't any water here, that won't work, now will it?" The mayor's voice rose. "And believe me when I say the dam's a sure thing. It *will* be built. Those horses will have to be removed or they'll die. And with no water, this ranch will become more useless than it is now. If Ida was smart, she'd unload this worthless rock-scrabble. It's no good to anybody, just a bunch of boulders and canyons. How's Nate going to help with it when he's in jail?" He slapped his hat across his thigh. "I don't even know why the hell I'm bothering."

Kate wondered this as well.

"I'm just trying to help," he continued as if reading Kate's mind. "But I guess Ida Springfield really ain't my problem. It's just that Frank was a friend, and I felt obligated to do something now that he's gone. Listen, I just came here to talk. Can we sit down a minute?"

Don G raised his leg to the left front tire of the mayor's Ford Ranger and showered it with a handsome stream of urine. Now mixed with the dust from Ida's dirt road, the pee-paste would attract every male dog from here to Red Lodge.

"Goddamn dog." Winford kicked some gravel in Don G's direction.

"Sitting down is a good idea," Stokes said, massaging the muscles in the small of his back.

Kate led her guests to the front porch and went inside to bring out another chair. She used the excuse of the weather being too beautiful to stay indoors, but the fact was she felt uncomfortable inviting these two men into Ida's cabin.

"I know you plan on talking in Ida's place at the meeting tomorrow," Winford said. "You and that Gregory woman and Pete Bear Walks Slowly will speak against the dam."

"And the Nelsons," Kate reminded him.

"Right, the Nelsons. How could I forget?" Mayor Winford said.

"The Nelsons." Stokes snorted, causing the mayor to cackle at some private joke.

"I'm prepared to make an announcement at the meeting offering to donate my land for the mustangs' new home," the mayor said.

"In exchange for what?" Kate could see the swap for dam support coming a mile away. But instead of feeling angry, she was encouraged. If the mayor and George Stokes had gone to the trouble of coming up with a plan to relocate the horses, then maybe the election outcome was not the foregone conclusion they professed. But maybe this was just a political move to prevent the loss of votes in the next mayoral election. In any event, Kate was fairly certain that Stokes' study of the Winford ranch consisted of what he was told by the mayor.

Kate also wondered if Frank Springfield's death had caused these men to fear for their own safety, now that the spokesman of their team had been murdered. There might be more to this situation than anyone was telling or knew. Kate was beginning to doubt that it was simply a case of Sonny Porter's finding out about his wife's affair and murdering her lover and leaving him without his pants as a warning.

"In exchange for nothing," Winford said. "I'm concerned about the horses. Ida's trying to make me out to be some bad person who only represents the ranchers, but that's not the case."

"How about the other concerns?" Kate said. "How about the Crow teepee-project and the Nelson farm? Those two businesses employ several people."

Stokes couldn't remain silent any longer and piped up, "The Nelsons are selling their place, so that's not an issue anymore. And James Brown Bird will just have to find a different type of wood for those damn tents. He's too goddamn picky. Everyone has to give a little in these cases."

Kate noticed Stokes' alligator-skin boots and wondered what the mayor's buddy was "sacrificing" for the cause. "When I spoke to Ed and Lucy Nelson, the idea of selling out was no more than just that, an idea," Kate said.

"I just came from their place and made them a good offer." Mayor Winford folded his arms across his stomach as if the idea of the Nelsons selling the farm was no longer in question.

"*You're* buying their farm?" Kate was aghast.

"I want to expand my ranch, and I've been looking

at that place for some time."

"You've been busy, Mayor. But if I were you, I wouldn't make any announcements at the meeting tomorrow without talking to Ida." Kate was sure that Ida would refuse his offer. Kate was also not about to speak to Ida on the mayor's behalf. "If you're serious about this, you should make a trip to Red Lodge and visit with Ida tonight. I don't plan to act as peacemaker or messenger between you and Ida. And I do plan to speak against the dam tomorrow."

Stokes rose from his chair and stormed off the porch.

Mayor Winford sat for a moment longer, his knuckles turning white as he gripped the arms of the chair. Then he gave her a steady look and finally said, "For a meddling outsider, you're a bit too sure of yourself, Ms. Caraway. I'll talk to Ida, like you suggested. Thanks for your time." Then he followed Stokes to the pickup.

Kate walked after them and before Winford could back the truck out, she said, "Any word on Frank Springfield's murder?"

The natural redness in George Stokes's face brightened, and Winford shoved the gearshift into reverse. "I wouldn't know. That's not my job."

As Mayor Clyde Winford pulled away, Kate noticed the fresh streaks of liquid on the tires of the mayor's truck and smiled at Don G for completing his spray job.

Chapter Eight

Determined to keep her promise to Ida, Kate decided to take another look at the place where she had found Frank's body. She could also give Jack his daily call while she had the chance. Grabbing her cell phone, she hoped the increase in elevation would provide a connection.

Kate welcomed the ascent on the grassy side of the mountain, remembering her slide down after last Friday night's storm. Dried footprints left by the investigators led directly to the spot. Whoever stabbed Frank in the back either sneaked up behind him, which seemed impossible on this sparsely covered rock, or it was someone Frank knew and was not concerned about turning his back to. If the latter were the case, did Frank come out here with someone and have an argument? Whatever reason they were here, they didn't want Ida to know, otherwise they would not have driven in the back way. They had not driven out here together, either. Frank's truck was found in an isolated canyon beyond the lake. So his killer had to have arrived and left in another vehicle. Ida's ranch was too far in the middle of nowhere for someone to have simply walked away.

Kate thought again about Ida's theory. Maybe Sonny Porter did follow Frank and kill him here on the ranch. That might explain Frank's missing pants. But why would Frank come here after his rendezvous with

Porter's wife? Maybe Frank and Imagene met here, and Sonny followed them. The time seemed wrong for that scenario. Frank was murdered early in the day, around noon, not the normal time for lovers to meet. But maybe they were grabbing whatever time was available.

Kate sat down on a lichen-covered rock. She punched the call button on her phone and received an AT&T logo. Jack's voice mail answered.

"This is Jack. Leave a message, and I'll get back to you."

"Keep those baseball boys in line. All's well here. I'll try you again later. Love you."

Kate looked out across the valley at Ida's lake below. It covered about two acres and looked out of place between the steep mountain walls. Two turkey vultures soared over the adjacent mountain, drifted downward, and disappeared as quickly as they arrived. As Kate watched their spiraling descent, she spotted the back road out of the canyon. It followed the edge of the lake. From this vantage point, it would have been impossible to see Frank's pickup. That's why Kate and Ida did not notice it the night they were watching the horses under the full moon.

Kate climbed down from her perch and walked to the water's edge. A slight breeze drifted across the surface of the water, creating dancing, undulating ripples. An old, wooden pier sat high above the water's surface, more evidence of the recent drought. Fighting evaporation, a thin ribbon of water trickled from the creek, feeding the only watering hole on the ranch. Ida had reason to worry. If any alteration was made to the larger river's flow, the trickle would disappear overnight. Unless water could be trucked in, this harsh, arid country would no longer support a herd of wild mustangs.

Then Kate noticed that the hoof prints that pocked the perimeter of the lake were accompanied by deeply rutted, extremely wide tire tracks. The tracks followed the water's edge next to the pier. She took a closer look. It was clear that the tracks were not made by the slick, thin tires on Ida's small truck. Whoever had driven here had sunk into the soft soil and had spun the tires before gaining enough traction to drive out. The tracks appeared recent, no more than three or four days old. Friday's rain had washed away the tread pattern, but the large width of the tire prints was still evident. Kate walked out to the edge of the pier. Many of the boards were rotten—wide gaps revealed dark water below. This rickety structure jutted out into the lake about forty feet. As Kate approached the end, she felt the entire pier give. It was only a matter of time before the structure would collapse completely.

Kate squatted carefully and looked across the water. Why had Frank been on Ida's ranch? If these tracks were from his pickup, why did he drive to the lake in full view, and then drive around the canyon wall and hide the truck? Maybe these tracks weren't from Frank's truck. Had it not rained, it would have been easy to determine. But it was still worth a try. Kate eased her way off the pier. She studied the tracks closely. She pulled out her cell and snapped several photos. Then she followed the tracks from the lake around to the half-moon-shaped canyon. It was a short walk. Frank's pickup had been parked under a mesquite tree just off the road. As Kate approached that area, she noticed one set of tire tracks now joined by several others—patrol cars and a tow truck most likely—but the wide tracks of the vehicle parked under the tree appeared to be the same width as those next to the lake. What had Frank Springfield been doing near the water?

A gust of wind from the north brought a chill to the air. As Kate zipped up her jacket, a strong scent of decay overcame her. She covered her nose with her sleeve and hiked from the canyon to where a small valley had opened up. Her sudden presence sent a flock of turkey vultures into the air. There seemed to be too many birds to be scavenging on the body of a small rodent. Kate swallowed hard as she peered beyond the slope of the road and down into the embankment.

Blotted from at least two days of decomposition, the body lay on its side in a tuft of tall grass. Kate fought back tears as she edged closer. The cause of death was painfully apparent. And as realization took hold, smoldering anger exploded from Kate's body like a volcano. All the anger she had held inside since she had discovered the elephant slaughter near her Kenyan camp finally erupted—the outrage over number 405, the elephant they called Ginger because of the reddish, gold tint that ran down the top of her trunk; the fear and guilt of having to leave her camp and the country she had come to love; the claustrophobia from living in a big city; the lack of control over her life and what she wanted it to be. Kate turned her head away from the body and heard a shrieking cry bounce off the canyon wall and spread across the valley with the wind. It was a few moments before she realized it was the resonance of her own scream. The anger she'd held back finally erupted. She picked up rocks and one after another, flung them at the vultures that had perched in a nearby tangle of scrub oaks waiting for a chance to return to their feast. When her arm finally gave out, Kate collapsed in the dirt and cried out months of agony.

After several minutes, she pulled herself together and walked back to the corpse for a closer view. There was no doubt in her mind—it was the stallion Ida called Randy, the one Kate had seen the first night she was here. As best she could tell, the horse had been shot at least four times, probably with a high-powered rifle. The wounds were large and gaping. It tore her heart to think of this majestic animal, proudly protecting his band from an intruder the night she and Ida had climbed the mountain. *Where are those mustangs now?* Had another stallion stepped into the role of alpha male? Kate knew little of wild-horse behavior. Was this species as altruistic as the African elephant? When attacked, the older members of the elephant herd were known to run toward their attackers, putting themselves between the younger members of the herd and danger. When the alpha females were killed, which was often the case due to their large tusks, the herd became lost in structural disarray as well as in grief. They floundered, unable to recover and maintain their social order.

Kate climbed out of the ditch and scanned the valley below. To her relief, she saw no other corpses and prayed this was the only one. Then a startling thought crossed her mind. Was someone trying to scare Ida? If so, when had the shooting occurred? Sometime on Saturday afternoon when the three of them were in town, or early Sunday morning when they went to Billings to pick up Nate? The rest of the time, Ida had been here and would have heard the shots. But someone had to have known about their movements, and in this secluded ranch, rimmed with mountains and canyon walls, that seemed impossible.

Kate ran back to the cabin, ignoring the jarring pain in her ankle. She grabbed Ida's things and was at the sheriff's office in half an hour.

Chapter Nine

Kate thought she had released every ounce of anger
that had fermented in her gut, but the sheriff's reaction
to the dead mustang told her she was wrong. A lifetime
of cultivating patience kept her from trashing the officer.

"These animals are a threatened species, Sheriff, and
killing one is a crime."

Sheriff Phillips sat up a little straighter in his chair.
"I know it's a crime, Ms. Caraway, but I have a murder
on my hands right now that's taking up all my time."

Kate wanted to tell him that he didn't look too busy
at the moment, but since a small amount of decorum
remained, she instead suggested that an investigation
might be worthwhile. "This was the second killing on
Ida's ranch in less than a week," she reminded the
sheriff, "even if the second victim was a mustang. If I
were you, I'd get out there and see what's going on."

"Don't tell me how to do my job. I have a deputy
out right now running down a lead on Nate Springfield.
As soon as he returns, I'll send him over to Ida's ranch."

"Someone's seen Nate?" Kate said. She could have
kicked herself for losing her temper. She needed to stay
on good terms with this man, if for no other reason than
to learn how things were proceeding.

"I didn't say that. The rental-car company called.
Nate rented a car on Thursday, the day Frank was
murdered. Nate was supposed to return the car late

Saturday afternoon, but hasn't yet. I've issued a warrant for his arrest."

"For not returning a rental car on time?"

"For murder."

"And may I ask what motive do you think Nate had for killing his grandfather? All you know is that he may have been in Frank's truck on Thursday."

"And that makes Nate the last person to have seen Frank alive. Those two were at odds with one another. That's a well-known fact. Nate was always weaseling money out of Frank."

"You think Nate killed Frank over money?" Kate sat down in a folding chair across from the sheriff's desk and rested her head in her hands.

"Nate sneaks into town without telling anyone. He goes to see his grandfather and tries to bleed him for money again. They have a heated argument and Nate kills him. Simple."

Too simple, Kate thought. "Why would Nate have to sneak into town? He was coming to Two Horse anyway."

"Lot of reasons. Something came up, and Nate needed money quick."

Kate couldn't believe what she was hearing. "They meet on Ida's ranch and have an argument? Then Nate kills his grandfather and takes off?"

From the look on his face, Kate knew even the sheriff did not believe his own absurd scenario. But sitting here playing "what if" was a big waste of time.

"Are you checking any other leads? Frank had a reputation for fooling around with other men's wives. How about Imagene Porter? I've only been here four days, and I've heard from more than one person that Frank was having an affair with that woman. Where was

Mr. Porter on Thursday?"

"Sonny Porter was in Billings at a cattle auction."

"And Imagene?"

"She was with him. Stick to what you know, Ms. Caraway. Talk all you want at that meeting tomorrow. That's why you're here, even though our situation is really none of your business. Leave this investigation to me."

His snicker spoke louder than his words, and Kate laced her fingers together to keep from grabbing a paperweight and flinging it at him.

"I want to know who killed that horse and why. If you don't find out, I will."

"Listen, Ms. Caraway. Ida's a cantankerous old woman. It wouldn't be the first time someone tried to get back at her."

"What do you mean? Someone killed that horse as a pay-back?"

"Ida's been a pain in our ass as long as I can remember. It's a wonder she hasn't landed in jail for all the times she's taken the law into her own hands. Like busting in at the council meeting with a shotgun. I should have arrested her on the spot, but I felt sorry for that sister of hers. If I had arrested Ida, I'd have to account for Veda as well. And just last year Ida got into a confrontation with another rancher over the sale of some of her cattle. I won't go into details, but she threatened to remedy the situation by burning down his barn. It's no wonder after years of thunder-clapping her way around, that someone might have given her a taste of her own medicine. A lot of folks are angry. Ida's been shouting about protecting those mustangs as if they were the only thing of any value here in Carbon County. Someone might have just gotten sick of listening to her and decided to do something."

"If that's the case, Sheriff Phillips, then Ida isn't the only one in this corner of Montana with a misplaced sense of law and order."

Kate stormed out of the office and almost ran into Deputy Lucas coming down the hall.

"Sorry, ma'am." He tipped his hat.

"Lucas!" Sheriff Phillips shouted. "Did you locate that rental car yet?"

"Not yet."

"Then do something useful for a change so I can justify paying you. Go out to Ida's and have a look at that dead horse. And tuck in that goddamn shirttail." Then Sheriff Phillips stood up, reached across his desk, and slammed his door shut.

Out of courtesy to the young officer, Kate pretended she had not noticed the flush of embarrassment on his face at being dressed down by his boss. They walked outside and stood for a moment on the front steps.

"I'm afraid I put your boss in a foul mood."

"Not your fault. This is my first job in law enforcement. Phillips wasn't keen on hiring me, but he had a debt to pay to my Uncle Will, the county commissioner, so here I am. What's this about a dead horse?"

Kate explained to Deputy Lucas where he could find the stallion. "I'd say he's been dead about two days."

"I'll look into it." He started to his patrol car and turned around. "Any time you want to visit the sheriff is fine by me. When he has someone to take his mind off my idle time, I'm able to escape his wrath for a spell." He tipped his hat and drove off.

Kate walked across the street and into Ruby's. Even though it was late Monday afternoon, the atmosphere in the cafe was pretty much the same. Being the only eatery in town, it was the gathering place for food, companionship, and, gossip. She slipped in unnoticed this time. The TV was bolted to a wooden platform on the wall above a stack of supply crates. It was tuned to some talk show. The show's theme was "Children who are pushed too hard to excel, and what happens to them."

Kate immediately thought of Mike Chambers, the young pitcher for the Cubs' minor-league team, whom Jack was visiting in Des Moines. Maybe that was Mike's problem. Major-league pitchers didn't develop overnight. The process, the skill, the training, the desire—it all started at a very young age when boys joined Little League. What started out as a chance to play ball and have fun often turned into an intense competitive pursuit of a dream, not necessarily the child's.

The talk-show host's guest was a child psychologist. She was seated next to three young people, who were obviously subjects of the theme. The expert spoke of rebellion as one of the main symptoms resulting from pushing children in a direction not of their choosing. Was Mike Chambers finding life as a potential major leaguer too stressful? Was he fulfilling his parents' dreams or his own?

Then Kate thought of Nate. He was a young man whose parents had died while he was a boy. He grew up in the middle of a hateful relationship between two of the three people he had left as a family, his great-grandmother and his grandfather, both of whom were eccentric beyond imagination. Kate wasn't even sure who Nate's legal guardian had been. Ida said he had spent much of his time with her and Veda. And was it true what Sheriff Phillips had said? Had money been an issue? Attending college in another state was obviously expensive. Who had been paying for Nate's education? Had he really been a financial drain on Frank as Sheriff Phillips claimed?

Kate perused Ruby's menu for something meatless. She settled for an egg-salad sandwich and ordered it to go. Before she stopped at the hospital, she would pick up meals for Ida and Veda, including ice cream and root beer. Veda might not have an appetite, but a little temptation couldn't hurt. Kate prayed that Veda was feeling better. Not only did Kate need to probe further into Ida's life, she needed to deliver the news about the dead mustang and about the warrant that had been issued for Nate's arrest. A chicken-fried steak wouldn't be enough to soften those blows, and Kate hoped to gain some type of encouraging information before she left town. It was late afternoon, but Kate had one more stop. She used the phone in the diner and called Ida at the hospital.

"How's Veda?"

"The same," Ida said. "Are you having any luck?"

"Luck might not be the right word. I want to run by the Brown Bird place for a quick visit, but I wanted to check with you first. I might not get there for a couple of hours."

"You worry too much. We're fine."

Ida was right. Kate could not do much to help with Veda, but she was determined to do everything possible to find Nate and ameliorate some of Ida's worries. If Meg was right, and Jim and Rachel had been together on

Thursday, the day Nate was to arrive in Two Horse, there was a better than good chance that the two young people had been in contact with Nate, regardless of what Lucy Nelson had said.

The cashier brought Kate's bill. Kate asked for directions to the Brown Birds' home.

"James Brown Bird?" the cashier said as she handed Kate her change.

"That's the one," Kate said.

"Easy. You take the road north of town about three miles and then turn left on Pryor Range Road. It's the only way to the place. The Brown Birds are about half a mile down on the right. You'll spot it with no problem. James's place looks like an Indian campground. Teepees everywhere. He makes them. If you're interested in buying one, you better do it soon. As soon as they start building that dam, James is gonna have to find a new hobby to bring in extra money."

"Thanks for the directions, and for the advice," Kate said and placed a couple of dollars in a tip jar that contained a small amount of change and a happy-face drawn on a used meal ticket taped to the side of the jar. Underneath the face was written, "Tipping isn't a place in China."

The cashier was right. The Brown Bird place brightened the entire landscape. There were a dozen or so handsome teepees dotting the front of the property, and James Brown Bird had hung a banner along his fence, advising people to vote against proposition number 503. The banner read, *Dam Bad Idea–Vote NO and Save Our Land and Forests*.

Kate drove down the long drive toward a small prefab house with so many add-ons that it looked like a small shopping center. She parked in front of an enormous canvas-covered pavilion erected behind the residence. More than a dozen other vehicles were parked in front. Kate wondered if all those people were here to purchase a teepee. Out of the corner of her eye, she noticed Pete Bear Walks Slowly standing at the front of a large group seated at several tables set up under the pavilion. She suspected that the gathering had something to do with tomorrow's meeting and the election next week.

Kate was glad Pete was here. She needed to speak to him about Nate, a subject that was sure to be unpleasant. Nevertheless, she had to find Ida's grandson. Whether or not Pete approved of Nate seeing his daughter, there was a good chance the two young people had been together recently.

Pete glanced at Kate as she walked in and indicated with a nod for her to have a seat. Things were winding down. Pete reminded everyone of their responsibility and assignments and encouraged them to make sure their neighbors came to town to vote.

The meeting broke up and everyone gathered around a table covered with bumper-stickers and fliers. Pete approached Kate.

"You have quite a gathering here. It's encouraging," Kate said.

"Yeah, well, like they say, don't count your chickens. Are you here to see the teepees?"

"I wish I had time. Veda's sick and in the hospital in Red Lodge. I'm on my way there now. And I'm sure you've heard about Nate," Kate said.

"I have," Pete said. His jaw clenched as if those last two words were all he planned to say on the subject.

"I need to find him soon. Do you think he could be with your daughter? Ida said they were friends."

"My daughter is none of your concern." The congeniality of Saturday night's visit was gone.

A tall, slender man in his late forties joined them before Kate had a chance to respond. Pete introduced James Brown Bird, the owner of Crow Teepee Company.

"Nice to meet you, Mr. Brown Bird," Kate said.

"Pete told me about you. You're here to help Ida and Karen with those mustangs. I hope you can sway some votes in our direction."

"I plan to do what I can. I must apologize. I didn't know you were having a meeting. I came to speak with your son."

"Jim?" James looked around and when he spotted his son, waved him over. "What's my boy been up to?"

Kate looked at Pete. He seemed anxious to know as well. "I guess you've heard that Nate Springfield is in a bit of trouble," Kate said.

Pete spoke first. "We know. The sheriff was here earlier looking for Nate."

A younger version of James joined them.

"Jim, this is Kate Caraway, the lady who will speak on our behalf at the meeting tomorrow. She's concerned about Nate. I'll let you two visit. Pete and I have to finish up here."

Pete did not look all that willing to leave, but James ushered him to a group that was planning their final strategies.

"I wish I could help you, Dr. Caraway, but, like I told the sheriff, I haven't seen Nate in several weeks."

Kate wished she could have spoken with Jim before the sheriff, before Jim had rehearsed his story. Kate knew he was lying. She rarely used her academic title. The only person from Two Horse who had called her "Dr." Caraway was Nate when he had attended her lectures. Kate was certain the two young men had spoken to one another very recently.

If Kate planned to get more information, she'd have to gain Jim's trust. She needed to make Jim understand that for Nate's own benefit, he needed to come out of hiding.

"Nate's been in Two Horse since Thursday. It's fairly evident that he'd been with Frank on the day he was killed. Ida's worried sick, and even though it looks bad for Nate, he needs to be found so we can help him. I'm not suggesting Nate turn himself in, at least not now. I'm sure he has a good reason for staying away. I just want to talk to him and reassure his great-grandmother that he's all right. I promise I won't go to the sheriff."

Kate saw the first sign of uncertainty in Jim's eyes. She knew he was struggling with the need to help his friend and the promise he had obviously made to keep quiet.

"How about Rachel Bear Walks Slowly, I mean, Martin? I know that you three are close friends—"

Jim turned white. He swallowed hard and looked around until he saw Pete.

"What is it, Jim? For God's sake if you know something about Rachel and Nate, please tell me." Kate followed Jim's stare and saw Pete glaring at them from across the pavilion. "Let's walk over to Ida's truck. I'll write down my cell-phone number. I know service here is intermittent, but I'll also give you my phone number in Chicago. You can also leave a message there if you need to contact me."

As they stepped outside and away from the crowd, Jim's mood eased somewhat.

"Okay, no one can hear us." Kate gave Jim a stern, but sympathetic look. "I know that you and Rachel were together on Thursday. You were seen in town. Is Nate with Rachel?"

"No. They broke up a while back. She won't have anything to do with him." Jim glanced over his shoulder and then looked back at Kate. "Pete gave Rachel a hard time about dating Nate."

"Why?"

"It's not that Pete has anything against Nate. It's just a Native American thing. Pete said Rachel and Nate were too involved. Rachel's still in high school, and Pete doesn't want her getting serious with someone who's not Crow."

"From what I hear, Rachel was supposed to be in rehab. You were with her last Thursday. You must have known that she'd run away."

Jim brushed his long hair back from his forehead. "She told me she had been released. I just picked her up and gave her a ride. She was hanging around the gazebo in town with a bunch of girls and I stopped to talk. Then she asked me to take her to a friend's house on the reservation. I didn't know she had run away."

"How can you be so sure Nate's not with Rachel?"

"Rachel's pissed at Nate because he didn't stand up to her father. Listen, Dr. Caraway, I really don't know where Nate is. I need to get back. I have work to do."

"Who's Rachel's friend? The one you took her to see?"

"Don't know. I just dropped her off at the entrance to the reservation's RV park and left." As he turned to

129

walk away, Kate called him back and handed him her number. "Tell Nate to call me, please. Nate's the reason I'm here. He trusted me enough to want me here in Two Horse. I'm sure that with a little encouragement, he'll want to see me."

Jim stuck the card in his pocket and hurried back to the tent.

****

It was after eight when Kate peeked into Veda's room. Both sisters were asleep, but Ida's eyes shot open with the squeak of the door. She jumped up from her chair and motioned Kate back into the hallway. "Let's go to the cafeteria. Veda finally fell asleep."

Kate was happy to see that some of Ida's color had returned. "How's our patient?"

"She's not out of the woods yet. The doctor's afraid of this turning into pneumonia. Veda's fever is down some, but not gone. Seems she's had some sort of bug for some time. She's been coughing a lot lately, but I thought it was just a wintertime thing."

"I have a chicken-fried steak for you and a bowl of chicken soup, ice cream, and root beer for Veda."

"You did good. Let's find a freezer." Ida pulled the carton of ice cream out of the sack and stopped at the nurses' station. "Bruce, be a sweetheart and keep this cold for me, will ya?"

"You're lucky it isn't chocolate," the guy named Bruce said. "It wouldn't last two minutes with us here."

"Thanks. Kate and I will be in the cafeteria if Veda wakes up."

"A friend of yours?" Kate asked.

"Bruce and I go way back. Like way back to when Veda checked in earlier. I think he has a thing for old ladies."

"While I've been taking care of business and Veda's been recovering, you've been flirting with the nurse?"

"Hey, I'm old, but I ain't dead. I'm also hungry." She reached for the chicken-fried steak. "I'll eat it cold."

Kate found them a table near the window, and Ida dove into her meal. Not wanting to deliver bad news so soon after Ida had recovered from her slump, Kate stalled. "Coffee? Black, right?"

"Yep. Then sit down and quit catering to me. I want to know everything you found out."

Kate returned with two cups of charred-smelling coffee that the vending machine spat out. She decided to level with Ida. "Did Mayor Winford contact you today?"

"Nope."

"He told me he'd come by."

"Well, he hasn't. What's up?"

Kate related the events of the afternoon. Everything except for finding the dead mustang.

Ida ranted on for several minutes about Mayor Winford's asinine offer to move the horses to his property. Her shotgun made its way into her soliloquy, along with a detailed explanation of how and where the buckshot would find its way into Clyde Winford's and George Stokes's backsides.

Kate sipped her coffee and listened while Ida let off steam—refueled by the high fat-content of her meal, no doubt. Kate had known this woman for only a short while, but that was enough time to learn that Ida handled life's problems better when she was in an agitated state with adrenaline shooting through her veins. For the last twenty-four hours, Kate was afraid that Ida's depression might send her to her bed. Now Ida was fiery and fit-to-be-tied, especially after learning that Jim Brown Bird most likely knew where Nate was hiding but didn't want to say.

"Just let me get ahold of that boy, and I'll have it out of him, or I'll take it out of his hide."

"Jim also told me that Nate and Rachel broke up because Pete told her stop dating Nate since he wasn't Crow. But Pete's wife isn't Crow either, right?"

"Yeah, ever since Lila left, Pete's blamed everything that's gone wrong with his family on the fact that she wasn't Crow. But that man's blowing in the wind where Rachel's concerned. He has no more control over that girl than a goddamn fart." An elderly couple sitting next to Ida and Kate moved to another table across the room. "Pete thinks all of Rachel's troubles will disappear if she'd take her heritage seriously. That part about Nate not being a Crow is just a goddamn excuse. It's because Nate is a Springfield." Ida acted as though that last remark was funny.

"What else?" Ida said as she squinted her eyes at Kate. "Spit it out, honey. You know something. What is it?"

Wasting words to soften the blow would be an insult to someone like Ida, so Kate leveled with her. "Someone killed Randy, Ida. I found him this afternoon on the side of the road near the canyon by the lake. He had been shot several times. It must have happened sometime on Saturday, probably when we were in Two Horse having breakfast.

Ida wiped her mouth with her napkin and threw it on what remained of her meal. "Would you mind checking on Veda? I need to step out for some air. I've been breathing too much of this hospital shit."

Chapter Ten

The evening temperature had already dipped into the thirties. Kate stood on Ida's front porch, sipping some of Ida's Southern Comfort, grateful for the opportunity to be alone on the ranch. Solitude was Kate's lifeline to sanity. While living in Kenya, all the sounds of survival—weaver birds chirping mating calls, African wild dogs howling warning of an intruder, a hyena's curdling screams during a feeding frenzy—had aroused instinctual feelings buried somewhere deep inside, giving Kate justification for living among nature's best. The sounds of the city grated on Kate's nerves—her only solace came while being isolated in some library nook or sitting up in the stands at Wrigley Field. There was something about ballpark sounds that made sitting among forty thousand people comforting. At times like this, being away from Jack brought on despair deep enough to cause a panic attack. Kate sipped the whiskey and focused on her breathing.

Kate fed the dogs and carried in enough firewood to get through the night. Luisa Miller and Carmen were curled up in the living room, while the other three dogs were still prowling. Tomorrow Kate would address Two Horse's voters and give her input on why building the dam was not the only solution to water shortage. If she learned anything at all while living in Kenya, dealing with the National Park Service in Africa and the local government, it was the art of negotiation.

An out-of-town scientist spewing research statistics or lecturing on the preservation of natural resources as the only sensible way to live would not impress her audience. She would lose them before she even warmed up. She'd have to convince them that there were other, less costly alternatives, that living *with* nature's gifts would be beneficial to everyone. Were there other water sources? Was irrigation from the Pryor River a possibility?

Kate had brought with her a short video produced by the Texas Parks and Wildlife Department on the man-made wetlands in the Trans-Pecos region, an arid section of Texas not too dissimilar to Carbon County, Montana. The video described a compromise among farmers, ranchers, and environmentalists who had solved the water shortage problem to the satisfaction of all factions. An inexpensive irrigation system brought water from the Rio Grande River. Wetlands were then formed for wildlife and a new water supply for the agriculturists was created. It was a win-win situation. That project had been instituted more than twenty-five years ago and was now a model for other successful ventures. Kate's research team in Kenya had used similar designs with as much success. But the Maasai people, who draped themselves in colorful blankets, decorated their bodies with beads and paint, and drank cow's blood, were not relatable as an example for Montana ranchers.

Texas and Montana ranchers had a common link. Much of the cattle in Montana could be traced back to stock driven north from Texas on the Great Western Cattle Trail in the late 1800s. If Kate had had more time, she could have brought a representative from the Texas

Parks and Wildlife Department to explain the irrigation project in person. One good old boy tended to listen to another good old boy. Instead, Kate hoped an exaggerated Texas drawl, and her cowboy boots would be convincing enough. If some of the ranchers were interested in developing dude ranches and cashing in on the tourist dollars, maybe she would not be booed out of the meeting room.

Kate's reverie was broken by the sudden, chilling sound of a coyote howl echoing in the canyon. Before she could tell from which direction the call came, the howling turned into a yapping ruckus. Luisa Miller and Carmen flew out the door and around the barn. The barking grew louder, and Kate realized that what she mistook for coyotes were the Springfield dogs. Kate hoped that the pack was not hot on the trail of a deer or had tangled with a badger. Or worse yet, a skunk. Having to bring Ida more bad news would be awful.

Kate held her breath and listened to the yaps and high-pitched squeals go back and forth at the base of the mountain. If it was a deer the dogs were after, by the time Kate got there either the deer would have escaped or her efforts at preventing its capture would have been in vain. The sounds were not exactly predatory, but more like a nighttime romp. Nevertheless, for the sake of the pursued as well as the pursuers, Kate traded her glass of Southern Comfort for the flashlight, which hung on a hook by the kitchen door. She headed behind the barn to scout the area.

Don G was the first to greet her. He scampered up looking too pleased with himself. Kate shone the light over his matted fur, looking for signs of a fight. Seeing none, she breathed easier. The other four mutts arrived, panty, and equally devoid of battle wounds.

"You dogs are coming inside tonight. I'll not be responsible of your demise while Ida is away. She has enough to worry about."

Rigoletto paused, looking over his shoulder as if contemplating whether or not to obey Kate's command. Kate spoke in a sterner voice to override any thought Rigoletto had about bolting. The scruffy yellow lab tucked his tail and reluctantly followed the others into the house.

Kate lit the wood in the fireplace and turned off all the lights except for the lamp near the sofa where she planned to read through Ida's notes one more time. Her canine companions had settled into their nighttime routine. Two dogs sprawled on Ida's bed and two on Veda's. With more blankets from the hall closet, Kate hoped to coax Luisa Miller into sleeping on the floor next to the sofa rather than on Kate's legs. She thought about sleeping on one of the beds, but the idea of wrestling for the covers with two dogs instead of one didn't appeal to her.

Kate dozed off around midnight and shortly thereafter was awakened by the lack of circulation in the lower part of her body. She rearranged the blankets on the floor to accommodate a five-foot-four person rather than a forty-pound dog. She snapped off the lamp and let her sleeping companion have the sofa. Like a regular nighttime visitor, the wind kicked up and roared so loudly it sounded like a freight train circling the cabin. For the next couple of hours, Kate tossed in and out of a shallow sleep, alternating between dreams too similar to the day's events and the knowledge that she was not really asleep at all. Finally, her busy mind shut down, and she dropped into a paralyzing slumber.

Suddenly Kate's eyes shot open with an unexplainable knowledge that things were not right. She instantly thought of Jack and froze, feeling that something bad had happened to him. Then the thought quickly disappeared. Her fear was closer, more immediate. Someone was in the cabin. But that was impossible. An intruder would send the dogs into frenzy. Except for Luisa Miller's snoring, the only other sound Kate heard was the wind. Her mind told her that her fears were unfounded, but her instincts shouted danger. Kate lay still and listened. She forced her hearing to pick up something—a creak of a floorboard, a rustle of fabric, anything. There was nothing.

The silence remained, hanging in the air like a heavy curtain. Kate had learned the hard way not to ignore her instincts. She slipped her arm from under the blanket and wrapped her fingers around the fireplace poker lying nearby. Pulling her weapon close to her body, Kate rolled over onto her stomach and rose to her knees. The kitchen door was the only other door in the cabin leading to the outside, and although it wasn't near the bedrooms, Kate doubted that someone could sneak into the back of the house without alerting the dogs, even with the noise of the wind covering the sounds of the intruder.

Then Kate saw him—a bent shadow cast across the kitchen doorway and up onto the bottom of the refrigerator. Luisa Miller's tail thumped on the sofa and in her slumber, she let out a friendly whine. Either the dog was dreaming a pleasant dream, or her olfactory sense had picked up a familiar smell. Kate felt it must be the latter.

"Nate?" Kate called out.

"Dr. Caraway?"

Kate sat back on her heels and brushed her hair from her eyes. "Shit! Are you trying to send me to an early grave?"

Nate walked out of the kitchen, came into the living room, and slumped down in the chair next to the fireplace. Even in the dark, Kate saw that his normal fresh-scrubbed appearance was disheveled. He looked as if he had not slept in days. Luisa Miller woke up and hopped into his lap.

"Why are you sleeping on the floor?"

Kate ignored his question and pushed the dial-button on her watch—four twenty-three. "It's bit early for a visit, Nate, but I'm glad you're here."

"I couldn't very well show my face during the day. Jim convinced me to come see you. He told me about Aunt Veda. Please tell me that she's okay."

"The last I heard, her fever was down, but her condition is still tentative. Where are you staying?"

"I can't tell you. Don't try and talk me into turning myself in. I won't. Not right now, anyway."

"Why don't you get cleaned up? And I'll make us some coffee— make that breakfast." He hesitated, and Kate added, "I'll help any way I can, Nate. I know you didn't kill your grandfather, but we need to talk about this."

"I just came to Two Horse to help." He buried his face in his hands. "I let her down." He stopped suddenly as if he just realized who was seated across from him. After all, he had known Kate for only a short time. Their relationship was that of student and teacher. He drew in a breath and appeared to swallow his emotions.

"Your great-grandmother doesn't feel you let her

down. She's just worried about you."

"I'm sorry, you're right. I need a shower, and I am hungry."

Kate wanted to say more, but decided to wait. At least he was here. Showered and fed, Kate hoped he'd pull himself together enough to give her more information.

Three of the dogs were standing at the door, so Kate let them out for an early morning inspection of their territory. Then she turned her attention to cooking and had breakfast on the table by the time Nate stepped from the bathroom. He walked into the kitchen, toweling the moisture from his hair. Seeing Nate shaved and dressed in clean clothes gave Kate a brief moment of hope, as if a hot shower could wash away life's misfortunes.

"So, you keep a set of clothes here?" Kate handed him a cup of coffee.

The light returned briefly to his eyes and he chuckled. "No, these are Aunt Veda's jeans and Gram's sweater." But just as soon as he spoke, Nate's hangdog expression returned. Unsure of what to say next, he sat down at the kitchen table and shook his head.

Kate set a plate of biscuits and eggs in front of him and stood by the kitchen door watching the bright reddish glow rise over the horizon. Kate wondered if "red sky at morning, sailors take warning" applied in the mountains of Montana. She had barely finished half her coffee when Nate refilled his plate, pausing as he spooned a second helping of eggs out of the pan.

"Go ahead. It's too early for me to eat," Kate said.

"What did you do to these scrambled eggs?"

"Like 'em?"

"Oh, man. You put Ruby's to shame."

139

"It's a wonder what a little garlic, onions, and cheese can do to a chicken embryo. Listen, Nate, you were around earlier this evening. The dogs were excited about something or someone, someone familiar, someone they knew."

Nate looked up from his plate but remained silent.

"Nate, you knew I was here. If you came because Jim convinced you to talk to me, why did you wait until four in the morning? Why did you sneak into the cabin?"

Nate pushed his plate away and rested his elbows on the table. "I didn't know how you'd react to seeing me. When I talked to Jim earlier, it made sense to contact you. Then I'd about decided that maybe it wasn't such a good idea. So much has happened. I changed my mind and came to the cabin for—for food and was trying to leave before you woke up."

"The sheriff thinks you killed your grandfather over money. And he has evidence that you were with Frank on Thursday morning, the day he was killed."

"What evidence?"

"The police found your boarding pass in Frank's pickup. How did that happen?"

"As soon as I left the airport, I accidentally ran into Grandpa. He motioned for me to pull over, so we drove into the McDonalds, and I got into his truck. We talked for a couple of minutes. Then I left."

"The sheriff said you asked Frank for money several times and he recently told you he wasn't going to give you any more."

"Sometimes I hate being from a small town. Everybody knows your business, or thinks they do. I've borrowed some money from Grandpa in the past. He didn't like the idea that I chose to go to college in

Chicago. It's expensive and I'm barely able to make it. He thought I was being irresponsible and I should have gone to school closer to home, somewhere here in Montana."

"You and your grandfather just had a casual conversation?"

"Having a casual conversation is something the Springfields don't know how to do. Grandpa was in one of his moods. I knew as soon as I got in his truck he was going to start in on me again about living in Chicago. But that wasn't it. He was really furious over The Nature Conservancy idea."

"I didn't think Frank cared about the ranch," Kate said.

"He didn't. In fact, he always referred to it as a worthless piece of wasteland. He knew the ranch would come to me when Gram died, and he used to always laugh at that, saying that Gram would be leaving me an albatross. So when he started in on me about The Nature Conservancy deal, we got into a bad argument pretty fast. He told me that I'd regret giving the ranch away. He even said that once the land was mine, he'd be willing to help run it, sort of like being my partner. He said he had some new ideas on how to make the ranch profitable. I told him I didn't believe in owning land for the sake of owning it. He called me an idealistic idiot. He didn't like the stewardship idea just because Gram liked it. They're the two most stubborn people I know. And they're so much alike. It's either their way or no way. Living between those two is too much sometimes. I made the mistake of telling Grandpa that, and he blew up and told me to get out of his truck. The whole argument was so stupid, but it reminded me that living in Chicago for now was a good idea."

Kate noticed for the first time the sagging skin under Nate's eyes and sickly pallor of his complexion—the signs of stress that a shower and much-needed meal could not remove. Kate's maternal instincts kicked in as she reflected on everything Ida had revealed about Nate's troublesome childhood. She searched for the right words to convince Nate to trust her and follow her advice. None came. And Nate had told her nothing she could use to help him.

"Why was Frank in Billings?"

"He didn't say, but he seemed anxious to be somewhere. To tell you the truth, I was glad that he was in a hurry. Otherwise, he wouldn't have let up on me so easily."

"Why didn't you tell Ida that you were already in Two Horse? We all drove out to the airport to pick you up."

Nate carried his empty plate to the sink. He turned on the water and let it run until it was hot enough to clean the dishes. "Sorry about the mix-up. I keep trying to get Gram to get a phone, but I'm sure you know how stubborn she is. Anyway, I've got to go."

"Nate, we have to talk." Kate stepped in front of the door as if to bar his exit. "If you're innocent—" A look of horror flashed across Nate's face. "—and I believe you are, you can't hide out forever. The sheriff knows you rented a car on Thursday." Then Kate remembered her grim discovery earlier that day. "You need to be careful. The sheriff and his deputies are combing Ida's ranch, looking for you."

"I know," Nate said. "But they won't find me. I grew up here. I know every inch of this land. I'll be okay."

"This afternoon I found the body of the stallion Ida called Randy. Someone shot him near the place where the police found Frank's pickup."

"Have you told Gram?"

"Yes. It was a miserable thing to have to tell her with everything else that's going on. I wasn't sure how she'd react, but she took it in stride."

"Don't misread my great-grandmother, Dr. Caraway. She loves these horses. The only reason she didn't explode in a fury is because Aunt Veda's sick. One time she caught some tourist who had wandered off the main road to take pictures of the horses. She chased him off with her shotgun. Aunt Veda and those mustangs mean more to Gram than anything. It's hard to explain." He paused before his next words.

Kate waited, but was disappointed.

"Thanks for the breakfast."

Before Kate could respond, Nate trotted back to the bathroom and returned with his dirty clothes rolled up and tucked under his arm.

"Leave those. I'll clean them."

"I didn't ask you to come here to take care of this crazy family." He walked past her and onto the back porch.

"What shall I tell Ida?"

"Tell her not to worry. And as soon as I take care of some things, I'll come back. I promise."

"The longer you stay away, the worse the situation will get."

"I don't think so. I think I know who killed Grandpa, but I'm not safe until I can prove it first." Nate waved over his shoulder and was gone.

Over her second cup of coffee Kate thought about

what Nate had said. Why had Frank suddenly changed his mind about the ranch? If he had no interest in the property, what was he doing here the day he was killed? And if he was suddenly interested in the land for any reason, its need for a steady water source made his opposition to the dam a conflict of interest. Had Mayor Winford viewed Frank's possible change of heart as a betrayal? If so, was this motive enough for Winford to have killed his old friend? Except for a jealous husband, Mayor Winford was the only other suspect Kate could come up with.

Kate chided herself for letting Nate leave so easily. She should have insisted on some answers. Why had he sneaked into town several days before his planned arrival? If that reason was linked to Frank's murder, then the situation must have been brewing long before Kate had come to Two Horse. If Nate knew who had killed Frank and planned on exposing the killer, he was in more danger than Kate had thought. One thing was for sure, Nate was not safe here on the ranch, especially if the deputy sheriff was following up on his promise to investigate the killing of the horse. At least she had had a chance to warn him. She was grateful for being a light sleeper, otherwise, she wouldn't have heard Nate enter the cabin.

Then a thought struck her like a slap across the face. Kate set her coffee cup on the table and rushed into Ida's room. She pulled open Ida's sweater drawer. As she slid her hand under the clothing, she let out a string of expletives that sent Luisa Miller running for the backdoor. No matter her good intentions and warnings, she might as well have handed Nate Ida's .38.

Chapter Eleven

The meeting was still an hour away, but anxious citizens from Two Horse and Carbon County were already pouring into the council chambers. It looked as though every pickup in the county was trolling for a parking place. Most drivers gave up and parked wherever they could squeeze in. Kate parked behind the medical center and ran across the street to the phone booth. Relieved to see it vacant, she called the hospital.

Ida answered on the first ring. Her voice was coarser than usual, but what frightened Kate was its lack of vigor.

"How's our girl?" Kate asked.

"She's got pneumonia. We had a rough night, but she's sleeping now."

"What's the prognosis?" Kate knew better than pretend that the situation wasn't serious. "And how are you doing?"

"Fair, at best—for Veda that is. But these young doctors don't know shit. They fly in the room for two minutes, have a quick look, make notes, and fly out faster than a pigeon fleeing a hawk. They don't tell you nothing, because they don't know nothing."

"Have you had any sleep?"

"Not much, Veda was cranky most of the night."

"If Veda's resting, that's a good sign. Try to get some sleep yourself."

"Easier said than done. We've got company."

Kate's heart leapt in hopes that Nate had reconsidered and decided to visit his great-grandmother.

"A woman who had her female troubles yanked out joined us across the curtain. Either she's overjoyed at the thought of her new life with her hormones under control, or she's a TV junkie. I swear, the next time the bitch dozes off, I'm going to flush that little back button thing down the toilet."

"You mean the TV remote?"

"Whatever."

"Ida, Nate paid me a visit last night, or early this morning I should say." Ida was silent, and Kate had learned that silence from Ida was not a good thing.

"Ida?"

"I'm listening."

Kate told Ida about the conversation with Nate, and asked Ida if she had any idea what things Nate felt he had to fix. Ida had a way of pulling pat answers from her well-stocked repertoire. And her response was one Kate had heard before, how Nate was a great kid and would never do anything wrong.

"Ida, I believe what you say, but Nate's in a lot of trouble. You need to help me out here if I'm to find out what's going on. Nate was with Frank on the day he was killed. The sheriff believes they had a fight over money. But Nate's assured me that wasn't the case."

"Ever since Nate left, Frank's been spouting off about his ungrateful grandson. The sheriff listens to rumors like everyone else. Reece's life insurance took care of Nate and he's also got a full scholarship. Besides, Nate knows that if he ever needs anything, he can come to me."

Kate felt like banging the receiver against the phone-booth window. Everything everyone told her sounded rehearsed. "Ida, listen to me. Nate admitted borrowing money from Frank in the past. Now please, what mess could Nate have gotten himself into that brought him to Two Horse on Thursday?"

Again silence.

Kate reciprocated.

"I don't know, Kate. I just don't know. But I know Nate didn't kill Frank. I did my best to try and let Nate and Frank develop their own relationship. Frank seemed to care about the boy, but he was never here long enough to make it matter. I still don't know how Nate turned out so normal. Every adult in his life has been nuts, except for Reece, and he went and got himself killed in some desert, fighting over some country that I'd never even heard of. I wish I could tell you more, but I don't have any more to tell." Ida drew in a breath and changed the subject. "I want to be at that meeting today, but I can't leave Veda."

"Don't worry about it, Ida. Speaking of the meeting, did the mayor ever come see you about relocating the mustangs?"

"Naw. You must have scared him off. You're getting the hang of living in Two Horse."

"Give some thought to what I said about Nate. I'll see you at the hospital as soon as the meeting is over. And I'll stay with Veda tonight. You need to go home and rest. Leave a message at the sheriff's office if you need anything."

"Yeah, right. At the sheriff's office where all the morons hang out."

Kate hung up the phone just in time to see the

longest funeral procession she had ever seen heading through the middle of town. The first car, which was not a limousine, pulled in front of town hall. Kate was taken aback when she saw that the procession was a Crow caravan led by Pete Bear Walks Slowly and James Brown Bird, Sr. Several men who were standing around their pickups started a series of mock war cries. Dread and despair washed over Kate. It was a good thing Ida wasn't here.

Kate slid more change into the slot and dialed Jack's cell. The Cubs were playing a night game at Wrigley. Whenever Kate was out of town, Jack spent every waking hour at the ballpark. As she listened to it ring, she swallowed two ibuprofen. Jack finally answered.

"How was Des Moines? Were you able to visit with your young pitcher?"

"Yeah, not that I did much good. I'm getting lonely. How much longer?" Jack chuckled.

"Can't say. Lord knows what the hell's going on here. The ranchers and the Crow who work for the teepee company are squaring off as we speak. What did you mean, 'you didn't do much good'?"

"Chambers wouldn't tell me much. He was having serious doubts about whether he could help the organization. Man, he had a classic case of depression. He feels guilty about letting everyone down, especially his parents. But he's not the sort of immature kid who expects life to be handed to him. And believe me, I've dealt with my share of those. Anyway, he asked for a couple of weeks off to think things over. I thought he'd go home, but he has some friends in Montana, near Billings. There's some kind of retreat happening there that he wanted to attend. I put him on the plane myself yesterday, but I made it clear I wanted to hear from him every day. The guys in the front-office aren't going to look kindly on this."

"You should've sent him to stay with the Springfields a few days. That would surely take his mind off his troubles."

"Last time we talked, you'd found a dead guy. I hope things have gotten better."

"No more dead people. Just a dead horse and a very sick lady. And Nate's disappeared."

"Disappeared?"

"The boy is wanted for questioning in Frank's murder, and Ida has bigger problems than saving horses. Her sister, Veda, is in the hospital with pneumonia."

"Better come home, Kate. Don't make me come get you."

Kate laughed. "You better not. You have your own crazy family to manage."

"My family members earn too much money to go around doing crazy shit—well, most of them anyway."

"How's Kenya?"

"Smart. She only limps when I'm watching. Kate, be careful."

They talked for a few more minutes, then Kate said good-bye and hung up. Guilt grabbed her before she opened the phone-booth door. She trusted Jack more than anyone on earth, yet she avoided telling him that Nate had come to the cabin and left with a gun. Had she wanted to keep Jack from worrying, or to keep from discussing the possibility that she might have misjudged Nate Springfield? Right now, she wasn't sure. She vowed the next time she talked to Jack, she'd fill him in, get his insight on the situation in Two Horse, and apologize for not being more trusting. But for now, she had the town meeting to deal with.

The day had turned blustery and the brightness of the morning had been replaced with swollen, low-hanging clouds. Kate grabbed her briefcase with her notes and flash drive with the video. As she walked across the town square to meet the gathering crowd, raindrops started to fall. Kate heard Karen Gregory before she spotted her standing with Pete and James. Karen held a sheet of paper and was waving it in the air like a flag. James grabbed the paper, read it, and shook his head. Pete stood there listening with his arms folded across his chest and his jaw tense. Several members of the Crow tribe walked over and turned their attention to what Karen was saying. Kate couldn't make out the words, but the angry look on Karen's face and James's look of disbelief told Kate that an unexpected development had occurred, one that apparently did not favor the environmentalists.

"Bad news?" Kate said when she approached the group.

Karen turned around, her face almost as red as her hair. "Do you want to tell her, or shall I?" Karen asked Pete.

"Our mayor's adjusted the agenda," Pete said to Kate. "And you're not speaking anymore."

Kate couldn't believe what she was hearing. "Can he do that?"

"He just did," Karen said and took the agenda from James. She handed it to Kate.

"Since this agenda was set before Ida recruited you, the only way you could have spoken was during Ida's scheduled time. And since Ida won't be here, Mayor

Winford scratched her name. That means you were scratched as well," Karen said.

"Can't I speak during someone else's time?" Kate looked at Pete.

"That's possible, but that call is strictly up to the mayor. He doesn't have to allow it. In fact, there was no guarantee that he would have allowed you to speak during Ida's time," Pete said. "Of course, with Ida here, he probably would have allowed it rather than incur her wrath, or have to cut the meeting short to avoid a riot."

Kate looked at the agenda. "Karen, you're speaking toward the end. I could go over my notes with you, and you could incorporate them into your talk. My video is on a flash drive."

"I've got my laptop," Karen said. "Let's find a place where I can look at it before the meeting."

"My house isn't far," James said. "If you left now, you'd be back before your scheduled time. My wife's at home. I'll give her a call and tell her you're coming."

"It's worth a try," Karen said. "Let's take my truck. I'm parked around back."

As Kate and Karen rounded town hall, three men came out of the sheriff's office next door. Mayor Winford and George Stokes were in a head-to-head discussion. Winford was firing comments at Stokes, and he nodded with impatience, looking as if he'd heard this too many times before. Sheriff Phillips took up the rear and glanced back at Kate. He tipped his hat and smiled— a smile that gave Kate the willies.

On the way to the Brown Bird place, Kate told Karen about Winford and Stokes's visit on Monday, about the mayor's offer to relocate the horses to his ranch, and Stokes's assessment that the new site would be able to sustain the herd.

"Any conclusion like that would take several weeks of study," Karen said. "Stokes is an idiot. He'll do whatever the mayor tells him. Those four guys were tight: Winford, Stokes, Sheriff Phillips, and Frank Springfield. I called them the Two Horse Social Club. Frank was the only one of the mayor's entourage who had any brains."

"An interesting mix."

"That's an understatement. You've got the head of our local government, the head of the local law enforcement, and the local head honcho of the National Park Service, all who on the surface appear to be concerned about the environment, plus a favorite son returned after a long absence."

"What was Frank Springfield's role in the social club?" Kate asked.

"Besides having an evangelical gift with words and being a longtime friend of the mayor, he had a knack for making things happen. I haven't been here that long, but the story I get is that Frank returned at the mayor's request. Sort of became a spokesman for whatever cause Winford assigned to him. In fact, Frank ran the mayor's last campaign."

"From a pipeline worker in Alaska to a public relations man in Two Horse. Sounds like a man of many talents.

"Actually, Frank boasts of being a project engineer."

"Did you know Winford has also offered to buy the Nelson farm?" Kate said. "Lucy and Ed are giving it serious consideration." She studied the agenda again. "Weren't the Nelsons scheduled to speak?"

Karen looked out of the corner of her eye at Kate.

"Yeah, why?"

"Because they're not listed here."

"Shit. The mayor really has been busy."

****

Martha Brown Bird greeted Kate and Karen from the front steps. "Come in, please. You can work in the den."

"Thanks, Martha," Karen said.

Karen watched the video while Kate sketched out notes. Once they decided on their strategy, wrapping up the details went quickly.

"We've got about an hour before my time slot," Karen said. "I'll call the Nelsons to find out what's up. Even if they decided to sell their farm to Winford, their presence at the meeting couldn't hurt."

"Good idea. I need to have a word with Jim."

Kate found Jim under the tent directing a skeleton crew of teepees assemblers. He was watching a young woman as she traced patterns on a large piece of cream-colored hide that was stretched over a frame that looked similar to one used for stitching quilts. When he noticed Kate coming toward him, he grabbed a bottle of soda from a bucket of ice and motioned for her to join him at a bench under a grove of trees. The look on his face told Kate that he wasn't happy to see her.

"Thanks for getting my message to our friend," Kate said. "He came to see me early this morning."

Jim sat his bottle on the bench and stared off into the distance.

"He didn't tell me much, but at least I was able to reassure Ida that he was okay," Kate continued.

Jim shrugged his shoulders. "I told him to turn himself in. But I've known Nate a long time, and he's pretty stubborn."

"Do you know what kind of problems he's trying to correct? He was adamant about fixing something before he came out of hiding. Does it have anything to do with Rachel?"

"I told you Rachel hates Nate."

"Was Nate upset about their breakup?"

"He doesn't talk much about things like that." Jim stood up and looked toward the work area. "Listen, I need to get back on the job. Most of our people are at the meeting, and there's a lot to do. I don't know what Nate's got going. He tapped on my window last night, right out of the blue. He wanted to know how to get in touch with my older sister. Then I told him about you wanting to see him. We talked for a while and he left."

"Why did he want to see your sister? Are they close friends?"

He turned and looked directly at Kate. "Beats me. He barely knows Jackie. She's lived over at St. Francis Xavier's for the last eight years. She's a nun."

Before Kate could digest that last bit of information, Karen tooted on the horn, pointed to her watch, and motioned for Kate to hop in the truck.

"Coming," Kate called. "Guess what? Since Nate is not able to help with tomorrow's gathering, Jim's agreed to be of service. He's bringing a couple of his buddies, too." She winked at Jim.

"That's great, Jim," Karen yelled out the pickup window. "Be at Ida's tomorrow morning at nine. We need all the help we can get."

Jim dropped his Mountain Dew. Kate hadn't worried about Jim refusing. A person couldn't talk unless their trachea was flooded with air. Jim seemed to have lost his breath.

Kate sprinted across the yard and hopped into the pickup.

"This just might work," Karen said and gunned the motor. They sped toward the road that led to the highway. "Mayor Winford and his redneck, screw-the-environment cronies may have shot themselves in the foot over this one. The information you gave me is just what we need. And these people here may find it easier to swallow if it came from me rather than an outsider, no offense."

"None taken," Kate said, as she buckled her seat belt. Karen's excitement had escalated, and the faster she talked the faster she drove.

"Besides, the election next week will be close. They may talk like they have it in the bag, but they don't. Otherwise, why were they willing to relocate the mustangs and purchase the Nelson farm?"

"Why, indeed?" Kate said. Was Mayor Winford simply a man who hated to lose? Or was he playing it safe, as Karen suggested, by pulling out all the stops because he no longer had his friend and spokesman to advise him? Whatever the reason, Kate didn't have a good feeling about Winford's motivations.

"What?" Karen said in response to Kate's prolonged silence.

"I don't know. There's been too many unexpected events recently. Frank's sudden interest in Ida's ranch, Nate's unusual behavior, the killing of the stallion. And the Nelsons' change of heart about selling their farm. And now the mayor's offering to take Ida's horses. There's got to be a connection."

"And Frank's murder. Don't forget about that."

Yes, Frank's murder, Kate thought. Was that the connection? The question resonated in Kate's mind. The loudest voice of the social club was murdered after he apparently changed his mind about Ida's ranch. If what Nate said was true, that Frank had offered to help run the ranch once it came to Nate. To be successful a ranch needed a good water supply. If Winford thought Frank's sudden desire to keep the ranch in the family was a betrayal, then the dam itself was really more important to the mayor than simply satisfying the ranchers of Carbon County. And what had caused Frank to change his mind? Why was he on Ida's ranch the day he was killed? If she could find the answers to those two questions, maybe Kate would have her connection. But so far the task seemed impossible.

All the unanswered questions left Kate feeling less than enthusiastic. Maybe it was good that Karen was going to do the talking. The thought of Nate being desperate enough to take Ida's gun and risk everything to right a wrong made Kate's initial role as environmental spokesperson seem unimportant. Swaying a scant number of votes would not solve the Springfields's problems now, especially with Nate as the sheriff's number-one suspect. Suddenly Kate's priorities shifted. She knew Nate was innocent. She had to find the real killer. But where should she start? Murder usually proved to be close to home, intimate. Kate thought of Imagene Porter. She might have an alibi, but if Frank was a talker, maybe he let something slip about whatever scheme he had going. For now, Kate kept her thoughts to herself. She did not want to douse Karen's enthusiasm.

"Did you talk to the Nelsons?" Kate asked.

"I called. No answer."

Kate and Karen entered the town hall just as James Brown Bird recapped his presentation. His projected gross from Crow Teepee Company of Two Horse this year was close to four-hundred thousand dollars. Even though his employees were all from the reservation, money in tribal members' pockets would be money spent in Two Horse. If the dam flooded the land along the river north of town, cutting off access to necessary timber, the company would fold and thirty-six people would lose their jobs.

Pete Bear Walks Slowly spoke next about the cultural aspects of James's company. Construction of these Native American structures would become a lost art if the Crow people were not given the opportunity to continue the craft and pass it on to the next generation. This drew snickers from a group of ranchers congregated on one side of the room. Pete glanced at his opposition and reaffirmed James's claim that financial stability of the company would benefit the town. Plus, five hundred visitors had come to Crow Teepees so far this year. If people were willing to add Two Horse to their tourist stops, many businesses in Two Horse would benefit in the long run. Then he reminded them of how the once-dusty town of Red Lodge had been transformed to one of the hottest ski locations in the state.

While she was standing at the back, Kate overheard two men agree with Pete's assessment. "That dude ranch near Red Lodge is booked year-round, and they're building more facilities," said a scruffy looking fellow to the guy sitting in the next seat. "Hell, I got two hundred head of cattle, and it's touch and go every year. I just might add another bunkhouse or two and turn my place into a dude ranch. Teach my ranch hands some manners.

Then find some city folks who want to come to my ranch and do the shit work and pay me for it. I'd rather sit around a campfire singing cowboys songs and drinking wine with some rich folks than fall into bed dog-tired every night smelling like cow shit." He snickered.

The other guy nudged his friend in the ribs. "Yeah. You could call your place Two Horse Trails, or Cowpoke Spa and Resort."

"Or how 'bout Separate-a-Fool-from-His-Money Dude Ranch?"

"I like Home-on-the-Cow-Shit-Range." Both men chortled at their jokes, but Kate didn't miss the dollar signs in their eyes.

Chapter Twelve

Karen spoke after Pete, and it was clear that the young woman's enthusiasm had not waned during the wait for her moment in the spotlight. She seemed to be in her element, and spoke with a fervor that commanded everyone's attention. Kate thought about Karen's rickety, aluminum trailer and how much she must have to give up to live and work here. Every word the young park ranger spoke came from the heart. Karen had started by thanking everyone for taking time from their busy lives to come and listen to a bunch of experts who acted like they had all the answers. The crowd mumbled an appreciative laugh and nodded in agreement with her candor.

"The truth is," she continued, "there's no one here who knows, proof positive, what's best for Two Horse. All we can do is gather as much data as possible, analyze it, and hope for the best. But it's equally important to look at the past. There's not one of us here who doesn't see that we've screwed up Southern Montana. I'm sure no one wants to continue down that road. Scraping out a living here is harder than trying to make corn grow from a rock. We've exploited our resources and used up too much of what God's given us without thinking of what we'll do when it's all gone. So instead of fighting over what's left, let's consider ways we can make those resources last by working together as the level-headed

Montanans that we are."

A round of polite applause and murmurs of agreement came from at least half the people in the audience. Karen continued, using Kate's information, which offered viable alternatives that cost less than damming the Pryor River and causing some people to come out winners and others losers. Karen showed segments of Kate's video and concluded, cautioning everyone about making decisions now that they would regret later. Karen had their attention. Heads were nodding. But before Karen called for questions, a lanky man suddenly stood up, pushing his chair back so hard it tumbled over.

"The only regret I have is sitting here listening to this bullshit." He jabbed his sweat-stained cowboy hat into the air emphasizing each word. "I need to be out working my ranch. Every hour I'm not there is time wasted. I don't need to be talked to as if I were an idiot. We all know about limited resources. We all know about mistakes of the past. But we also know that ranchers need water."

Another rancher stood up. "I'm trucking in water daily just to keep my cattle from dying. I don't need to gather no damn data. The drought's all the data I need."

Mayor Winford banged his gavel and pointed to the men causing the outburst. "Buddy Gill, you and Chester shut up and sit down. You'll have your say-so when it's time. Now, do what I say, or I'll remove you from the list of speakers."

"You do that, Mayor, 'cause I've said all I want to say." Buddy edged his way through the row of people. By the time he reached the aisle, he had gathered more steam. He looked over at a group of Crow sitting together on the other side of the room. "You can build those teepees out of any damn wood. To hell with them being authentic. I ain't gotta choice. I can't compromise. I need water."

"Don't you tell us about compromise. We've compromised all the way down to our tribe's dignity," said a man Kate had seen the day before at the Brown Bird meeting. The mayor continued to bang his gavel, but the sound was lost in the uproar. The entire crowd was now on its feet—ranchers, Crow, and environmentalists—shouting threats and obscenities. Several men grabbed and shoved at one another, ripping shirt collars. Before the mayor could slam his gavel again, punches were thrown, and chairs began to fly. Kate ducked as a seat cushion flew over her head. Pete managed to grab James Brown Bird's arm just as he was about to connect his fist with Buddy Gill's jaw. Suddenly, gunshots rang out, and the angry citizens of Two Horse hit the floor.

Sheriff Phillips stood in front of the mayor's desk with his pistol pointed at the ceiling. "I'll shoot the next man who throws a punch."

The crowd froze, not doubting the sheriff's admonition. Within five minutes, the sheriff and Deputy Lucas had removed half-a-dozen men from the town hall, and those who remained began straightening the furniture. Karen was still at the microphone, her red coloring having drained to a pale white. Mayor Winford wiped the sweat off his neck, and turned to Karen and said, "I want to thank this little lady for her concerns. You did a good job with that speech, Miss Gregory." His patronizing remarks brought Karen back to life. Then he made the mistake of adding, "We need to hear what the younger citizens have to say. They'll be voting soon." He chuckled.

As Karen stepped from the podium, she volleyed with, "I've voted here twice and neither time did I vote for you, Mayor." Her comment threw the crowd into a fit of laughter, but since Karen's back was to the mayor, he only caught a few words, and was smart enough to let the comment lie. He opened the floor for the allotted five-minute statements.

The next and final three speakers were hard-core ranchers who owned much of Carbon County and who collectively employed more than two hundred people. They spoke about saving their ranches, but also increasing their productivity, which would mean more jobs and more cash in the citizens' pockets—more, they said, than any tourist operations could bring in.

Karen leaned close to Kate and whispered, "What they've failed to mention is that most of their employees are illegals from Mexico working for next to nothing. The locals who work on those ranches get the high-paid positions of managers and foremen."

The town meeting closed with the ranchers having the last word. Pete and James were standing outside when Kate and Karen left the building.

"Out on bail already?" Karen said to James.

"No one was arrested," James said. "But I'd gladly spend a night behind bars for another shot at pounding Gill's face in. He's nothing but a loudmouth son-of-a-bitch that needs to be taught a lesson."

"Yeah, but you can't go to jail, James," Pete sighed. "At least not this week. We need you to keep the campaign going. Knock on doors. Make some phone calls. Get the word out." His declarations sounded good, but lacked enthusiasm. Quiet and contemplative, he was a difficult man for Kate to figure.

"What about the Nelsons?" Karen asked. "I think it's worth a visit to find out how serious they are about selling out."

"They never really fit in here," James said. "To tell the truth, it surprised me when Ida recruited them to help with our cause. It's true the dam would ruin them, but they always struck me as the kind of people who like to keep to themselves."

Kate agreed with James's assessment. Lucy Nelson and her cherished collection of Royal Doulton figurines, Wedgwood coffee service, and Early American parlor furniture was definitely one of a kind in Two Horse.

They continued laying out strategies for the upcoming days. Pete had business near Red Lodge and would do whatever campaigning he could along the way. James, with Martha's help, would man the phone lines in Two Horse. And Karen would visit the Nelsons.

As they were dispersing, Pete said, "Anyone heard from Nate?" The question was directed at the group, but he looked directly at Kate when he spoke.

Rather than lie, and say that she hadn't spoken to Nate, Kate held her tongue and said nothing.

James finally spoke. "I've known that boy all his life, and I can't figure it. He's the only Springfield with any sense. I can't believe he'd kill Frank."

"He sure is acting guilty by hiding from the law," Pete said.

"I'd hide out too if the sheriff wanted me for a murder I didn't commit," Karen said.

"Even Ida hasn't heard from him?" This time Pete's question was definitely directed at Kate.

Kate could handle this question without lying. "Ida hasn't heard a word from him, and I'm afraid this whole ordeal's taking its toll on her, especially with Veda in the hospital."

Pete's phone chirped. He checked the number and didn't look too pleased with what he saw. "Gotta go. Let me know what you find out about the Nelsons," he said to Karen. Then he left. James excused himself as well.

"Want to ride over to the Nelson farm with me?" Karen asked.

Kate was tempted out of sheer meanness. She'd love to see the look on Lucy Nelson's face when she opened the door to see Kate standing there. But Kate had no time to fool around.

"I think you're better off by yourself. Besides, I need to get back to the hospital to give Ida some relief. She's hardly left Veda's bedside."

"Those two are something." Karen shook her head. "You know Ida always talks about how Veda can't get along without her older sister, and there's no doubting that. But I think if Ida Springfield didn't have Veda to look after, she'd be the one to fall apart. I'll be at the ranch tomorrow morning around eight to get everything ready before our cowboys arrive. Thanks again for arranging all the extra help for the horse-gathering, and of course, for today. I think it went really well, considering. Take care."

As Karen turned to leave, Kate asked, "Do you know where I can find Imagene Porter?"

"Another colorful figure in Two Horse. She's across the street working check-out at Molin's." Karen waved and was gone.

Since Ida's coffee-can was almost empty and the

last egg had been used for Nate's breakfast, Kate needed no excuse to browse the grocery aisles. She walked across the street and entered the store. Walmart would be shamed. This place was huge—one long warehouse-type store, minus the florescent lights and flashing advertisements. Kate crossed through the dry-goods section and went into the grocery area. Molin's reminded her of the old A & P in Austin where her grandmother used to shop. The shelves were short, and you could see over the top and chat with whomever was in the next aisle. The wooden floor had buckled in places and the grain smoothed and barely visible. There were three checkout stands. Two were in operation, and Kate had no trouble picking out Imagene Porter.

"Jerry Mason, get out. You can't tell me you quit drinking beer. Lord knows, if that belly sags any more, you're going to need a forklift to move it."

"I quit when I run out and have to wait till payday," Jerry retorted. "And I seen the way you look at my body. You love it." Jerry grabbed his sack of groceries, patting his stomach on the way out of the store.

Imagene whistled as Jerry departed, then reached over to check-out her next customer.

"Imagene, keep flirting like that, and Sonny's going to wonder if you still love him," said a woman who had two grocery carts filled with dog food, cat litter, frozen TV dinners, and not much else. "Give me two cartons of Marlboro Lights."

"Well, Faye, since we're giving each other advice, if you didn't take in every stray in the county you could afford something better than TV dinners."

The two women laughed and continued slinging friendly insults. When Imagene had sacked the last of the

Kathleen Kaska

frozen dinners, she called out to the other checker. "Ben, I'm taking my break." She grabbed her cigarettes and lighter and headed for the backdoor. Kate followed.

Outside in back of the store, a picnic table, two plastic chairs, and an old gallon ice-cream bucket now full of sand and cigarette butts decorated the break area. Imagene had settled into one of the chairs and was inhaling deeply when Kate joined her.

"Imagene Porter?" Kate asked.

"That's me. My husband's the one who pays the bills—or doesn't—which is why you're here, right?"

"No, Mrs. Porter. I need your help with a problem. I've talked to several people and have gotten nowhere," Kate said.

"Have a seat." Imagene blew a plume of smoke out the side of her mouth. She was much younger than Kate had thought, probably in her late thirties or early forties. Dressed in tight black jeans with silver studs down the side and a low-cut tank top under her unbuttoned checker's smock, Imagene look like a female body builder in bling. Her platinum hair was piled on top of her head and held in place with a silvery sequined clip that matched her inch-long nails. Throw on some expensive jewels and clothes and she'd be a Kardashian. She took a final drag from her cigarette then snubbed it out in the ice-cream bucket, leaving the filtered tip smeared with a bright red lipstick-ring.

"Bad habit."

Kate sat down and introduced herself.

"Oh, I heard about you. You're Ida's friend. I heard Veda's in the hospital. How's she doing?"

"Not good. Her strep has turned into pneumonia, but she's holding her own."

166

"That's too bad. I like those two old gals. They give this boring town something to talk about. You had something to ask me?"

"I'm sure you've heard about Nate."

"That boy didn't kill no one. I can tell you that."

"I feel the same way, but the sheriff thinks differently. Something happened on Thursday, the day Frank was killed, and I'm afraid it involved Nate. I just need some answers." Kate paused and considered how to word her question, but it wasn't necessary.

"You're looking to find someone else that could have killed Frank, and you thought of me."

"Sheriff Phillips told me that he'd already spoken to you. I don't mean to pry into your personal business, Mrs. Porter, but—"

"Imagene. I didn't have anything serious going with Frank, in spite of the rumors. I'm a big flirt and so was Frank. Sonny, my husband, is big, quiet, and mean looking, so people think he's real bad. But he's also as exciting as a warm glass of milk. Hell, if I didn't have my job here at Molin's where I can jaw with folks, I'd go crazy. Frank was always coming in here and we'd go on about running away together. It was just crazy talk. He'd come in and say, 'Imagene, I'm on my way to Cozumel—going diving. Leave that stupid husband of yours and come along with me.'"

"Did you ever go?"

"Hell no! What do I know about scuba diving or any of that other crazy stuff he spouted off? It was just a game we liked to play."

"Did Sonny mind?"

"You know, Ms. Caraway, I could've run off with Frank to Cozumel or wherever, and Sonny wouldn't have missed me until the food ran out and there was no more clean overalls in his drawer. But I'm all talk and no action."

"You just flirted with one another whenever Frank came in for groceries?"

Imagene pulled another cigarette out of the pack, lit it, and inhaled. She squinted at Kate as if considering her next words. "It don't matter now. Frank and I used to meet for drinks over at the Dead Coyote. He'd talk about all these great deals he had coming down. Frank always had a get-rich scheme brewing. Most didn't pan out. We called a halt to everything about a month ago. But I never got between the sheets with him, and that's the god's-honest truth." She took another drag and let the smoke trail from her nostrils. "Sonny didn't kill Frank. We were both in Billings when Frank was murdered. But Sonny wouldn't have killed Frank anyway because my husband didn't care enough to."

"Did Frank ever talk to you about the dam?"

"All the time. That's all he would talk about. How his mother and all these ecology-type people were bound and determined to stop progress and ruin Carbon County."

"Was he afraid the dam would be voted down?"

"No way. He knew the dam was a sure thing, and I believed him."

"How's that? How could he be so certain?"

Imagene put her cigarette down in the plastic ash tray, removed the clip from her hair, twisted it for a tighter hold, and replaced the clip. Just as Kate was beginning to think that Imagene would say no more, she finally spoke. "Because something big was coming down. He said he couldn't tell me, but he was busting at the seams, like he knew this big secret. I've never known Frank to hold his tongue, but he wasn't talking about this one, at least not to me. I even saw him riding around with someone in an expensive, dark blue car. You know, one of those big machines that people who have too much money drive, a Cadillac or Lincoln, or something like that." She looked at her watch. "Break's almost over. I wish I coulda helped you more, but you're talking to the wrong woman." Imagene snubbed out her cigarette and stood up.

Kate waited.

Imagene gathered up her pack and lighter. "Good luck. If I hear of anything, I'll let you know."

"Why did you quit?" Kate asked.

"Quit what?"

"Meeting Frank for drinks at the Dead Coyote."

"Like I said, you're talking to the wrong woman." Imagene went back inside, closing the door behind her a bit harder than necessary.

Kate sat for a moment, hoping something would gel in her brain. Apparently Frank had dumped Imagene for another woman— one he was not flaunting at the local bar. Besides needling Nate's friends, Kate had another suspect to hound. Tomorrow promised to be a busy day.

Kate went back inside the store, bought the necessary groceries, and left. Back at Ida's, Kate unpacked the bags and gathered what she needed for an overnight stay at the hospital. She planned to do her best to convince Ida to go back home for the night.

****

Veda's face had lost the sparkle. Awake but listless, she seemed to be staring at nothing. Even Ida's voice was going unheard.

"The doctors had to put an IV in this afternoon. Veda stopped eating." Ida stood up and tucked the sheets around Veda. "So tell me how the meeting went."

Kate related the events of the day. Ida listened, letting out expletives now and then, but without her usual flamboyance. She was not even surprised that Mayor Winford had removed her name from the agenda. But she beamed when Kate told her Winford had not voiced his proposal to move the mustangs to his ranch, and she chuckled lightly when Kate told her about the riot.

"Pete and James plan to step up their campaign this week. I'd say the election will to be a close one," Kate said.

"You did what you could." Ida patted Kate's knee. "I've no right to ask you to do anything more." Ida paused. "But I need to know Nate's okay, and I don't want him to turn himself in."

"Hiding out makes Nate look guilty—"

Ida raised her hand as if to shield herself from Kate's words. "Nate's not guilty, but when that sheriff seizes on something, he's like a dog on a bone. I couldn't handle it if Nate was thrown in jail."

"Running from the law puts Nate's life in danger."

Ida didn't respond.

"Who else could have killed Frank? Think, Ida. I came to a dead end with Imagene Porter this afternoon. Seems she and Frank met for drinks on occasion until Frank found another girlfriend, but that's all. Besides, Imagene and Sonny have an alibi. Any idea who the other woman is?"

"Could be anyone. Frank wasn't picky."

"Frank's murder must be connected to the election, especially since Randy was killed. But then why would the killer strip off Frank's pants? That sounds like a jilted lover or a jealous husband." Ida sagged back in her chair. The look of exhaustion on her face worried Kate. "Ida, go home tonight and get some real sleep. If you're rested, you can think better. Come back in the morning, and we'll put our heads together and try to figure this out."

Ida agreed. She gave Veda a kiss on the cheek and told her to behave herself.

Kate handed Ida the keys to the pickup and could not wait any longer. "Ida, I didn't tell you this earlier, but Nate has your gun. When I was gathering your clothes last night, I found the pistol in your dresser drawer. After Nate left the cabin this morning, I checked the drawer. The gun was gone."

"Fine, just fine," Ida said as she left the room.

The curtain between the two hospital beds was partially drawn, enough to give the two patients privacy and a view of the TV. The hysterectomy patient had the only remote-control and was flipping channels. She was considerate enough to have muted the sound. Veda was watching as the TV screen flashed channels.

Veda began to doze, so Kate pulled a yellow legal pad from her bag and started jotting down the facts as she knew them.

Kate glanced at the TV screen. Something had finally caught the other woman's interest. The History Channel was airing a feature on the history of the automobile, with film footage from the first half of the century. Suddenly, the volume came back on, and jolted both Kate and Veda.

"Sorry, sorry," the voice from the other side of the curtain said. "I didn't know it was up that loud." She muted the TV.

"It's okay," Kate said. "No harm done."

Veda was now wide awake and staring at the TV. Kate went back to making notes. All of a sudden, Veda screamed and started pulling at her oxygen tube. Kate grabbed Veda's arms and tried to calm her, but Veda only kicked and fought harder.

"Could you please ring the nurse, ma'am," Kate called to the other patient.

"Yes. Oh, my. I'm so sorry."

By the time help arrived, Veda had kicked the blankets off the bed and pulled the oxygen tube completely out. Kate had kept a hold on the IV to prevent Veda from removing that as well.

Two nurses came in and took over while Kate tried to calm Veda. One nurse held Veda's legs, while the other held her shoulders down. The neighboring patient had turned off the TV but continued to mutter apologies.

"Should we give her a sedative?" the nurse holding Veda's legs asked her colleague.

"I think she'll be okay. Are you all right, ma'am?" she asked Kate.

"I'm fine" Kate said. "I think the sudden noise of the TV frightened her."

Veda had calmed down, and the nurses released her. They replaced the breathing tube and straightened out the bed covers. There were tears in Veda's eyes. "Veda's hurt," she said. "Ida's gone."

"It's okay, Veda," Kate whispered. She reached over and held Veda's hand. "Ida will be back in the morning." Before they left, Kate asked one of the nurses to pull the curtain completely around Veda's bed.

"Would you like some orange juice, Veda?" Veda nodded and Kate put the straw to Veda's lips. She sipped a little of the juice. The tears were gone, but the fear in Veda's eyes remained.

Kate was afraid, too. Not about what she had just seen, but because of what she had not.

Chapter Thirteen

The early part of the evening went without incident. Veda fell asleep again with the help of a mild sedative added to her IV. Kate lay on the bedside cot and stared at the ceiling. Her mind, unable to rest, raced over the day's events, but making sense of everything that had happened was a useless effort. Sleep was as far away as next week. Kate gave up and decided to call Karen. It was late, but she chanced that Karen might still be awake. Karen answered on the second ring and sounded as wired as Kate.

"How did it go with the Nelsons?"

"I only talked to Ed. Lucy wasn't feeling well."

"Another migraine?"

"Hey, you've been here less than a week and you know more about what's happening than I do. Yes, another migraine."

"Are they selling the farm?"

"Looks that way. Ed seemed pretty dejected. He says the stress of running the place is affecting Lucy's health. But I think if it were up to him, he wouldn't sell. Something else has got to be going on."

"What do you mean?"

"I just talked to them less than ten days ago and they were both hell-bent on saving the family farm. Lucy was gung-ho about speaking at the meeting, and now they're ready to sell. It doesn't make sense."

"Maybe she's really having health problems. I'd like to talk to Lucy again, but I'm not one of her favorite people."

"Maybe I can find out something. I'll call Meg Little Coyote. If the Nelsons have a secret, Meg will either know, or know how to find out. See you tomorrow."

At around one-thirty in the morning, Kate felt like asking the nurse if she could hook Kate up to a drug-cocktail IV, too. How anyone ever rested in a hospital was beyond her. The activity in the halls never stopped. The hospital staff went about their duties with all the noise and bright lights necessary to complete their tasks. Veda slept fitfully. Whenever it seemed she had fallen into a restful sleep, a nurse would walk in to check on her patient's condition. Then Veda would wake with uncontrollable coughing that took several minutes to subside. Each time this happened, Kate sat up next to Veda until she fell back to sleep.

The last such interruption occurred around four o'clock, after which Kate finally fell asleep. She dreamed she was searching for a phone to call Jack. She needed to tell him that Nate had headed back to Chicago and that he had stolen a gun. But every time she found a phone, she dialed the wrong number. Pete Bear Walks Slowly appeared with his cell phone and handed it to her, but then Kate forgot the number while she dialed. She went back to Ida's truck to dig the address book from her backpack. When she returned, Pete had disappeared, taking his phone with him. Her frustration grew into an intense fear that Jack was in trouble. Then, just as the sun was beginning to brighten the room, Kate was awakened with the smell of coffee—good coffee.

"Rise and shine. I brought you a muffin and some

caffeine," Ida whispered. She placed her hand on Veda's forehead, then pushed Kate's legs over and sat down on the cot next to her. "I went to that fancy coffee-shop in Red Lodge. I had to wait in line. And the goddamn place had a menu."

Kate sat up and inhaled the familiar aroma. "This is Breakfast Blend, right?"

"How the hell did you know that? Some frisky gal wanted me to choose from three different coffee flavors. What do I know about flavors? I told her to give me something black and strong."

"Starbucks."

"No. Breakfast Blend. You said so yourself."

"I mean the name of the coffee shop—it was Starbucks." Kate sat up and drew her knees to her chest to give Ida more room.

"Whatever. Hell, I just sprinkle some instant coffee in a cup and pour on the hot water. I don't need all that fancy shit."

After reporting the evening's events, including Veda's TV-induced outburst, Kate turned the vigil over to Ida. Veda's color looked better, but her breathing was raspy, and her coughing spells had increased.

****

Yesterday afternoon's swollen rain clouds had emptied themselves during the night and then dissolved, leaving behind a fresh, cool smell of spring. When Kate arrived at Ida's ranch, a string of empty horse vans were parked next to Ida's barn. Karen walked the last horse from the back of a van. Three men stood nearby saddling their mounts. A fifth horse was already saddled. Kate assumed it was hers. Two of the men were strangers to Kate. The third, to Kate's surprise, was Pete Bear Walks

Slowly. The other two turned out to be Meg Little Coyote's sons, Ted and Daniel. Just as Karen completed the introductions, Jim Brown Bird, Jr. pulled up driving a company truck and towing a horse van. A young, dark haired woman sat next to Jim. A young man wearing a baseball cap rode shotgun.

"Sorry we're late. We had a hard time getting Ned into the van. I think he's claustrophobic. Hi, Karen." The young woman waved at everyone and walked up to Kate. "I'm Julie Brown Bird, Jim's sister."

Kate shook her hand. Julie was shorter than her brother, but tall for a woman. Her eager smile told Kate that Julie differed from Jim in another way—Julie was a talker.

"That's Clayton Farley. Jim said that he and I would be enough. But I knew that Clayton was just bumming around, so I called him to help."

"Shut up, Julie," Clayton called from the back of the van, rubbing sleep from his eyes. "Just because you're so chipper in the morning doesn't mean everyone else is."

Judging by the way Clayton blushed when Julie said his name, Kate guessed that, despite the young man's whining, he'd follow Julie on just about any mission she cooked up.

Kate walked up to Jim and thanked him for coming.

"Yeah, well, I didn't have a choice, did I? You're kind of pushy, you know."

"That's what I've been told."

"Come on, guys. Let's get going. I need to have the park's horses back as soon as possible," Karen said impatiently.

Kate noticed for the first time that Karen's usual

broad smile was absent, but figured it was probably because the park ranger had been awake several hours arranging last-minute details for the gathering. The three latecomers quickly saddled their mounts, Clayton and Julie teasing one another and laughing, while Jim said very little.

Twenty minutes later, all eight riders were trotting around the base of the mountain and into the canyon on the other side. Kate's horse, a spotted palomino gelding named Salty, was so light on his feet that he seemed to bounce on air. Kate rode up next to Karen to thank her for the horse. As she neared, Kate suspected that Karen's grouchy mood was due to something other than an early rise.

"Thanks for Salty," Kate said.

"He's a sweet one. My favorite. I knew you'd like riding him," Karen said, trying to resurrect her usual cheerfulness. "Last night, I hadn't planned on bringing him. He tends to get skittish when it thunders. But that storm wasn't too bad. When I checked on him this morning, he was eating well, and I had no trouble getting him into the van."

"He's beautiful," Kate said, patting her steed on the side of his neck. "What's wrong?"

"I'm fine," Karen said.

"No, you're not."

Karen glanced at Kate and sighed. "Just as we were loading the horses, Stokes drives up and gives me a load of shit for using park horses and equipment."

"But I thought this was planned weeks ago," Kate said.

"It was. I sort of had to go over his head, and he's been on my case ever since. I don't know how long I'll be wearing this uniform." Karen took off her cap and ran her fingers through her hair. "We've never gotten along. I kept watching him during my presentation yesterday. I could tell he wasn't happy with my ideas. But then, he's not happy with anything I do. He refers to me as the 'girl,' even in front of the others."

"Sounds like he feels threatened," Kate offered. "You know—a young, smart woman with better ideas than his."

"Maybe. I was thrilled to get this assignment. It was my first choice—to be here working with the mustangs. If I get transferred, no telling where I'll end up. Somewhere in Oklahoma counting prairie dogs, maybe. But I'm here today, and that's all that matters." Karen nudged her horse and trotted off.

Kate wondered how such a young woman had become so wise. At Karen's age, Kate had rebelled against everything out of pure stubbornness, spurred by an immature sense of rights and freedom. Kate followed Karen's lead and focused on the task at hand, one that up until this moment, she had not realized how much she was to enjoy.

As many times as Kate had ridden, she'd never quite gotten used to the size and power of these animals. Sliding her boot into the left stirrup and swinging her right leg over the back of the horse always seemed easy enough. But once in the saddle, a strong bonding occurred. Every nuance communicated a message, the twitching of the horse's ears, the raising and lowering of its head, and the expression in its eyes communicated things the rider needed to know.

Salty flicked his ears and nodded his huge head as Kate patted his neck once more. He looked back over his shoulder and Kate saw an approving look on his face. She slacked the reins, gently squeezed her thighs and took Salty into a trot and then a gallop. He seemed content to follow Karen's horse. And until Kate could acclimate herself to being in motion four feet off the ground, she was more than willing to accommodate him.

Everyone else, except for Kate, was obviously an experienced horse person. Julie and Jim were riding their own horses, and riding was part of the job for Karen. Meg's two sons looked more comfortable on horses than off. Although Pete's horse was huge, at least sixteen hands, Pete's bulk gave the perfect appearance of a barrel balanced on a saddle.

On the way into the canyon, Karen briefed everyone on the game plan. The goal was to herd the mustangs without causing injuries or undue stress. Once the herd was spotted, Karen would lead her posse around the mustangs in single-file, without getting too close. If they were feeding in the narrow west canyon, the plan was to herd them in one large group up to the road, and then into the corral located in the pasture near Ida's lake. That would be fairly easy. But if the mustangs were spread out across the entire valley, the morning would be more adventurous. Instead of simply herding them as a group, the riders would have to double-up and take one mustang at a time. Once all eighteen mustangs were corralled, the riders would split up. Pete, Jim, and Clayton would herd the horses into the squeeze-chute. Then Karen, Julie, and the Little Coyote brothers would handle blood-sampling and examinations. Kate would document the horses' behavior. If everything went as planned, the work would be completed shortly after the noon hour. If the horses were uncooperative, they would be there all day.

But the first thing on the agenda was to view the body of the dead stallion. The stench was much stronger today and everyone covered their mouths and noses as they approached. Pete dismounted. "It was a rifle, all right." He turned to look behind him. "The guy was probably perched up on that outcropping."

"How could anyone kill such a beautiful animal?" Julie said, not expecting an answer.

"More than 'how,' 'why'?" Karen added.

"And 'who' is going to be impossible to figure out," Pete said. "Everyone around here totes a rifle. And Ida pisses off so many people in Two Horse, the line of suspects would stretch from here to Billings."

"I can't believe someone would do this to get back at Ida," Karen said.

"Things have gotten tense around here. With Frank's murder and Nate on the lam…well, let's just say anything could've happened." Pete climbed back on his horse. "I, for one don't like being on this ranch. We need to stay heads up."

They rode off without anyone saying another word. Pete's warning and the fact that a man had been stabbed to death on this ranch less than a week ago stifled any attempt at joviality. Being in the shadow of the cliff where a sniper had recently perched caused the warmth of the morning to disappear as well. Kate kept looking over her shoulder, as did the others.

They continued on to the west canyon, but the area was devoid of horses. Karen suggested they split up to save time. She instructed Kate, Julie, Jim, and Pete to head east and follow a deer trail up over the canyon and into another valley. The others would follow her. They would take the narrow, rocky trail down along the creek.

Jim wasted no time speaking up. "Why don't Clayton and I swap? His cantankerous gelding doesn't like to be separated from Julie's horse."

Julie winked at Clayton. The blush spread and covered his face in seconds.

"Fine with me," Karen said. "Jim, you, me, Ted, and Daniel will take the path along the creek." She handed Pete a walkie-talkie, and everyone headed out.

Clayton and Julie rode up ahead, teasing one another and laughing. Kate took that opportunity to talk to Pete privately. He was a complex man and hard to figure. Despite his previous curt words concerning his daughter, Kate was encouraged by his presence. "Do you really think someone killed Ida's stallion out of meanness?"

"Several years back, Ida shot a rancher's steer." Pete guffawed. "It had repeatedly wandered over to her property. She almost ended up in jail. But things were settled, and she paid for the steer and that was that."

"But that was a long time ago."

"Around here people hold grudges. Some of my own people work themselves into a fury over things that took place a hundred years ago when the Crow lost most of their land. I'm just saying what I said earlier. Ida attracts trouble."

"Don't you think it had something to do with the dam? If her ranch was established as a protected area with help from The Nature Conservancy, a lot of people who wouldn't make money in the tourist industry might want Ida to fail in that regard."

"Then why just kill one horse? Why not shoot the entire herd?"

What Pete said made sense. Except for harassing Ida, Kate couldn't see any viable reason for killing the mustang. It wouldn't even keep Karen from gathering sufficient data for the Conservancy. And with the election only a week away, anyone could realize that there wouldn't be enough time to have the preserve established, anyway. If the motive was to remove Ida's reason for opposing the dam, then the entire herd, like Pete said, should have been eliminated. And if truth be told, the presence of Ida's horses probably influenced no more than a dozen or so voters. The most influential people against the dam were the Crow with their desire to save their teepee business, and no attack was made against any of them. Every theory Kate came up with resulted in only more uncertainty and a plethora of questions leading in different directions.

They had traveled almost a mile and were nearing the valley when Pete's walkie-talkie crackled. "We're in luck," he said. "Karen's spotted the entire herd feeding down by the creek. She's going to head them toward the road. We'll make our way back and meet up with her, and head the horses off toward the lake."

They picked up their pace and arrived just as the mustangs were galloping up from the creek. As the wild horses turned toward the road, Karen and the others came into view. Kate was pleased to see a wide grin on Karen's face. It was apparent now how important this work was to the young woman. The first part of Karen's plan had been a success. Finding the herd had been easy. Kate hoped the rest of the day would fare as well.

Daniel and Ted Little Coyote went to work. Their job was to stand sentinel on either side of the corral keeping the gate wide open and closing it as soon as all the mustangs entered. If a stubborn mustang or two managed to circumvent the corral, there was no way to escape the area because of the bordering rocky landscape. Pete followed the alpha mare closely. If they could corral her first, the other horses would be prone to follow. With Jim and Clayton galloping into the herd, the rest of the group stayed behind to keep the mustangs from turning back and bolting in the opposite direction.

Having found her comfort zone, Kate was finally in rhythm with Salty's gallop. An overwhelming sense of power and freedom overcame her. The idea of having horses at her camp in Kenya had never crossed Kate's mind, but she now realized they would have been a great asset. Following an elephant herd on horseback would have been much less intrusive than maneuvering a jeep through the thorny grassland of the Amboseli.

All of a sudden two young stallions, a bright roan and a dapple gray, turned and bolted quickly, jolting Kate out of daydream. Anticipating their movements, she darted toward them to keep them from breaking free from the rest of the herd. Julie jerked her mount around, and both women headed down the road to cut off the runaways and force them back to the corral. Dust rose in a swirl, momentarily clouding Kate's vision. If she and Julie did not get in front of the two mustangs, they would dart toward the trail leading into the narrow valley, and herding them back would be impossible. Kate kicked Salty's flanks and pulled the reins to the right. Her horse flew into full gallop without any further encouragement. Julie swept to the left, and the race was on. Wild mustangs were hardy animals, but they were no match for the domestic horses and riders cutting and turning on a dime.

Soon Kate and Salty nosed past the two rebel mustangs. Then as the dust cleared, she saw, with a shock, that the road left no room for error. It sloped sharply down about ten feet into a ravine. If Salty stumbled or took a step too far to the right, rider and horse would tumble down the incline. Kate crouched in the saddle and with a tight squeeze of her thighs asked Salty to give all he had. He responded instantly, and they were now a good twenty-five yards ahead of the mustangs and back in the center of the road. Julie managed to pull ahead as well. Kate risked a glance at the truants. The look of freedom that moments ago had glowed in their eyes had turned to terror. They knew their escape route was now blocked. Kate glanced at Julie and gave a quick nod, indicating the next move.

Julie pulled her horse to a sliding halt in the middle of the trail entrance. Kate darted back to the road's edge. If the mustangs decided to leap over and down the embankment, severe injuries were sure to result. The roan turned and headed in Kate's direction as soon as he saw Julie blocking the trail. Kate cut back and forth, praying that her bluff would work. If the mustang continued to charge her, she'd give him plenty of room to keep from endangering Salty or herself. But there was no time for further strategies. The roan met Salty head-on, and both horses reared up on their hind legs. Kate grabbed the saddle horn, trying her best to stay aboard. The roan bucked and stamped, forcing Salty back to within inches of the drop-off. Salty stood his ground.

Just as the mustang surrendered the challenge and turned away, Kate felt the ground crumble beneath her horse. Salty lunged forward. Kate saw the fear in his eyes. He began sliding backward. She leapt from the saddle and flipped the reins over his head. Without her weight, the gelding regained his footing and with one hop was back on the road. Both stood there for a moment, catching their breath. Kate ran her hands down Salty's back legs. Except for a couple of minor scrapes, Salty appeared to be okay. Kate remounted.

"Great job!" Julie shouted. She trotted to Kate, stood up in the saddle, and gave Kate a high-five. "You're a natural on that horse."

"Salty did all the work. I was just trying not to wet my pants," Kate said, spitting dust from her mouth.

They galloped back toward the corral, keeping the two tiring stallions in front.

As they approached the group, Julie took off her cowboy hat and waved it in the air, announcing mission accomplished. A brilliant smile had spread across her face. Kate chuckled to herself, wondering what it was about horses that seemed to exhilarate women riders. Julie was having the time of her life, and her excitement was contagious. Now that the danger had disappeared, the adrenaline pumping through Kate's blood carried elation rather than fear. The idea of staying on Salty forever seemed delightful. Being outdoors and inhaling the raw essence of nature created an excitable flutter in Kate's stomach. She wondered what the hell she was doing back in Chicago. The ache to return to Kenya was the strongest since she and Jack had come back to the United States. The flutter of excitement then turned into a flutter of anxiety. Jack was committed to his new job in Chicago for at least two more years, and the only trip Kate would make was back to the city.

Most of the herd had entered the corral. The alpha mare was circling inside the enclosure, her nostrils flaring, alarm in her eyes. Another crucial moment had arisen. If she did not settle down, the other horses, as they approached the corral, would sense her fear and attempt to flee. As the other females, and some of the younger colts followed her inside, she appeared to calm somewhat. And the rest of the herd seemed to settle down as well.

Kate watched the horses circle inside the corral. Communication seemed to spread rapidly through the herd. Even the two young stallions whose escape Kate and Julie had thwarted earlier appeared to relax among the older mares. Seeing them all gathered together, drawing comfort from one another, convinced Kate, more than ever, that these animals had to be saved. If they were tenacious enough to survive in this harsh climate and desolate terrain where little else could, they had the right to be here unfettered and free. Kate felt a deep sorrow for what they were now putting these horses through, especially after the recent loss of their dominant male to a sniper. Who was going to replace him? The two young stallions had the strength and aggressiveness for the lead role, but each lacked the experience to take charge. Kate looked back to see the last horse enter the corral. Ted and Daniel closed the gate.

Karen motioned for everyone to join her. "Let's all take a breather. Our work gets harder from here. We need to let the mustangs relax. This flimsy corral will not hold them if they panic and bolt again. And that might happen if we lead them into the squeeze chute while they're still worked up."

The squeeze chute looked like a rundown version of a single racehorse starting gate. Once inside, the horse had little room to move. Karen had to work quickly to draw blood and make a brief examination. The horses' right ears would be tattooed by a quick-freeze method that would allow for easy future identification. While Karen was arranging her equipment, Kate joined Clayton and Julie.

"I haven't had this much fun since I untangled a young cheetah that had wrapped herself up in some sheets drying on a line," Kate said.

"I've always wanted to see Africa," Julie said. "Is it as wild as it looks on TV?"

"Africa is a feeling," Kate said then paused. "It's an emotion that can only be experienced in person. I'll never forget the first time I went to Kenya. As soon as the plane touched the tarmac, I almost started crying. I felt like I was finally home after a very long absence, even though I'd never been there before. It's really kind of hard to explain."

"That's neat," Julie said. "Man evolved from that area of the world. I guess it felt like you'd come back to your roots."

"Those are some long roots," Clayton said.

Kate laughed, "Right, eons long."

"Nate always liked your lectures. I think you really made an impression on him," Julie said.

"You and Nate must be good friends," Kate said. To include Clayton in the conversation, Kate added, "I hear you and Nate are buddies, too."

"We all hung around together. But Nate and Jim have been best friends since they were in first grade," Julie said. "I can't believe what's happening. There's all kinds of rumors that he killed his grandfather for some money."

"I've heard that too," Kate said.

"Nate wouldn't even step on a bug," Clayton responded. "We used to laugh at him and call him a

Buddhist. When we were little, he was always telling us how every living thing is linked to us, and stuff like that, and that if we broke the link, we'd die. What's going to happen to him, Ms. Caraway?"

"The longer Nate stays away, the worse his situation gets. I'm afraid he knows who killed his grandfather and he may be trying to protect that person."

"Sounds like something Nate would do," Clayton said. "He always took up for anyone in trouble."

Julie looked at Clayton, and her expression hardened. She reached down and ran her fingers through her horse's mane. "That's Nate, all right. Looking out for everyone, even when it's against his best interests." Then she rode away to join the others.

Chapter Fourteen

Kate tied Salty to the trailer-hitch of Karen's pickup. Then she hopped up on the cargo bed for a good perch to view the horses. Using her shorthand version of note taking, she began documenting the captured horses' behavior while Karen and Ted started the testing. Julie labeled and arranged the blood samples as Karen handed them to her. Each vial showed the horse's ID number, and Julie entered that number on a document set up on an iPad. The data would be fed into a computer later, and DNA comparisons would be run against the other herd at the Pryor Mountain Wild Horse Range.

Kate's analysis was less biological, but just as informative. By simply observing how the horses responded to one another, the herd's infrastructure could be determined: which ones nurtured, which ones sought comfort, which ones spooked easily, and where they stood in the social hierarchy.

They had just released the tenth mustang from the squeeze chute into the corral to rejoin the others. Jim trotted behind the young aggressive roan, ushering him into the chute. All of a sudden, shots rang out, echoing throughout the canyon. The roan spooked, rose up on his hind legs, and came down on top of Jim, knocking him off his horse and into the rope forming the fence. In a moment's flash, Kate saw all the terror of the day's ordeal in the roan's eyes. Fear had turned to anger, and the animal let out an earsplitting cry. It trampled Jim's foot, then reared again and came down on Jim's back and shoulders.

Kate dropped her clipboard and leapt off the truck. Ted reached Jim first and grabbed him by his right arm to pull him away. "Stop! Don't touch him! His back may be broken!" Kate yelled.

Pete and Clayton shouted and waved for the horse to back away, but the gesture made the situation worse. It was as if the horse, after backing down from its captors once, was now standing his ground. He lunged and kicked at Pete like a rodeo bronco that had just bucked its rider. The alpha mare had had enough as well and started trampling the fence on the other side of the corral.

"Let them go! Let them go!" Karen shouted to Clayton and Daniel to open the gate. As soon as the mare saw the opening, she darted for freedom. The other horses followed in a frenzied mass, hooves thundering so loudly that the second round of shots almost went unnoticed. In a matter of seconds, most of the herd had escaped the enclosure. The young stallion was out of control, darting out in every direction. He bolted toward the table where Julie had set the vials of blood samples. Karen grabbed the morning's work only moments before the horse's hooves crashed down, smashing the table into splinters. He then circled the perimeter of the enclosure, leapt over the fence, and was gone.

Jim was still conscious but not for long. Pete and Ted carefully untangled Jim's legs from the rope. Kate and Karen dragged over a long, flat board that had been part of Karen's work table. Kate saw the bony protrusion under Jim's thin T-shirt. His clavicle had been snapped in two. His ankle was probably broken as well. But mostly, Kate feared a spinal cord injury. Keeping his neck as straight as possible, they rolled Jim over and onto the board. A deep gash over Jim's left eye bled profusely. As Kate pressed a cloth to the wound, Jim passed out.

They lifted Jim into the bed of his pickup. Ted and Julie clambered in beside him. Pete hopped in the driver's seat and took off. The plan was to get him to the medical center in town where EMS could rush him to the hospital in Red Lodge. The others stayed behind.

An eerie silence replaced the noise and confusion. But the sense of danger had not dissipated. Kate scanned the canyon walls, shading the sun from her eyes.

"Did you hear the second shots?" she asked.

"After that horse came at me, I didn't hear anything but voices singing at my funeral," Daniel said.

"I heard the shots," Clayton said.

"The echoes in these canyons make it pretty tough to tell where they were coming from," Kate said.

"The shots were from different guns. The first rounds were from a rifle and the second a pistol," Clayton added.

"A pistol?" Kate asked. "Are you sure?"

"Positive." Clayton took off his baseball cap and wiped his forehead with his sleeve. "Do you think we're safe here?" He glanced up at the top of the cliffs.

"If someone was trying to disrupt the testing, I'd say they saw they succeeded and have probably left," Kate said. "If that was their purpose."

"I managed to save the blood samples," Karen said. "With your notes, I might be able to complete a probable pedigree chart."

"I feel like a sitting duck," Clayton said, looking around.

"There's not much else we can do now. Let's get out of here," Karen said, placing her vials in the ice-chest. "Daniel, could you water the horses and then get them loaded? I'll take Pete's van and drive his drive horse back, and you can take one of the big vans with our mounts. We'll leave the other van here and come back for it tomorrow."

Kate walked over to Salty. To her surprise, he backed away from her. She untied him and stepped back to give him a chance to calm down.

"The gunshots spooked him. But he'll be okay in a bit." Karen stroked his mane. "I can leave Salty with you, and you can put him in Ida's barn tonight if you want. We'll pick him up when we come back for the van."

"If I water Salty, do you think he'd be up for a trot through the canyons?" Kate said. "I'm sure I won't find anything, but I'd like to take a look all the same."

"Sure. He'll be fine. Are you sure you should go riding around here by yourself? I'd like to go with you, but I need to get these horses back. They're needed for trail rides this evening, and I'm sure Stokes is hoping I'll be late so he can rag on me again."

"I'll be okay," Kate said. "I'm not going far, just to where the trail splits."

"How bad do you think Jim was hurt?" Karen said.

"Despite the blood, the cut on his head was shallow. That roan did some pretty nasty damage to Jim's clavicle and foot. But what I'm really worried about is his neck and back."

"I'll try to get over to Red Lodge and check on him after I finish with the horses," Karen said.

"I'll be at the hospital tonight with Veda. Drop by or call me later." Kate said.

Kate walked Salty to the lake and let him drink. She discussed her plan with the horse as he slurped some water. He twitched his ears. "Don't get excited, boy. The adventure's over. I hope. We're going to take a nice, leisurely ride around the property, and then you can rest in Ida's barn."

Kate adjusted the saddle and took another look at Salty. She pulled her scarf from around her neck and dipped it in the water. Then she sponged off the scraped area on the side of the horse's leg.

Karen walked up behind them. "We're ready to go. How does he look?"

"Except for that scrape, he's fine," Kate said.

Karen looked Salty over, agreeing with Kate's assessment. "Be careful."

Kate watched as Karen, Daniel, and Clayton drove their mounts out of the valley and disappeared around the mountain. Standing there alone, Kate started to doubt her decision to scout the property. If a mad gunman or two were still around, Kate, like Clayton expressed earlier, would be a sitting duck as she rode between the narrow canyon walls toward the open valley. Salty draped his big head over Kate's shoulder and whimpered as if to reassure her that a quiet ride would be just the thing to turn the tides on the disappointing morning.

"Okay, Salty, if you're game, so am I." Kate climbed back in the saddle, feeling the pain in her ankle return after a short respite. Before circling back through west canyon down to the creek path where they had found the herd, Kate decided to follow the road to the back boundary of Ida's property to only other entrance to the ranch. Whoever was shooting must have come in from there in order not to have been seen.

Kate passed the trail to west canyon. After about a quarter mile, she saw that Ida's road cut a straight path to the county road. Not knowing what she'd find, if anything, she rode Salty a little farther. But the road gave up no clues.

Kate retraced the path back through the canyon and picked up the trail that followed the creek. After a few hundred yards, the canyon opened to a valley speckled with every color of the rainbow. Wildflowers stood in profusion, along with purple gayfeathers, rose-colored paint brushes, and yellow primroses, all mixed together like a Monet canvas. Kate imagined what this lush valley and creek-side trail would turn into if the dam was built. With no water supply, most of the vegetation would disappear, transforming this area into a wasteland.

A flood of memories suddenly assaulted Kate, memories of another water-starved place—this one in the western part of Texas. Guadalupe Mountains National Park was a huge limestone rock that looked like the hull of a ship rising out of the desert floor. And just beyond its massive stern was an astonishing oasis, McKittrick Canyon. In the fall the entire canyon was painted with contrasting colors almost too brilliant to be real—red madrones and big-tooth maples mix with the deep greens of Douglas firs and pinyon pines. A spring-fed creek flowed through the canyon, providing sustenance for a diverse mix of life. Kate and Jack had hiked the lower canyon trail several years back. They had vowed to return for a complete through-hike over the mountain wall and into Dog Canyon, abutting New Mexico. That was ten years ago.

Kate had an urge to call Jack, but she knew it would be impossible from this canyon. Even if cell-phone service was available, playing telephone tag with her husband sucked. Being alone sucked. But wasn't it less than a week ago when she bolted from Chicago? From Chicago, yes—she had desperately needed to get out of the city—but not away from Jack. She wanted him here so they could enjoy this scenery together. She needed him here to ease her anxieties. But baseball season had just gotten underway, and the only traveling he would be able to do for the next six months was with the team.

Salty snickered, reminding Kate to get moving. They trotted out of the canyon. As they reached the road, Salty showed signs of fatigue. Not used to this much riding, Kate felt her back and leg muscles tighten in protest. She decided this would be a good place to rest before heading back to the lake. But before she dismounted, the crack of a rifle shot sounded and the rock behind Kate shattered, sending shards and fragments flying. Salty reared, but this time Kate was not quick enough to grab hold and stay in the saddle. She tumbled backward, somersaulting over the horse's back and landing face down in a thick tuft of wild gamma-oats. With her breath knocked out and not knowing where the sniper was perched, she rolled under a sage bush and prayed her breath would return before she passed out. As dizziness subsided, Kate listened for more shots. None came. She glanced around for Salty, but he was nowhere in sight. She lay there for several minutes then heard a vehicle approaching from the back road.

Kate did not intend to give the sniper another chance and scramble for better cover. Hidden by an embankment below the road, she stayed low and scampered toward the trail from where she and Salty had detoured. A low, overhanging rock looked to be good cover. As she wedged herself in as far back as possible, she heard a car door slam.

"Ms. Caraway," a familiar voice shouted from the road. "Are you okay? Karen Gregory called about someone shooting on Ida's ranch," Phillips shouted. "I drove up around the bend in time to see you tumble off your horse. Ms. Caraway?"

"I'm here. I wasn't sure who you were." Kate crawled out of hiding. "Do you see my horse anywhere?"

"No, he's gone. Are you all right?" The sheriff walked down and offered his hand to pull Kate up to the road. "Karen said shots were fired twice while you were working with the horses."

"Right. Clayton Farley's well-tuned ear heard rifle shots and then shots from a pistol." Kate brushed the dirt from her jeans and walked upwind of his cigarette smoke. "And just now, someone shot at me. You didn't happen to see anyone?"

"I saw a guy running along the top of the cliff, but it's too steep to climb," Phillips said, pointing to an overhang about fifty feet below the top of the mountain—a shelf-like slab of rock, perfect for someone to sit and watch the goings-on down below. "I have no idea how to get up there, and I'm not going to break my neck trying. There's no way I could've gone after him. But now we know he's here. Besides, I wanted to make sure you were all right. I told you that boy was dangerous."

"What are you saying?"

"Nate's already killed his grandfather. He's desperate, and I figured he was hiding out on this ranch. Now I know for sure."

"You're telling me it was Nate. That's absurd. Why

would he shoot at me?"

"We'll find out as soon as we bring him in. You want a ride back to Ida's house?"

"No thanks. I'll walk." Kate's recuperation from Friday's fall had been erased by her tumble from Salty's back.

"That's not a good idea."

"I need to find my horse."

"I know you refuse to believe that Nate's dangerous. But if I were you, I'd keep an eye peeled. Nate's desperate. He's killed once." The sheriff let his statement hang then snubbed his cigarette against the rock with emphasis, paused, then flicked it away. He got back in his patrol car and drove off.

Kate picked up the remains of the cigarette, wrapped it in a leaf, and stuck it in her pocket, a gesture stemmed more from annoyance than her concern for the environment. She ran her fingers through the dirt to remove the tobacco stench then started walking gingerly toward the corral. She could feel her ankle beginning to swell and was relieved to find Salty where she hoped he'd be, munching grass near the remains of the testing corral. He turned his head and watched her for a moment as she walked up to him, then resumed chomping.

"How could you snack at a time like this? Weren't you worried about me? Let's get you back to the barn for a proper feeding and brushing. I'm sure you'd like to be rid of that saddle. Then I need to tend to my own injuries."

Kate picked up the reins. Out the corner of her eye, she saw movement on top of the mountain where she and Ida had watched the horses. At first Kate thought a family of goats had scaled the rocky hill. Then she recognized three of Ida's crazy dogs watching her from the precipice. They must have come up from the grassy slope side. Still, she was stupefied at how they had made it to the top. As Kate walked around the mountain's base toward the barn, the dogs scurried down to meet her. Kate watched their descent. Sure enough, they had taken a well-used path that Kate had failed to see when she climbed down that night after the thunderstorm. Then the realization struck. This must have been the path Frank took up the mountain on the day he was murdered.

After taking care of Salty, Kate showered and rummaged through the medicine cabinet in search of something to coat her skinned knees. She unscrewed a bottle of Mercurochrome that looked as old as everything else in the cabin. The plastic cap cracked and crumbled in her hand. There was enough of the reddish-brown liquid to do the job. After spreading it on her cuts and scrapes, she threw the messy remainder in the trash. Kate waited for the liquid to dry, then put on a clean pair of jeans and a T-shirt. She rewrapped her ankle with a clean bandage. Her hair was still wet, so she let it hang loose over her shoulders. A look in the mirror told her that her visit in Two Horse was becoming unsafe. Her right cheek was scraped and the cut near her right ear still bled a bit. She pulled her hair over her ears and hoped she looked presentable enough to visit a convent.

Kate made a cheese sandwich and let an ice pack cool her ankle while she ate. Twenty minutes later, she secured the elastic bandage, slipped on her boots, and stepped out on Ida's front porch. In another two hours the sun would sink behind the Pryor Mountains, and the air would chill to near freezing. Shadows began dancing images across the hillside. The tall pasture grass waved in the wind and scrubby pinyon pines painted spiky silhouettes along the side of Ida's barn. Kate thought of Nate and what the sheriff had said. Surely, Nate hadn't stayed on the ranch after Kate's warning. But he knew this place well. There were several caves he could've hidden in. Maybe the sheriff was right. Maybe Nate was here. But the sheriff was dead wrong about Nate's shooting at her.

Kate was brought out of her ruminations by Rigoletto and Don G, who were engaging in a tug-of-war over an old piece of rubber. Their growls were escalating into an angry tiff. She walked over, clapped her hands, and shouted at the dogs to break it up. Rigoletto let go of his hold. Don G, now victorious, scampered around Kate daring her to take away his prize. Then Kate noticed that the object was not a piece of rubber, but a small, leather pouch of some sort. Despite having been dragged through the dirt and gnawed on, the pouch looked new. Kate squatted to Don G's eye-level and whistled for the dog. He trotted over to just within her reach and then took off before she could grab him, shaking the pouch in his mouth as if it were a dead squirrel.

"I don't have time to play, Don G. Give me that!" Kate raised her voice. Knowing he was now in trouble, the dog dropped the leather pouch and scurried into the barn.

"Chicken!" Kate called out, as she picked up the pouch and shook off the loose dirt. She went inside, found one of Ida's old kitchen rags, and wiped off the dried mud and dog slobber. It was a leather cell-phone case with the initials F.C.S. embossed on the top flap.

Kate looked at her watch and, without wasting any more time, headed up the mountain for another look via the newly discovered dog path. Sheriff Phillips had not said anything about having found Frank's cell phone. *Why would he*? Kate thought. Just because she had found the body, Phillips was under no obligation to share with her whatever other evidence he had collected. If Phillips had overlooked the phone case, maybe he missed the phone as well. There was no sense searching the place where Kate had found the body. The sheriff's investigators had already combed that area. Instead Kate confined her search to the trail area itself. Dog tracks interspersed with deer tracks led all the way.

Once she reached the summit, Kate quickly surveyed the area. She peered into the crevices and between the boulders as best as she could. Seeing nothing, she headed back down.

Frank must have made that climb in order to make a call. Why else would he be up on the mountain with his cell phone? The morning of his death, Frank had tried to talk Nate out of deeding the ranch to The Nature Conservancy. Nate had told Kate that Frank was anxious to be on his way. He must have headed straight for the ranch, but why? Kate scanned the vast property. For all its simple beauty and rugged terrain, it was not of much value to anyone, except Ida and Nate. Had the realization of losing the ranch caused Frank a change of heart? Or did he come looking for something and found it, something that warranted an immediate call, something that could not wait for the trip back to town? That would mean Frank had come here alone. But he had not been alone, whether he knew it or not. Someone had killed him soon after he made his last call.

Kate hurried back down. As she started Ida's truck, Don G peeked out from the barn. Kate made eye-contact, and the dog turned tail and ducked back inside. Then she remembered the dog's stash. Kate turned off the engine and followed him into the barn. It didn't take her long to find it. The dirt around an old plow blade had been disturbed. Kate brushed some dirt away and there was the cell phone, along with one of Veda's red tennis shoes and an old, long-stopped Timex watch. The phone was covered in dust, but otherwise in good shape. Don G must have brought it in before Friday night's storm. And it was the same brand as Kate's. She went back into the cabin and hooked up it up to her battery charger.

Later today, Kate would punch the redial button on Frank Springfield's cell phone. If she was lucky, she'd know the last number he called.

Chapter Fifteen

Kate vowed hereinafter to avoid afternoon coffee at Ruby's. She set her Styrofoam cup on the phone-booth shelf, half expecting the overcooked brew to dissolve the cup any second. "You sound tired," she said.

"Not tired—frustrated." Jack sighed. "I've spent the whole day in meetings trying to save Mike Chambers's ass while he's somewhere on some kind of retreat trying to get his head straight," Jack said. "He hasn't even called me. I know it's only been three days, but I told him to stay in touch."

"Didn't he give you the name of the place he's staying?" Kate asked.

"No, and I didn't ask. I should have pressed him, but the boy was so bummed out when I took him to the airport, I thought he was going to cry. It was my idea to bring him up to Chicago. If he screws up, I guess…well, I screwed up too."

"Quit doubting yourself. You were looking out for Mike and the team's best interest. Those guys in the front office are looking out for the bottom line. If you help Mike decide what's best for him, even if it isn't baseball, you've done the right thing," Kate said.

"I wish you were here. I'd sure like to see you across the table from me at Shaw's Crab House wearing that red sleeveless sweater and those tight black pants. What do you call them?"

Kate laughed. "You mean capri pants?"

"Whatever. You've got the best butt in the world."

"You know, I could use a decent meal and a nice bottle of wine. And I'd be glad to dress up like your dream girl. All my clothes are starting to smell like smoke and horses. Speaking of smell, grab Kenya, and tell me what she smells like."

It was Jack's turn to laugh. "Hang on."

Kate heard him call their greyhound. The sound of claws clicking across the hardwood floor came through loud and clear.

"Okay, here she is. Uh, oh. She no longer smells like a desert flower. More like a corn tortilla."

"She needs a bath. I don't think it can wait until I get back. Do you have time to take her in?"

"I'll try to do it tomorrow. Any word on Nate?"

"Actually, he paid me an early visit on Monday morning. I didn't tell you the last time we talked, because he sneaked Ida's gun out with him before he left the cabin."

"And you didn't want me to worry? My worries started as soon as you left."

"We also had an accident at the horse gathering this morning."

"Okay, I'm sitting down. Spit it out."

"Someone hidden up in the hills above fired several shots while we were taking blood samples. The mustangs spooked and broke out of the corral. We had managed blood samples on only half the horses. One of the young men got trampled, and he's in the hospital. Then, after everybody had left, I rode around to see if I could dig up anything, and someone shot at me."

"Kate, that's not what I'd call an accident! Listen to

me—"

"Wait. You need to hear the rest. Sheriff Phillips was on the ranch investigating the earlier shots, and he told me that he saw Nate leaving the area."

"Nate?"

"He claims it was Nate who shot at me," Kate said and listened to the silence, giving Jack time to take it all in.

"I know you don't want to hear this, but I also know that it's crossed your mind. I can hear some doubt in your voice. You haven't known that boy for all that long. He comes into your office after hearing you lecture and begs you to come help his great-grandmother. You get to the ranch, find his grandfather's been murdered, and then Nate does a disappearing act. I know you think no one can size people up like you, but don't ignore your uncanny intuition. You tell me not to doubt myself. You should listen to your own instincts."

"I'm not sure of anything right now, Jack. Except I know it wasn't Nate."

"If I knew I could get away with it, I'd come to Two Horse and bring you home. Just be careful. Call me tomorrow and leave a message if you don't get me live. I'll be busy getting the boys ready for the series with the Braves."

"A tough team, best of luck. What was the name of that creek running through McKittrick Canyon?"

"What the hell made you think of that? Pratt Creek, maybe? Does that sound right?"

"It does. We've never done that through-hike, have we?"

"And if you're not careful—" Jack's voice softened. "—we never will."

****

The school bell rang at St. Francis Xavier School and a rush of children followed. Kate watched for a moment. Most of the students boarded here, and many were from the reservation. A priest stepped from the main entrance carrying a canvas bag of baseball equipment. Some kids were waiting for him on the field next to the school.

Kate went inside where Mother Katrina was waiting in her large, but unpretentious office. A crucifix hung over her desk and a vase of silk sunflowers sat on the end table. Otherwise the office of the convent's Mother Superior was austere.

A huge picture window flooded the room with natural light. And the vast Big Horn Canyon in the distance made any other decoration unnecessary.

"I had to place my desk so my back would be to this window, otherwise I'd never get any work done." Mother Katrina wedged her round body into her swivel chair. She indicated for Kate to take the chair in front of the desk then came directly to the point. "You said when you called you wished to visit Sister Jacquelyn."

In habit and wimple, the only clue to the nun's age were the creases around her steady green eyes—about sixty, Kate guessed. "Yes, Mother. I'm sure you've heard about all the trouble in Two Horse. Nate Springfield is wanted for the murder of his grandfather. Nate disappeared a few days ago. Every day he's missing makes his situation worse. I need to find him soon."

"We've heard about what's happening in Two Horse. Do you suspect Nate killed his grandfather?"

"No, I don't. I think he's protecting someone, maybe even the killer. Nate was with a friend a couple of days ago. He said Nate was coming here to talk to Sister Jacquelyn."

"Nate was here early this morning." Mother Katrina paused at the surprise on Kate's face. "We have no secrets here, Ms. Caraway. Nate spoke with Sister Jacquelyn and then left. Of course, we had to call the sheriff." She paused again. "It had been a crazy day. It's Parents' Week, and we've had visitors arriving since early Monday morning. Besides the regular school curriculum, we have others coming to study here—programs that run in coordination with the seminary. Then as soon as Nate left, Sister Christina caught two of our girls smoking in the loft in the chapel. Um…I'm afraid I didn't get around to calling the sheriff until around noon."

Kate noticed a wry grin before it quickly disappeared.

Mother Katrina rose from her desk. "I'll call in Sister Jacquelyn."

"Mother, does Sister Jacquelyn know that her brother is in the hospital?"

"We received the call about Jim a couple of hours ago. A broken collar bone, broken ankle, and several stitches. They say he's doing fine, though."

"Thank God."

"And thank you. We heard how you handled the situation."

Ten minutes later, Sister Jacquelyn came in, following Mother Katrina. The younger nun's beauty shone. Her wimple created a white glow around her dark, stunning face. The resemblance to her two younger siblings was immediately apparent. The three women sat in a small sitting area away from the Mother Superior's formal desk.

"Mother Katrina and I have discussed Nate's situation. We weren't aware of Frank Springfield's murder until Nate told us what had happened. He said he didn't kill his grandfather. We believe him. He came here on behalf of a friend, Rachel Bear Walks Slowly. However, we agree with you that he should turn himself in, and if it weren't for Rachel, he probably would have by now."

"Pete's daughter? I knew she was involved."

"Nate rushed home from Chicago because Rachel had called him, pleading for his help. She had run away from the drug rehabilitation center," Sister Jacquelyn said. "Apparently, she wanted money to leave Montana. When Nate refused to give her any money, and instead tried to talk her into going home, Rachel disappeared. Nate's been looking for her. He's afraid she may harm herself. She tried to commit suicide last year. Nate hoped that if he found her, we'd take her in for a few days. He feels responsible for Rachel's taking off again. He's determined to find her."

"How he plans to do so while he's hiding out himself is beyond me," Mother Katrina said. "He is a smart boy, but I'm afraid he inherited the Springfield stubbornness."

"Have you told Sheriff Phillips everything you've told me?" Kate asked.

The two nuns exchanged glances. Mother Katrina answered. "We told the sheriff Nate came here for help. And that he said he didn't kill Mr. Springfield but was afraid no one will believe him. We also told the sheriff that we advised Nate to turn himself in. We didn't mention Rachel."

"We didn't think it was necessary, since the sheriff didn't ask about her," Sister Jacquelyn added. "And he was a little upset that we waited so long before calling him."

"I'll bet," Kate said.

"We explained to him that we needed the time to pray for God's guidance to do what was right." Mother Katrina responded with a smile.

"And he bought it," Sister Jacquelyn added, receiving a wink from her superior.

"We're very fond of Nate. He attended school here. We've prayed many times that he would come back one day and teach," Mother Katrina said. "When he was here, he mentioned your name several times, Ms. Caraway. Nate trusts you. We'll pray that you find him before the sheriff does."

"I hope I can. Unfortunately, the sheriff has more manpower than I have."

"The sheriff's not the only one who's looking for Nate," Sister Jacqueline said.

"Pete Bear Walks Slowly came to see us soon after Nate left," Mother Katrina said. "He was quite angry."

"He's convinced Nate is the reason Rachel left rehab," Sister Jacquelyn added. "He believes they're together. He said he knew Nate was up to something as early as Saturday morning."

Something clicked in the back of Kate's mind. Niles, the sheriff's janitor, had delivered Nate's note on Saturday morning while Kate, Ida, and Veda were out having breakfast. Pete said he had been to Ida's that morning. He must have gotten there after Niles, read the note, and taken it. That explained why they hadn't seen the message when they returned to the ranch.

Mother Katrina looked at her watch. She stood up and walked Kate to the door. "I'm afraid we're needed elsewhere, Mrs. Caraway. Good luck with finding Nate. We'll keep you both in our prayers."

Two minutes later, Kate was staring through the windshield of Ida's truck, thinking she, not God, would have to be the salvation of two troubled young people. At least she now knew Nate's reason for changing his plans and arriving early. But that knowledge only made the complex situation even tenser and had given Kate an added burden—a burden she did not need.

Not yet ready to leave, Kate sat in the truck and contemplated the new information she had just received. She knew Nate to have a profound sense of honor, and an almost idealistic view of right and wrong. After a few more years of maturity, Nate's principles might help him choose a path in life that could bring positive change. Kate suddenly understood why she had been so easily been taken in by Nate's plea for help. Maturity and principles didn't necessarily guarantee a level head. She and Nate were two peas in a pod. But at least Kate might one day have a chance to return to her camp in Kenya if she chose. But the way Nate was going, he might not have any choices at all.

The setting sun glowed scarlet in the western sky. Kate needed to get back to the hospital and check on Ida and Veda and, now, Jim Brown Bird. But she took the keys from the ignition and walked over to the baseball field instead. The sights and sounds of the game might relax her and give her some direction.

She made her way up to the top of the rickety bleachers when she heard the priest call, "You're awfully brave to sit up there. Most people just bring their lawn chairs and watch from alongside the dugout."

Kate looked around. Even her best imagination did not reveal a dugout.

The priest laughed and pointed. "The bench over by the fence—that's our dugout. My name is Father Rick. We're just finishing batting practice. Sorry you weren't here earlier."

"So am I. I'm Kate Caraway. My husband played for twenty years. There's something about the sounds of baseball that relaxes me."

"I know what you mean." He walked around the fence, climbed up, and joined her on one of the few spaces that had not succumbed to rot. "Sports are important to young people. Like religion is to the soul. You can't develop the spirit if you ignore the body. Are you one of the parents?"

"No, I was here visiting Mother Katrina and Sister Jacquelyn."

"How did you escape so early? There's still some sunlight left. People don't usually get away from Mother Katrina without being coerced into some chores. You know us Catholics. We're great at using guilt to our advantage."

"Don't I know it?" Finally, Kate could laugh. "I guess I'm what you call a raised-Catholic. But I've recently come back to church."

"Congratulations. What brought you back?"

"Antonio Banderas."

"Excuse me?"

"Ever see the movie *Desperadoes*?"

"The one where Antonio wipes out a slew of bad guys single-handedly in a bar?"

"Actually, it was a bookstore/coffee-shop, covering

for a drug operation."

"Right. That's the one. So, you saw the light in that film?"

"Well, I was always judging too much, taking everything too seriously. And the entire concept of confession; it seemed too hypocritical, too easy. You know—sin, confess, sin again. Then I see Antonio go to a church before the big shoot-out. A priest asks if he wants to go to confession. Antonio replies something like, 'Not now, Father, I would just have to come back again later.' Something just clicked for me." Kate watched the kids on the field line up. The young man who had pitched batting practice was now instructing them on running bases.

"Yes, I remember that part now." Father Rick grinned. "We confess our sins with the intention of never sinning again, but we know that sinning is a part of being human. Besides, the Lord said, 'It's mercy I desire, not sacrifice.' I just wish it was as easy for other Catholics to return as it was for you."

"That wasn't the real reason I returned to the church," Kate said.

"I didn't think so." Father Rick turned and looked at Kate.

"I shot a man and sort of felt bad about it later," Kate said.

The priest threw his head back and started laughing so loudly the kids on the field turned and looked. Tears streamed down his face. He leaned over and grabbed his side. Kate watched in dismay. At first she wanted to cry. She had been carrying this like a heavy anchor. But instead, for the first time in months, she was able to let go of what had happened in Kenya. As her tension eased, tears of laughter streamed down her face as well.

Father Rick sucked in a much-needed deep breath. "Confession's good for the soul."

"Is that what I just did?" Kate said.

"I don't know, but you sure look a hell of a lot better. I watched you climb the bleachers and you looked like someone walking the plank."

"I didn't get to see much batting practice, but your coach looks like he has a pretty good arm when he's not holding back for the kids," Kate said.

"He's not our regular coach. I am. He just volunteers occasionally. We'd like to have him full-time, but he has a real life, so to speak." The disappointment in Father Rick's voice was slight, but too apparent for Kate not to notice. "See that graded area beyond the parking lot? We're building a new sports complex. Nothing fancy, just new baseball and football fields, and volleyball and tennis courts. We have a new benefactor, and we're very grateful for his financial support. But to tell the truth, we'd rather have him than his money."

Kate looked at the priest. He was watching the kids leave. Then he nodded toward the young man who had pitched to them. "He's the one who is footing the bill for the sport complex. But he's struggling. He seems to have heard God's calling, but he's not ready to accept it. His other life offers great possibilities as well. You may be able to relate to that."

"How's that, Father?"

"You said your husband played baseball for quite a while. Did he ever make it to the majors?"

"Sure did. He spent his whole career with the Chicago Cubs."

"You don't say. It always surprises me how small a

world this is. That's Mike Chambers, our volunteer coach and our benefactor. He's a pitcher in the Cubs' minor-league system. They gave him quite a bit of money to sign. He gave some of it to us. Enjoy your visit, Ms. Caraway. If you see Mother Katrina heading your way, run. I'd better go pick up those balls in the outfield. We need them." Father Rick climbed down the bleachers and trotted away.

Chapter Sixteen

Kate returned to the truck and sat on the bumper. She still did not know where to find Nate, and she was now looking for a missing teenage girl, but at least she had found Jack's missing pitcher. She called Jack, but got his voice mail. The news was too good to leave a message, so she hung up. She then called Ida at the hospital to see if she needed anything. Kate was about to hang up before Ida finally answered.

"I'm on my way, Ida. I've got some info. If we put our heads together, maybe we can figure out how to find Nate, or at least have a better idea where to look. Can I bring you anything?"

"Veda's on life support," Ida's voice was thin and raspy. "She had a bad stroke about two hours ago. Not long ago I had one of those living wills drawn up for both of us. I'm turning off this damn machine in the morning."

Kate was crestfallen. Every comforting thought that popped into Kate's head would sound trite. "I'm on my way," were the only words Kate could speak.

She hung up the phone as Sister Jacquelyn walked out.

"My word, Ms. Caraway, are you okay?"

"I just spoke to Ida. Veda's had a massive stroke. I have to get to the hospital right away."

"I'm going with you. I was on my way to see Jim. I'll drive. You're in no shape to. Just give me two minutes."

Sister Jacquelyn returned shortly, hopped into the driver's seat, and the two women took off. Kate rolled up the window to keep from choking on the dust. As soon as they hit pavement, Kate lowered the window to breathe in some fresh air.

"I probably should've asked," Kate said. "Ida might have wanted a priest to administer last rights."

"Ida and her sister aren't Catholic. Nate converted while he attended high school here. I think that sort of teed Ida off. But if she wants some kind of last rights for Veda, I'm sure there's a chaplain at the hospital."

"I don't know how to thank you for all the information and help, Sister Jacquelyn."

"You know, that title still sounds funny to me, not while I'm at the convent, of course. But whenever I'm away, especially when I'm at home, I still want my family to call me Jackie. You can too, if that makes you more comfortable."

"Thanks, Jackie. Do you really think Rachel Martin is suicidal?"

"I only know her from my sister Julie. By the time Julie and Rachel got to high school, I had already graduated. But according to Julie, Rachel is a very high-strung girl. Everything is a crisis. I think she was diagnosed as chronic depressive. That makes me think Nate's assessment of the situation is probably accurate. We also called Rachel's mother after Nate's visit. The poor woman was frantic. She feels responsible, too. She's afraid Pete will challenge her custody rights. Knowing him, he will."

"Pete was at the horse-gathering this morning. I knew something was bothering him—something closer to home than the building of the dam."

Sister Jacquelyn drove the old pickup like she did it every day. Within forty minutes, they were at the hospital in Red Lodge. "How about if I have a talk with Jim while you're with Ida?" Sister Jacquelyn suggested. "If he's seen Nate and knows where he is, I'll find out. Jim can't lie to me, especially while I'm wearing my habit."

"You're a godsend. I mean really," Kate said.

"I'll drop you at the front door and park the truck. See you inside."

When Kate pushed opened the door to Veda's room, Ida was sitting on the bed beside her sister, braiding her hair. The only sound was a steady beeping from the ventilator.

"She likes two braids instead of one, like me," Ida said. "She puts one in each of her shirt pockets."

Kate went over and put her hand on Ida's shoulder.

"I'm not a Christian woman, Kate. I never have given much thought to what happens after we check out. The only praying I've ever done over the years is that Veda goes first. The thought of her living in an institution is unbearable. It hurts like hell, but my prayers are being answered."

Veda looked as pale as the bed sheets. Ida had made the nurses remove the IV.

"What can I do, Ida?"

"Sit down right here. I need two things. Find out the time of sunrise. That is Veda's favorite time of the day. She loves hiking up the mountain and watching the sun come up over the east canyon wall. She's been bothered with arthritis the last few years and hasn't been able to make the climb. Sunrise is when I want to turn off that awful machine."

"Sure. And if it makes any difference, Ida, I know you're doing the right thing." Kate sat down on the chair next to the bed.

"And the other thing is—find Nate." Ida finished the second braid, tied it off with a small rubber band, and straightened both braids in perfect symmetry. She looked at Kate. "You said you had some news about Nate."

"We don't have to—"

"I'm almost done here. I've taken care of Veda. Julie Brown Bird came in and told me about what happened on the ranch. Things are getting hairy. I need to find my great-grandson. Let's talk. Where's that yellow notepad of yours?"

Kate pulled it from her backpack. "I've got two more pieces to the puzzle. Unfortunately, they seem to make the situation more uncertain. I was at St. Francis' today. I found out why Nate hasn't come forward. Rachel Martin left drug rehab last week and called Nate for help. When he got here and tried to talk her into going home, she bolted. It seems Nate may be afraid she'll harm herself, and he feels responsible. He most likely wants to find her first."

Kate told Ida everything Sister Jacquelyn had discovered.

Ida listened. "And what's the second piece?"

"After the gathering was disrupted, I rode around the ranch to check things out. On my way back, someone shot at me. It was very near where the stallion was killed. The sniper probably used the same perch."

Ida picked up Veda's hand. "I don't think she can hear us, do you?"

"Ida, we can wait and talk about this later."

"No, we can't. We can't wait. If we do, Nate might end up dead." Ida kissed her sister's hand. "And then where would I be?"

"I don't think Veda can hear us," Kate said, her voice sounding shallow to her own ears.

"Go on, then. Talking about this helps," Ida said.

"Sheriff Phillips was on the ranch investigating the shots fired earlier during the horse gathering. He came to my rescue right after the sniper tried to pick me off. He said he saw Nate leaving the area where those shots came from."

"That's ridiculous," Ida said.

"I pretty much told him the same thing. Ida, if Nate's hiding out on your ranch, I'm afraid he's in a great deal of danger. Phillips is combing every acre looking for him. If he finds him—"

"I know. If he finds him, the sheriff might shoot Nate first."

"Pete is looking for Nate as well."

"I'll bet."

"Do you think Pete would help us? We're both looking for the same two people. Besides, he owes you one."

"What do you mean?"

"I'm pretty sure he's the reason you didn't get Nate's note on Saturday. He came to your ranch that morning while we were having breakfast at Ruby's. He probably saw the note and took it. I suspect he was afraid that if Nate got to town, he would contact Rachel."

"That girl's a pain in the ass. Nate always came to her rescue. And Pete knows that. Where his daughter is concerned, Pete loses all good sense. But I wonder why he took the note. He could have just read it and left it there."

"Unless he didn't want you to know Nate was here," Kate said.

"So he could get to Nate first? Talk to Pete's wife—Lila Martin is what she goes by now. What else have you got?" Ida said looking over at Kate's notes.

"I talked to Imagene Porter. She said Frank dumped her for another woman. We may have another suspect. Any idea who this woman could be?"

"Meg Little Coyote."

"*What*?"

"No, I mean, talk to Meg Little Coyote."

"I'm going to ask Karen Gregory to help me with that."

"Good. I like that little redheaded girl. And don't forget the Nelsons. Lucy's an odd duck, but Nate holds a big place in their hearts."

"Ida, the sheriff suspects Nate, and no one else. We have to figure out what Frank was doing on your ranch the day he was killed. Nate told me Frank tried to talk him into keeping the ranch in the family."

Ida stood and turned her back to Veda. "Bullshit."

"He said Frank even offered to help run the place."

"Frank was up to one of his tricks. It makes me spitting mad to know the bastard lied to his grandson."

"Well, whatever caused Frank to be on your ranch, he may have accomplished his mission. I found—rather Don G found—Frank's cell phone on your mountain. My guess is that he climbed up there to get a signal."

Ida turned and looked at Kate. "Have you told Phillips?"

"Not yet, but I'll have to."

"Yes, you will." Ida let go of her sister's hand and

pulled the sheet up under her chin, folding it carefully at her shoulders.

"I'll find out the time of sunrise," Kate said, feeling helpless. "Do you want me to be here in the morning?"

"No, honey. Say your goodbyes now. It's been me and Veda for most of our eighty-two years. That's the way she always liked it. You've got a lot of work to do. Get going."

"One more thing. Is there any safe way to get up on that slab of rock the sniper used? It's right where the trail splits."

"I know where you're talking about. You can drive right up to it. There's a road off that back road leading off my ranch. You'd never see it unless you knew it was there. Why do you ask?"

"I want to see if the sniper could have hit the mustang from that perch as well."

"Good luck."

Kate went to the bed, gave Veda's hand a gentle squeeze, then left the room. Sister Jacquelyn came around the corner with Julie and Karen in tow.

"It was like pulling teeth," Sister Jacquelyn said. "Julie and Karen took Mom to the cafctcria for something to eat. When I was finally alone with my little brother, I put the screws to him, and he caved. What's with the male loyalty thing? Anyway, I think I know where Rachel is. How's Ida?"

"Resolved," Kate said. "She's taking Veda off life support at sunrise."

"I'll go in for a moment," Sister Jacquelyn said.

"I'll go in too," Julie said.

"I'd like to offer my condolences," Karen added.

Kate waited in the hall, anxious to know what Sister

Jacquelyn had found out. She was studying her notes when Bruce, the nurse, stood up from behind the nurses' station. He rested his elbows on the counter. "You're Kate, Ida's friend. Thanks for coming and helping Ida through this. She's a real character. We've all grown quite fond of her. And thanks for staying with Veda last night. Ida hasn't slept at all while she's been here. She's made the right decision, though."

"I agree, but it's still a difficult thing to do. At least she got some sleep last night while she was back at her ranch. She seemed rested this morning."

"Ida wasn't at her ranch last night."

"What?"

"Before I came on duty at two this morning, I saw Ida driving through Red Lodge. And when Angie came on duty at five o'clock, she said she saw Ida at Starbucks. It's hard to miss her with that get-up she wears. Angie said Ida was having coffee with some woman who was sobbing. I guess Ida couldn't handle being too far from her sister." A buzzer went off and Bruce leaned over to check the room number. "Duty calls. If you need anything, let me know." He turned and hurried down the hall.

Kate stood there. Things started to come together. She couldn't waste any more time. A courtesy phone sat on a desk next to the nurses' station. Under the phone was a phonebook and Kate found the number she wanted. She was pacing when the three women came out of Ida's room.

"I know it's been a long, crazy day, but Nate's running out of time," Kate said. "I need your help. Jackie, when do you have to be back at the convent?"

"Not till tomorrow afternoon. Why?"

"I need you and Julie to arrange a meeting for me." Kate handed them the piece of paper with the name and phone number on it. "Karen and I will meet you back here in about an hour, and we'll see what develops."

"Where are you going?" Julie asked. "Do you have a lead on Nate?"

"Maybe, but first I need to solve a puzzle from the past."

****

The Red Lodge Library stayed open late on Wednesdays. Five minutes after Kate and Karen left the hospital, they were seated at a long table with several reels of microfiche in front of them.

"What are we looking for?" Karen asked as she threaded the film into the projector.

"The absence of something," Kate said. "We're checking for any newspaper stories about a fire on the Springfield ranch in the early 1950s. Ida said her kitchen caught fire. She said Veda was burned badly on her legs, leaving scars, and that's why Veda refuses to go into the kitchen. But there are no scars on Veda's legs. She kicked her sheets off last night, and I saw that her legs were smooth. It seems unlikely Ida would've been able to put out a fire by herself, especially if Veda had been injured. And the kitchen looks unchanged from its original construction. If there was a fire at Ida's cabin, the story should be in the newspaper."

"Why would Ida lie?" Karen asked.

"I don't know exactly," Kate said. "I think something else happened to Veda that Ida doesn't want anybody to know. It's probably irrelevant to the current situation, but Ida hasn't shot straight with me on a couple of things, and I'm wondering why, and whether she has something else she's trying to hide."

It didn't take them long to check every issue of the weekly *Carbon County Chronicle* from 1950 through 1954. There were no news stories or sheriff's reports on a fire or any other accident on Ida's ranch during that three-year period.

It was almost seven o'clock. Kate's hunger headache pounded too painfully to be ignored any longer. The muffin Ida had brought Kate earlier that morning was the last thing she had eaten. "I need food," she said as she popped two ibuprofen and grabbed her water bottle from her backpack. "Let's go pick up Jackie and Julie and find a restaurant."

"No arguments here," Karen said.

Before they left the library, Kate called Sister Jacquelyn and Julie at the hospital to let them know she was on the way.

"Nachos!" Sister Jacquelyn shouted when Kate arrived and mentioned food. "Sorry," she added sheepishly. "I love nachos. Our pious chef, Sister Hillary, would never even think of serving them. She turns out nothing but bland food at the convent. She either thinks spices are sinful or that we can't pray with digestive problems."

"Any suggestions?" Karen asked.

"There's a place called Big Mike's Bar and Grill just down the street off the courthouse square," Sister Jacquelyn offered.

Kate and Karen looked at their pietistic detective-partner with a mix of surprise and confusion. Julie laughed and shook her head.

"My friends and I use to make fake IDs when we were seniors in high school so we could party at Big

Mike's," Sister Jacquelyn said. "They've got a nice heated patio in back. Let's go."

Kate, Karen, and Julie had to hurry to catch up with Sister Jacquelyn. Her hard-soled nun-shoes clumped loudly as she flew across the hospital's tile floor.

The sound from Big Mike's jukebox twanged halfway down the block where Julie was forced to park. The four women piled out and headed for the bar and grill. Kate was propositioned twice as she elbowed her way through the crowded parking lot. *Sister Jacquelyn must be joking*, Kate thought. But when the nun held the door open for them to go in, a night among the most raucous folks in Red Lodge had become a reality. They walked down the narrow entrance hall and pushed open the swinging doors, which led directly to the bar. The bar noise ceased, as if instantly muted by some remote-control. Only George Straight singing about being on his way from San Antone and hoping to make Amarillo by morning could be heard. Their behabited guide strutted to the bar, grabbed four menus from a wooden pocket nailed to the wall, and made for the patio.

Everyone watched as the four women—a Crow nun; a short redhead wearing an NPS uniform; a tall, slender model-type; and a somewhat normal-looking woman with a limp—walked through the bar acting like they owned the place. Sister Jacquelyn was right. The patio was nice. And smoke-free.

"No one usually sits out here. I mean why would they, when they can smoke inside and get the added benefit of second-hand smoke as well?" Sister Jacquelyn sat back and let out a sigh. "I love being back in the real world. But twenty-four hours is about all I can take."

A waiter came and took their order: two plates of

225

veggie nachos, one each for Kate and Sister Jacquelyn; a cheeseburger for Karen; a chicken Caesar salad for Julie; and four Pepsis.

"Were you able to get in touch with Mrs. Martin?" Kate asked the Brown Bird sisters.

"We called several times, but the line was busy," Julia said. "At least she's at home."

"We're about to pay her an unannounced visit," Kate said.

The waiter brought their drinks.

Kate drained half her glass and continued. "Last night I stayed at the hospital with Veda so Ida could go home and get some rest. But according to Bruce, the nurse, Ida was in Red Lodge most of the night. He saw her driving around town at two this morning before he came on duty. Another nurse saw Ida at Starbucks. She was with a woman."

"You think she was driving around all night looking for Nate?" Karen asked.

"Maybe part of the time, I'm sure. But the woman Ida was with was crying. Who in Red Lodge would Ida be comforting?"

"Mrs. Martin," Karen responded.

"Exactly, Mrs. Martin, Rachel's mom. I'm pretty sure she's the person Nate has been staying with since he left Ida's on Monday morning, after I warned him about the ranch not being a safe place. While you three were in Veda's room, I talked to Angie the nurse who saw Ida at Starbucks. She described the woman as being anorexic-skinny, in her forties, and dyed-blond hair."

"That's Lila Martin, all right," Julie said.

"But why didn't Ida tell you?" Karen asked.

"I don't want to believe that Ida doesn't trust me,"

Kate said, "but that's the way it looks. Nate and Veda are her only family. Ida defends them like a mountain lion protecting her cubs. I'm here to do what I can to keep the dam from being built. Ida may want my help in finding Nate, but she's going to do whatever it takes to protect him. Give her credit, though. She did tell me to go see Mrs. Martin. Ida's a smart, cautious woman. She wants me to find Nate, but she's afraid of what I might discover when I do."

Two waiters pushed through the patio door, one carrying a tray of food, and the other a pitcher of Pepsi and a Margarita on the rocks, which he put in front of Sister Jacquelyn. "Compliments of J.D.," the waiter said to her.

Sister Jacquelyn turned pink and thanked the waiter. Julie tried to speak but let out a yelp instead as the hard toe of her sister's shoe met her shin. Sister Jacquelyn pushed the cocktail aside and refilled her glass with Pepsi. "Let's eat. I'm ravenous," she said, ignoring the quizzical looks on everyone's faces.

While they were eating, Sister Jacquelyn continued. "I need to tell you what I wormed out of my brother. When Nate got Rachel's frantic call, he booked the next flight to Billings. Then he called Jim and told him to pick up Rachel on Thursday morning and bring her to the mall near the airport. Nate made Jim swear secrecy on the rendezvous. Pete Bear Walks Slowly had forbidden his daughter from seeing Nate. And Nate is terrified of the man."

"Not surprising," Karen said.

"Things didn't work out the way Rachel had hoped," Kate said.

"You're right," Sister Jacquelyn continued, "Rachel

wanted money to leave Montana, but Nate wouldn't give her any. Rachel took off, leaving Nate sitting there in the mall."

"And no one has seen her since. That's not good," Kate said.

"No, it's not," Sister Jacquelyn agreed. "Nate was looking for her until he found out he was wanted for Frank's murder. And you were right, Kate, Nate was hiding out on Ida's ranch until Monday morning."

"This is all Nate and Jim's fault," Julie said. "I love Nate like a brother, but he should've known that when Rachel makes up her mind about something, Jesus Christ can't talk her out of it." She glanced at her sister. "Sorry. But Nate is just plain stubborn—always so high and mighty with his principles. And Jim shouldn't have kept quiet about this. Men!"

"Okay, we know Nate is no longer on Ida's ranch," Kate said. "And since Lila Martin was distraught, Rachel must still be missing. That means Nate is probably still looking for her. If I could just talk to Nate again, I might be able to talk some sense into him."

"What evidence does the sheriff have that Nate killed Frank?" Karen asked.

"Nate's boarding pass was found in Frank's pickup. When Nate didn't bring back the rental car, the sheriff had a warrant issued for Nate's arrest."

"If Nate met Rachel at the mall on Thursday morning, then when was he in Frank's pickup?" Karen inquired further.

"Nate ran into Frank on the way to the mall," Kate added. "They talked, or rather, argued about what should be done with the ranch. It seems Frank had a change of heart and felt the ranch should be kept in the family. But they didn't talk long. Nate said Frank was in a hurry to leave and he was agitated about something."

Kate looked at her notes and then at her watch. "It's nearly eight-thirty. Let's split up and see what we can find out. Julie and Jackie should go alone to visit Lila Martin. Try to find out what's going on there. What was she talking about with Ida? Has Lila been in contact with Nate recently? Karen, let's drive back to Two Horse. You can go and see the Nelsons. I don't care if it is late. Sound frantic and see what you can get out of those two. Something is also going on there. While you all are doing that, I'll try to find out more about what Frank was doing on the day he died."

"How are will you manage that?" Karen said.

"I'm not sure. But I know where to start. Anyone know where I can find Meg Little Coyote tonight?"

"It's Wednesday night. Try the medical center," Karen said.

"We'll meet later and compare notes." Kate picked up the bill and chuckled. "Someone paid our tab."

"It was probably J.D. back in the bar, crying over what he lost," Julie said.

"I'll add an ex-boyfriend to my prayer list," Sister Jacquelyn said. "When and where shall we meet?"

"Eleven o'clock at—" Kate paused.

"At the Dead Coyote," Sister Jacquelyn concluded.

"Lord, Jackie!" Julie threw her hands in the air. "You've been too cloistered."

"Nonsense, little sister. It's the only place open in Two Horse at that time of night."

"We'll meet at the town phone," Kate interjected. "But first let's go back to the hospital. I'll check on Ida and pick up her truck."

They threw a generous amount of cash on the table for a tip and left.

****

As Kate walked into Veda's room, Ida was hanging up the phone.

"It's all settled. I made arrangements to have Veda cremated. For Nate's sake, we'll have a little service when this is all over. They're going to disconnect the machines in the morning. The doctor said Veda could linger for a while, maybe a couple of days. Can you spend another night with the dogs?"

"Sure. But I want to check on some things tonight and see what I can turn up before I head back to your ranch." Kate wanted to ask Ida why she was holding back important information, information that could help Kate find Nate. But for the moment, she would let Ida have her secrets.

Karen left her pickup at the hospital and rode with Kate in Ida's truck. It was almost nine-thirty by the time they arrived back at Two Horse. The sun, long gone, had left behind a cool night—too cool for Karen to stand in the phone booth to call the Nelsons. Instead, Kate dropped Karen off at the Brown Bird's place. Martha was still at the hospital with her son, but James was home working in the shop. They decided not to tell James about Jim's admissions, fearing James would tell Pete. Karen had the Brown Bird house to herself. Kate drove to the medical center.

Both Two Horse patrol cars were parked in front of the shared building, so Kate pulled around back. She wanted to avoid running into the sheriff. As she drove up, her headlights caught the license plate of the only other vehicle in the back lot. It was parked in a small carport. The personalized plates read "FCS." It was Frank Springfield's pickup. Kate rummaged through Ida's glove box until she found a flashlight. She flicked it on. The batteries were weak, but it would do. The cab of Frank's pickup was locked. But through the window under the low beam of the flashlight, Kate saw that Frank Springfield had been a slob. The passenger seat—littered with stained coffee-cups, a paper sack that once held something greasy, a half-eaten bag of corn chips, an opened pack of Lucky Strikes, and various other travel-trash—looked like the inside of a garbage bag. A scent card hung from the rearview mirror. The floorboard was covered with various tools and enough dirt to grow a small tree. A work-boot stuck out from underneath the seat. How the sheriff had found Nate's boarding pass in this mess was beyond Kate. The pickup bed, though just as grimy, was empty. Whatever had been there was probably now locked up inside the sheriff's office.

Except for eating junk food, drinking coffee, and smoking, nothing in the truck had given Kate any indication of what else Frank had been doing on the day he was killed. She checked the tires. They were caked in mud. Kate thought of the deep ruts near the pier on Ida's lake.

Kate turned off the flashlight. Then on second thought, she flicked it back on to check the toolbox in the bed of the pickup. She expected to find it locked, but was surprised when the lid popped open as she pressed the latch. A strong moldy odor assaulted her nostrils. She shone the flashlight around the inside. The toolbox was empty. Just as she was about to close the lid, a glint of light reflected off something. Kate looked closer. In the back corner of the box was a shoe. She reached over, pulled it out, and was surprised that it was slightly damp. More surprising was that it was not an ordinary shoe. It was a dive-bootie and the zipper up the side had given the reflection. Imagene Porter had told Kate that Frank was a diver. *But where in this water-starved country could Frank have found a place to dive?* Kate thought. Then she remembered Ida's lake. Was that why he was on her ranch the day he was killed? If so, what had he been looking for? Someone had to have rented him scuba tanks. That should be easy to trace.

Kate closed the toolbox, put away Ida's flashlight, and went inside the building. There she found Meg Little Coyote slumped deep in an old, ratty lounge chair, reading the *National Inquirer*.

Meg heaved herself up to the edge of the seat and greeted Kate. "Hey, science lady, how's it going?" Then suddenly her cheeriness disappeared. "Oh my, I heard about Veda. How's Ida taking it?"

Kate sat down across from Meg. "Like you'd expect. But I think she's relieved. Her greatest fear was that she'd die first and Veda would end up alone. Though when Ida's through taking care of business, I think she'll have a hard time without her little sister to care for."

"Sad. Any word on Nate?"

"Not yet. I need some information. I was hoping you'd be able to help."

"If it's information you want, I'm the one who has it."

Kate didn't doubt that. She just hoped she could recognize fact from gossip. "I talked to Imagene Porter. It seems Frank may have been seeing another woman. Any idea who?"

"Hell if I know. Frank had women all over Carbon

County."

"But this one was recent and important enough to have pushed Imagene out of the picture. She seemed a bit peeved. My intuition tells me this new woman was more than an occasional pickup at the Dead Coyote."

"You think his new girlfriend may have killed him?"

"I don't know if there really is a new girlfriend. I'm just speculating. Where would Frank take a date, one that he didn't necessarily want to flaunt?"

"Um, let me think about that." Meg got up from her chair and walked to the vending machine. "Want some coffee? We got almond-amaretto cappuccino in here." She dropped in three quarters, and the machine spit out a sweet-smelling liquid.

"No thanks. I just drank a gallon of Pepsi. I'll be up all night."

"That'll do it." Meg sipped her coffee and leaned against the vending machine. "There's no place like that in Two Horse for sure. I'll have to ask around. See what I can dig up. Anything else?"

"This may sound like a stupid question, but are there any scuba-diving shops near here?"

"Not stupid at all. Haven't you heard the state's unofficial advertising logo: 'Dive Montana'?"

"You're kidding."

"Nope, there are two dive shops in Billings. Since Big Horn Canyon Dam was built, people have been diving in the reservoir. The limestone walls and caves we used to see from the road are now underwater and seen only by divers."

Kate jumped when her cell phone beeped in her backpack. She fumbled with the phone. Before she could say "hello," Julie's voice resounded in Kate's ear.

"You might want to drive back to Red Lodge," Julie said.

"Why? What did you find out?"

"Lots. You were right. Nate's been staying here, but he's not here now. And Mrs. Martin is frantic. She's ready to talk. In fact, she's ready to talk to the sheriff. We're stalling her until you can get here. Hurry."

"I have to pick up Karen, and then I'm on the way." Kate thanked Meg for her time and told her to call the cell phone number if she found out anything useful.

On her way from the medical center, Kate noticed a familiar figure stumble out of the Dead Coyote. He crossed the street and stepped up into the dark gazebo. Ed Nelson didn't look like the type to get shit-faced at the local honky-tonk. Strange things were starting to happen in Two Horse.

Whatever had caused Lila Martin to panic and want to call the sheriff had priority. Kate had to let this opportunity go.

Chapter Seventeen

When Kate drove up to the Brown Bird house, she found Karen waiting on the front porch. On their way back to Red Lodge, Kate told Karen about what Julie had discovered at Lila Martin's.

"Well, at least we know where Nate's been staying," Karen said.

"Did you find out anything from the Nelsons?"

"No one answered when I called," Karen said.

"I knew Ed wasn't home, but I wonder where Lucy is."

"What do you mean?" Karen said, turning the heater up a notch.

"He tied one on at the Dead Coyote tonight."

"Not Ed Nelson?! Now there's enough gossip-fodder for an entire month. The thing about living in a small town is that you expect people to act the way they always act. Then they do something out of the ordinary. Go figure."

"There's a lot of that going around lately. You think maybe Lucy and Ed had a fight over selling the farm then went and drowned their sorrows at separate bars of their choice?"

"Lucy's at home. She just didn't pick up," Karen said. "After I got no answer, I didn't want to waste time. So I called Clayton Farley. I leveled with him about the danger Nate's in, and Jim's role in all these clandestine activities. I told him he needed to 'fess up if he knew anything. He said he didn't, and I believed him. Like Ida, he suggested talking to the Nelsons. Clayton lives across the road from them. I told him I had just called and no one answered. He said all the lights were on, and not only that, he saw Lucy inside."

"Damn, I should've grabbed Ed when I had a chance," Kate said. "When he's with his wife, he clams up. I think Lucy may be the one who suddenly wants to sell the farm. We'll leave the Nelsons until tomorrow. Let's deal with Lila Martin tonight."

****

It was almost eleven o'clock when they pulled up in front of Lila Martin's house. Kate had taken Karen back to the hospital to get her pickup, and she followed from there. Julie's Honda was in the drive, as were now Ida's and Karen's pickups. The Martin house buzzed with activity. Kate knocked on the front door. Sister Jacquelyn answered. Once inside, she locked the door and led Kate and Karen into the kitchen. Lila Martin was standing at the kitchen sink, holding a washcloth full of ice-cubes to her eyes. Julie had her arm draped over the woman's shoulder and was murmuring words of comfort.

"Mrs. Martin, this is Kate Caraway," Julie said.

Lila put her ice-pack down, reached into the pocket of her jeans for a tissue, and blew her nose. "Ida told me about you this morning. She wanted to tell you that Nate had been staying here, but I made her swear she wouldn't. I'm so frightened. Rachel has never been gone this long. She's been so depressed lately. I can't seem to do anything to help. Sister Jacquelyn just told me that Rachel had called Nate and asked him to give her money so she could leave." Lila threw the tissue in the trash and reached for another one. "Every time Rachel gets in trouble, Pete blames me. He's been threatening to take custody of Rachel. He thinks I'm a lousy mother, and now, I suppose I am. My God, I'm not even sure if Rachel is alive." Lila pulled a chair out from the kitchen table, sat down, buried her face in her folded arms, and cried.

"Mrs. Martin, we're here to help if we can. Have you talked to Pete recently?" Kate asked.

"This afternoon," Lila said between sobs. "He was at the hospital with the Brown Birds and then came by here. He's sure Nate and Rachel are together, and that Nate has gotten Rachel mixed up in all this trouble."

"Did you tell him that Nate had been here?" Kate said.

"No, but he'll find out soon enough. He was so angry. I couldn't reason with him."

"Nate's been out looking for Rachel in Mrs. Martin's car," Julie said. "His rental car is hidden in the garage. Mrs. Martin has called all of Rachel's friends. No one has heard from her, or at least no one's talking."

"Rachel called me from the hospital the night before she ran away," Lila said. "She was strung out. She begged me to come get her. When I checked her into rehab, her counselor told me to expect something like this, but not to react. Rachel was hysterical, but I didn't believe she'd run away. Now it's been almost a week. I've called everyone I can think of, even Lucy Nelson, but no one has seen her. I've got to call the sheriff. What if she's hurt somewhere?"

"Lucy Nelson?" Kate asked.

"Lucy was Rachel's high-school mentor last year,"

Lila said.

Kate agreed with Lila Martin. At this point, the sheriff needed to be brought in. Lila would have to tell him she'd been harboring Nate Springfield for the last three days.

"Mrs. Martin, do you know where Nate is right now?"

"This afternoon, late, he drove over to Big Horn Canyon. There's a recreational area there. It's one of Rachel's favorite camping spots before she got involved with drugs. She was really into athletics and outdoor stuff."

"Did he say when he'd be back? He won't stop here if he sees our cars in your driveway."

"He's not coming back tonight. He was going to find a place to camp. I don't want to get Nate in trouble. He said he'd go to the sheriff after we found Rachel. But I guess the longer we wait, the worse it gets."

Kate thought of all the people, herself included, who were so sure Nate was incapable of harming anyone. Why then was she starting to doubt her own convictions about Nate's innocence? Maybe the truth was too ugly and hurtful for everyone to accept. As much as Kate hated to admit it, the only two likely suspects in Frank's murder, so far, were Ida and Nate. Ida had a motive and the opportunity, but she apparently lacked the means. Nate lacked a motive, unless money really was an issue. Facts and speculations were running rampant in Kate's head, not the least of which was Lucy Nelson's failure to mention that she once had a close relationship with Rachel.

With all the new puzzles pieces, Kate needed to restudy her notes and reorganize everything she had discovered, which meant a sleepless night.

"I can't tell you what to do, Mrs. Martin," Kate said. "I understand your situation. You're probably in trouble already for not calling the sheriff right away when Nate came here. There's not a person in this room who thinks Nate is a murderer, but the sheriff is looking for him. I'm going to try to find Nate as well. You do what you have to do to find Rachel. Here's my cell phone number. If you can't connect with me, you can get word to me through any of these women here. By the way, do you have a picture of Rachel?"

Lila Martin reached for her purse and pulled out her wallet. "Here's Rachel's school picture. She hates that picture." Lila forced a laugh. "I have to agree, it's not Rachel's best." Then Lila walked into the bedroom and came out with a framed photo of mother and daughter seated on the tailgate of a pickup. Rachel was wearing yellow overalls and a white sweater. Kate recognized Rachel immediately. She was the girl standing next to Lucy in the photo Kate had seen at the Nelsons.

Julie agreed to spend the night with Lila, and Karen took Sister Jacquelyn back to her parents' home. If Kate drove to the Big Horn Recreational Area campground to search for Nate, she would not even get there until after one in the morning. Chances were good he was not registered for a designated campsite. The effort would be fruitless. Instead, Kate drove back to the Springfield ranch to try to quell the onslaught of information swirling around in her brain.

As the pickup sputtered to a stop, the Springfield dogs came running from all directions. They circled the truck like a pack of wolves ready to pounce on their prey. Kate went directly to the barn, shooing her way through five ragtag canines. She filled their food bowls, rinsed out their water bucket, and refilled it and then went inside the cabin. She flopped down on the sofa. Every muscle in her body ached. So much had happened so quickly. Time seemed to have spiraled away in a vortex. The horse-gathering seemed like a week ago. It felt like only moments ago that Kate sat in the chair watching Veda as she slept. The realization that Veda would not return paralyzed Kate with sadness. How would Ida get by? Her sister had been Ida's entire life for the past eighty-two years. Kate took solace in the hope that Ida's anxiety might lessen with not having to worry about dying before her sister. But it would be small relief compared to the loneliness that was sure to follow.

Luisa Miller nosed the front door open, trotted in, and joined Kate on the sofa. The dog laid her head down on Kate's thigh and sighed. Kate thought of her greyhound, Kenya, and what a luxurious life she was now leading, after spending her first three years in racetrack kennels, how a bad racing injury had almost cost her her life, and how one Molly Gibson had cleverly planted the seed in Kate's mind that eventually grew to Kate and Jack adopting the dog. Kate had doubts then about owning another pet at this uncertain time in her life. But all doubts vanished once she imagined Kenya as her own. Those first weeks had been difficult. Kate had worried that Kenya might be crippled for life. Last September Kate sat with Molly while she nursed the greyhound out of the critical stage—packing Kenya's leg and hip in ice, injecting steroids to reduce inflammation to repair the damage, and comforting the dog until she finally fell asleep. At those times, Kenya had often rested her head on Kate's leg as Luisa Miller was doing now.

Kate looked around Ida's old cabin with its dark walls, simple furniture, and ancient record-player. She wondered what she was doing here. Her need to get out of Chicago and breathe mountain air had her running west—a rabbit fleeing a wolf—without much thought of what she might be getting into. The survival of a small band of mustangs seemed worthy of whatever influence and expertise she had. But within hours of her arrival in Two Horse, she had found herself searching for a murder suspect, enmeshed in the lives of two elderly women, and making enemies who wanted either to scare her out of town or kill her. Now added to her tasks was the search for a runaway teenager whom Kate had never met. Before her thoughts became any more overwhelming, Kate apologized to Luisa Miller and went to the bathroom to fill the tub. Rather than wallow in self-doubt, she'd use this time to soak out some soreness, and to rethink the developments of the last eighteen hours.

The hot bath helped. Now, sitting in her pajamas at the dining room table and listening to the bouncy music of *Carmen*, albeit on a scratchy record, Kate tore the scribbled pages from her yellow legal pad and started over. What did she really know for certain? Frank Springfield had been stabbed to death. His body had been on Ida's ranch the day before Kate arrived. Nate had changed his plans and come to Two Horse two days early after his one-time girlfriend, Rachel Martin, had called him. Nate's refusal to help her had caused Rachel to disappear. Nate had been searching for her while the sheriff had been searching for Nate in connection with Frank's murder. Ed and Lucy Nelson, Ida's allies in opposing the construction of the dam, had suddenly thrown in the towel and were planning to sell their farm

241

to the enemy.

Next, Kate listed other concerns that might lead to something. Frank seemed to be having an affair with a woman he didn't want to flaunt at his usual hang-out the Dead Coyote. Frank might also have donned his scuba equipment to dive somewhere in the area on the morning he was murdered. And Ida had been less than honest with Kate—holding something back—whether or not it was connected to Frank's murder.

None of this would help save Ida's horses. The BLM didn't want them. And the mayor wanted to relocate them to his ranch, a habitat that made the slaughterhouse a more humane option.

Hopefully, sleep would allow the churning mess in her brain to gel into something sensible in the morning. Remembering Veda, Kate set her watch alarm for half an hour before sunrise, then let the other four dogs in the house. Leaving Luisa Miller to her sofa, Kate curled up under a blanket on Ida's twin bed. She was asleep before the rest of the pack settled down.

****

The next morning, Kate stood on the front porch, closed her eyes, and wrapped her hands around a steaming cup of coffee. Living in these glorious Montana mountains for eighty-two years must have been a great preparation for the next life. Kate prayed that Veda would soon spread her goodness over this landscape.

Kate walked back inside, vowing to find solutions to the troubles in Two Horse before sunset.

Chapter Eighteen

Kate grabbed her cell phone and Frank Springfield's and went up the mountain via the dogs' path. It was about seven in Chicago. Jack was an early riser, and Kate couldn't wait to give him the news, or at least clear up his baseball-pitcher mystery.

"Hey!" Kate said when Jack answered.

"Hey, yourself. Your better half is ready. Give me the details," Jack said.

"I don't know where to begin. Yesterday was a blur. I didn't get in until after midnight, but I do have some news for you."

"You're coming home today, right?" Jack said.

"No, but you can stop wondering about your young pitcher."

"Don't tell me you found him?"

"He was pitching for another team."

"What?"

"Mike Chambers is staying at St. Francis Xavier School not far from Two Horse. I was there yesterday, following Nate's trail. I ran into a Father Rick at the school's baseball field. Evidently, Mike Chambers comes there often. Seems he's donated some of his new-found fortune to the school for a new sports facility."

"I'll be damned."

"That's not all. You were right. Mike is struggling with discovering his true calling in life. The boy wants to be a priest."

"No shit." Jack chuckled. "How can we compete with that?"

"Just give him some time. At least you now know what's been troubling him."

"You're a jewel. How about your situation?"

"Veda had a massive stroke yesterday. She was taken off life support this morning."

"Gee. From mustangs, to murder, and now this. How's Ida holding up?"

"Ida wants everyone to believe that she's a tough old gal, but she's going to be lost without Veda. I wish I could do more to help. I feel useless here. I was scratched from the town meeting's agenda, and I still haven't found Nate. And the fate of Ida's horses is as uncertain as the day I arrived. I might very well leave here having accomplished absolutely nothing."

"That's not your fault. You tried. It sounds like life in Two Horse is…just life in Two Horse. But you're not ready to throw in the towel and come home, are you?"

"Hell no. Actually, yesterday wasn't a complete bust. I know why Nate changed his plans and came to Two Horse early. I also know what he's been up to while he's been on the lam." Kate then recounted the Nate/Rachel saga, listening to Jack's sighs and muttered sounds of concern. "But I still don't know where Nate is, and I still don't have a clue as to who stabbed Frank and why."

"The problems in Two Horse started long before you arrived. Just try and stay focused on your initial mission. But you may have to face the fact that you've done all you can do."

"I know, but I just can't leave right now. If I haven't

accomplished anything by Monday, I'm coming home."

"I'll hold you to that. Be careful." He paused and Kate heard him sipping his coffee. "I wish Kenya and I could be there to help."

That thought caused a flutter in Kate's stomach. This country was too beautiful not to enjoy. Kate pictured the three of them driving through the Big Horn Canyon Recreational Area, traveling along without an agenda, enjoying each mile as it came.

"If I'm not run out of town, maybe we can add this place to our travel list. Wasn't it John Steinbeck who said that Montana was the state he loved most?"

"I don't know. But shall I put Montana before or after the McKittrick Canyon through-hike?"

"I have the travel bug, don't I? It doesn't matter. I just want you all to myself without the hassles and worries we seem to trail behind us."

"You got it. As soon as the season's over, we'll hit the road. Hey, Kenya has her own personal groomer now. His name is Javier. Javier LaFevre, of Javier's Precious Pets. He's booked weeks in advance. I was lucky to get a last-minute appointment with him."

"And how did you find this Javier LaFevre?"

"Well, if there was anything good that came out of Tuesday's game with the Astros, it was Javier. It was the bottom of the eighth. We were up by a run, and our starter was still on the mound. He threw a couple of wild pitches, and suddenly two runners are on, nobody out, and our slim lead was about to turn into a slim loss. I went to the mound to give him a break. There was nothing I could tell him. He's been around long enough to have heard it all. But I knew he had two high-maintenance dogs—what do you call them—Shih Tzu?

Anyway, I told him I had a dog that was starting to smell like a ripe corn-tortilla. He recommended Javier."

"Did the dog talk work?"

"For me, it did. I dropped his name, and Javier was willing to squeeze Kenya into his busy schedule. Next time, however, I need to tell him to go easy on the fufu scent. Otherwise, our little girl seemed pleased. She bounced out of the salon, tail wagging, a pink, curly ribbon attached to her collar, absent the corn-tortilla smell. Our pitcher was not so fortunate. He walked the next batter and loaded the bases. The guy on deck stepped up, and on the first pitch he sailed one over the ivy. We lost. Enough baseball. Now, can my fresh, uninvolved mind do you any good? Take a look at your notes. Think. Is there anything in your investigation that doesn't seem right?"

"The Nelsons. They're as out of place in Montana as those tourists we used to see camped in Amboseli dressed in designer safari outfits, drinking champagne in crystal flutes. After vowing to fight the building of the dam, Ed and Lucy did a hundred and eighty and now plan to sell their farm. I can't figure them out. But I know something is going on there. They seem prim and proper, but I saw Ed shit-faced drunk last night, and Lucy is angry at the world. I should have talked to Nate about them. But he was in and out in a flash."

"Okay. What else?"

"I keep linking Frank's murder with the dam controversy, but that doesn't fit with the murderer stripping off Frank's pants."

"You think it was a lover thing?"

"Frank had a reputation for screwing other men's wives."

"Okay," Jack said. "I'm writing all this down. His pants may have been removed to make the murder look like it was committed by a jealous husband."

"I've thought of that. Nate and Frank accidentally met up the morning Frank was killed. Nate told me his grandfather had been all worked up about something."

"That doesn't sound good."

"Nothing does."

"Kenya and I will work on it from this end."

"Thanks. I miss you two more than you can know," Kate said, and hung up.

Kate felt more motivated and encouraged than she had in twenty-four hours. She finally punched the redial button on Frank's freshly charged cell phone. The last number he had dialed before his murder came up. Kate pressed the call button and the phone began to ring.

"Hey. I'm not here. Leave a message." It was Nate's voice. So, Frank had called his grandson that day, but exactly when? Kate scrolled through the menu and discovered that the call had taken place at one-twelve p.m.—shortly before Frank was murdered. According to what Kate had learned, if Nate had been with Frank in his pickup on that Thursday morning, then why had Frank called again?

Before Kate could slide her phone into her jacket pocket, it rang.

"Kate, this is Meg. I just hung up from talking to my cousin, Lou Ann. She's a housemaid at the Country Inn, a small hotel on the way to Red Lodge. It's a place where folks go to celebrate when they're not up for driving into Red Lodge. It has a pricey restaurant and a dark, rendezvous-type lounge in back. She's working tonight. You ought to pay her a visit."

"She knows something?"

"It seems Frank Springfield had been meeting a lady friend at the inn. Lou Ann doesn't know who she was, but Lou Ann remembered seeing Frank at least three times having drinks with this woman in the lounge. One time they even moved their little party to one of the rooms."

"Was this recently?"

"Lou Ann said the last time she saw them together was last Wednesday evening."

"The night before Frank was killed, but that woman could have been anybody."

"I don't think so."

"What do you mean?"

"Lou Ann described her to me. I think I know her, but I don't want to influence your thoughts. Besides, you know how I feel about gossip. Talk to Lou Ann first and get back to me if you need to."

Kate would have gladly taken gossip at this point, but Meg was right. Kate needed to hear herself what Lou Ann had to say before any conclusions could be drawn. But first Kate needed to see Ida and make sure all had gone well. She'd stop at the Country Inn on the way back from the hospital.

"You did good, Meg. I'll call you as soon as I can."

****

Kate pushed the door open. The room was empty.

"They took Veda out a couple of hours ago. She's at the healthcare center next door," Bruce informed Kate. "We needed this room," he said apologetically. "Besides, the healthcare center is much nicer—quiet and peaceful. Veda can make the transition in her own sweet time. Ida's with her."

Kate wanted to give this big, burly nurse a hug. Instead, she thanked him and walked across the parking lot to the healthcare center. She found the room and knocked on the door.

"Come in," Ida said.

Startled, Kate almost backed out as soon as she opened the door. Both twins were lying side by side on the narrow hospital bed, looking like two skinny popsicles minus the sticks. Ida motioned for Kate to sit down.

"I'm not weird. My back hurts, and Veda don't mind," Ida said. "Tell me how you're doing. Then update me on everything."

"I don't know where to begin," Kate said.

"I'll get you started. You want to know why I didn't tell you about Lila Martin giving Nate shelter."

"Good place to start."

Kate listened while Ida explained that she had driven back to the cabin that night but was too antsy to sleep. She didn't feel like sitting around staring at the four walls. Wired on coffee, Ida said she drove around, hoping to find Nate. But on her way back to Red Lodge, she saw Lila Martin driving around like she was looking for a lost dog. Ida followed her to Starbucks just as the coffee shop was opening. Over a cup of coffee, Lila confided in Ida, knowing Ida was looking for Nate.

"At the time, I felt it was best not to let anyone know Nate was staying with Lila. Not only to protect Nate, but to protect her. She's so scared of Pete, it ain't funny. I wanted to tell her to grow a spine, but I kept my mouth shut for once. I did give you a hint, though. Remember? I told you to talk to her."

"You're right, Ida. I remember." Kate closed her

eyes and rubbed her temples. "I confess I was pretty peeved that you didn't tell me what you were up to. Karen, the Brown Bird sisters, and I all met at Lila's last night. At least I found out why Nate hadn't turned himself in. Lila thinks he may be staying somewhere in the Big Horn Canyon since he left your ranch. I will check there today. But I think I may have another murder suspect."

"Who?"

"Don't know for sure just yet, but Frank had been seen meeting a woman at the Country Inn. It wasn't Imagene Porter. Apparently, Frank had been with this mystery woman the night before he was killed. I'll talk to the hotel maid who saw them together. And I found Frank's cell phone. Don G had hidden it in his stash in the barn. He must have found it right after the murder— and before Friday night's storm. The phone was still in working condition."

Ida clambered out of the bed and stretched. Then she pulled on her lower lip. "If that's so, why didn't I see that phone when I found your sunglasses?"

"I had to rifle through Don G's pile of stuff. He'd hidden the phone under an old tennis shoe. It must've been a prize he didn't want to part with."

"You're some detective. I should have found that little prize myself." Ida stretched both arms around the right side of her body as far as she could, trying to get the kinks out of her back. Facing away from Kate, Ida grunted, "Did that phone tell you anything?"

"Afraid so."

Ida uncurled from her stretch and turned around to tuck in the sheets around Veda. "What?"

"Right before Frank was murdered, he called Nate."

"How do you know?"

Kate explained how she determined Frank's last call and the time at which it occurred. Ida was all ears.

"We need to find out what that call was about. It had to have been important for Frank to take the trouble to climb up the mountain for a cell signal. I know phone service is spotty here but I'll keep calling Nate until he answers."

Ida took a deep breath. "It gets complicated, doesn't it?" Suddenly, her knees buckled and she grabbed onto the rail of Veda's bed.

Kate jumped up and caught Ida before she hit the floor.

"I'm okay. Just a little dizzy."

Kate helped Ida to a chair and sat her down. "I'll call the nurse."

"No, please. This happens all the time when I don't eat. In fact, I can't remember when I've eaten last. They've got a god-awful cafeteria here that's even worse than the hospital's. Just bring me a donut or something?"

Kate felt like suggesting a bagel or a cup of soup instead, but knew she couldn't change eighty-two years of bad eating habits. She reached for her backpack, but Ida pulled a five from her pocket and handed it to Kate.

"Some coffee, too. And something for you."

"I'll be right back. But I'd feel a lot better if one of the nurses at least checked your blood pressure."

"And if it's high, they'd slap my ass in the hospital. And I wouldn't get my donut and coffee. What good will that do?"

Kate bought donuts, some plain and some with icing. Ida was right. After coffee and the first donut, color began to return to the old woman's cheeks. She listened attentively as Kate detailed her plans for the rest of the day. But Ida stopped in mid-bite when Kate said she was going back to Chicago on Monday.

"I feel like I've let you down," Kate said. "I'm not sure I was any help in saving your horses."

"Nonsense." Ida swallowed. "Karen told me how you handled the situation at the meeting. You came to plead our case, and even though they wouldn't let you talk on your own, you got our points across through Karen. We still got some time as far as my mustangs go. Even if the dam passes, I'll have more than a few months to decide what to do. But Nate's running out of time. If you could find him before the sheriff does—but, I guess that's asking too much."

"Nonsense to you, too. You've got me for three more days."

****

Lou Ann Blue Water was cleaning the rooms on the second floor of the Country Inn. Room 212's door was open and the TV was blaring. It wasn't hard to recognize Meg's cousin. They were cut from the same mold. Kate rapped hard on the door frame twice before Lou Ann turned and saw her. She motioned for Kate to come in. Then she quickly turned down the TV and closed the door.

"You're Kate. Meg told me you were coming. I'm the only one cleaning today. I'm not supposed to visit with people while I'm working, but it's not busy and no one should be nosing around. We can talk, but I've got to keep working."

"I understand," Kate said. "I've heard you recently saw Frank Springfield here with a woman."

"I don't know who she was, but I do know Frank.

And this woman wasn't his usual type. She was no barfly. She looked like she'd come from some church revival. Perfect hair, perfect clothes. Not the business type. More like some hoity-toity woman. The Brady Bunch's mom, except for the hair. It was shoulder length, that reddish-brown color. You know, like the color of an old plow after it's been sitting in a pasture too long."

"Auburn?"

"Yes, that's it, but with streaks of gray."

"She wasn't wearing a light-pink cardigan, was she?"

"A what?"

"A sweater."

"Sure was."

Kate shook her head.

"Surprised, huh? Me, too. I figured they were having some kind of business meeting until they slipped up to one of the rooms." Lou Ann looked up from tucking in the corners of a bed-sheet. "Remember now, I didn't talk to you, okay? I don't want people saying that Lou Ann Blue Water gossips."

"My lips are sealed. And thanks, Lou Ann."

"Tell Meg she owes me a six-pack of the good stuff."

"Will do."

Chapter Nineteen

Except for his dead naked butt, and back with protruding knife, Kate had no clue what the rest of Frank Springfield looked like. She pictured him with pixie facial features, somewhere between an Ida and a Nate. Try as she might, Kate could not imagine Lucy Nelson having a tête-a-tête with Ida's son. But how many other auburn/gray-haired, uppity women wearing a pink sweater lived in Two Horse? True, Lucy and Ed had been acting strange. Their sudden desire to sell the farm, Ed's stumbling out of the town saloon too drunk to drive home, and Lucy's failing to mention that she had a close relationship with Rachel Martin when Kate was frantically looking for Nate. Had Frank wooed Lucy to bring her over to his side for a few more votes? If so, what would have been in it for Lucy? Or had she been so bored with life in Two Horse that an illicit affair with Frank Springfield seemed exciting?

A little after ten, Kate walked into the second dive-shop in Billings. The first shop had no record of a Frank Springfield renting scuba tanks, but the manager of Billings Dive and Ski wasted no time coming to the counter after he overheard Kate explaining the situation to his clerk. The stitching on his shirt pocket read "Kevin."

"If you know Frank Springfield, tell that character his tank is overdue—a week overdue. And the overdue charge is ten dollars a day."

"I'm afraid Mr. Springfield won't be returning to your shop. He was killed last week in Two Horse."

"Oh, wow. Hey, was he that guy who was murdered in the Pryor Mountains? I read about that."

Instead of replying, Kate asked, "Did Mr. Springfield say where he was going to dive?"

"No. It was pretty strange. Most people who come here are recreational divers. They want to explore the walls of the reservoir. They usually do a two-tank dive. But this guy was in a hurry. He rented only one tank. And when I asked him where he was diving, he gave some smart-ass answer and told me to mind my own business."

"When did he come in?"

Kevin reached under the counter for his log book, found Frank's name, and ran a finger across the page. "Ten-thirty-five, last Thursday, and it was a twenty-four -hour rental."

"Did he say anything else about what his plans were?"

"No. He just grabbed the tank and left. Should I call the police?"

Kate thanked him and rushed from the shop. She climbed into Ida's truck, started the engine, and let it idle, while she considered what she'd just learned. If the dive equipment had been in the back of Frank's pickup, surely the sheriff would have checked with all the dive shops by now. But maybe there was nothing in Frank's pickup, except the dive bootie, which the sheriff had evidently overlooked. Kate glanced up and saw Kevin on the phone. Chances were, he was calling the Billings police. They, in turn, would contact Sheriff Phillips. Kate did not linger. She did not want to be anywhere near the dive shop when Phillips arrived. He would be furious if he knew Kate was one step ahead on this investigation. And she had not yet told him about having found Frank's cell phone.

Kate drove back through the city, piecing together the day of Frank's death. Nate and Frank had met at McDonald's around ten o'clock that morning, then Frank left immediately for Billings Dive and Ski and checked out the tank at ten-thirty-five. He made his last phone call at one-twelve that afternoon. And the medical examiner had set the time of Frank's murder at about thirty-six hours before Kate had found his body.

The Big Horn Canyon Reservoir was at least an hour's drive away. It would have been impossible for Frank to have dove in the reservoir, driven to Ida's ranch, and gotten there in time for his murder. So the reservoir did not factor. Kate had to face the realization she had been avoiding. Since Frank was murdered on the ranch, the only possible explanation was that he had been diving in Ida's lake. Except for the missing dive gear, the scenario fit.

It was a scenario that left an ache in the bottom of Kate's stomach.

Half-an-hour later, Kate was back at the first dive shop. She had everything she needed, except her dive-certification card, but a copy would do just fine. Kate reached into her bag to call Jack, but her cell phone was gone. She checked her pockets and walked back to Ida's truck. Not finding it, she asked to use the shop's phone to call Jack. As they talked, a copy of her card was printing off the shop's fax machine.

"I know you don't want to hear this, but the thing that keeps echoing in my head is, 'Keep it simple.' It doesn't sound like that murder was premeditated. At least it wasn't planned out very well. Too sloppy. I think you're tossing your net too wide." Jack paused.

"I hear you. It seems everything points to Nate. He met with Frank the morning he was murdered. Then he disappeared. Frank was killed with his own dive knife, that 'fancy knife,' as Ida put it. So maybe you're right. It wasn't premeditated. But still I can't come up with a motive, unless it's at the bottom of Ida's lake. Maybe I'll find something there."

Kate, for God's sake don't do anything rash. I don't like the idea of you diving alone. Get Karen Gregory to go with you."

"I will, if I can catch her. I'll call you as soon as I can."

Kate coasted up to Molin's gas pump on fumes. As she filled the tank, she began to question her next move. The day was warming up, but that created no illusions. It had been years since her last dive. Kate was on her second log book. Halfway filled, it brought her up to dive number seventy-six. But she had never dived in cold, dark water. She had never worn a wet suit. A dive skin was all that was needed in the sunny, warm waters of the Caribbean. For all her experience, this shallow dive was far from being a piece of cake.

"Hey, if you're trying to drain the station's gas supply, put that damn hose in my tank." A voice behind Kate jolted her out of her thoughts, and she noticed gas spilling down the side of Ida's truck. "And you never did replace those tires. That one looks low on air again."

Kate looked around and saw the GS&E's black truck parked in line for gas. Lloyd Stenson was already pulling the air hose over to Ida's truck. "Hope you don't mind me saying so, but I don't think Montana is the state for you."

"How's that?" Kate said, replacing the gas pump.

"Well, for one thing, you don't like mountain roads, and for another, Montana ain't any scuba Mecca." He nodded at the equipment in the bed of the truck.

Kate laughed. "You're right. I've been here less than a week, and every morning, I wake up thinking that I took a wrong turn out of Chicago. Maybe I need to have my head examined. But I also need to find out what's at the bottom of a lake, and this is the only way."

"Wish it was that easy for us." Lloyd squatted down with a tire gauge, checked the air pressure, and inflated the tire a bit more. "We have to rely on our equipment to do the seeing for us, and as sophisticated as it is, we're never a hundred percent. But we've done our best and we're heading home. Mayor Winford's bringing in the drilling crew right now."

"Oh, I remember now. Your truck was on the mayor's ranch a few days ago. You were the guys who were surveying his pasture, the one that borders the Nelson farm."

"That was us, all right. We're all finished and done earlier than we expected."

"Easy job?" Kate asked, thinking she sounded a bit too curious.

"Canceled job. We had another survey scheduled— another piece of property the mayor was interested in us looking at, but that job was canceled."

"So the mayor's ready to drill some water wells?" Kate said.

"Don't know about water, but there's a strong possibility he's got enough natural gas under that land to keep Carbon County aglow till the next century. Listen, this tire needs to be patched, if not replaced. You got a slow leak here."

"Natural gas?" Kate said.

"Yes ma'am, a strong possibility. Can't say more. Here's my partner now. Gotta go. Hope you find what you're looking for."

Natural gas. It all made sense now. If the mayor had a huge reservoir under his land, chances were good the Nelsons did as well. Kate was certain that the Nelsons were not privy to the real reason Clyde Winford wanted their farm. However, Kate still was not sure why the Nelsons were so unhappy and eager to sell. Even if the dam proposal passed, they would still have plenty of time to determine their course of action. And if the mayor had made them a great offer, shouldn't they be happy with their good fortune and early retirement? But maybe it had nothing to do with any of that. Maybe Lucy Nelson wanted to get out of Two Horse for another reason.

Then the picture became clear, like a stiff wind blowing away a fog. Just six months ago Mayor Winford had talked his old buddy, Frank Springfield, into coming back to Two Horse permanently. Frank, who knew the area well, Frank, the project manager on the pipeline, Frank, who all of a sudden had developed an interest in his mother's ranch.

Could the canceled surveying job that Lloyd Stenson mentioned been on Ida's ranch? Was that why Frank was poking around there on the day he was murdered? If Frank *and* the mayor both had their sights set on Ida's place, too, then Clyde Winford was removed from Kate's list of suspects. He needed his friend alive.

The closer Kate came to the solution, the farther away she wanted to be from Two Horse, Montana.

Kate walked to the town phone to call Karen Gregory, but it was in use. After waiting several minutes, Kate gave up headed to Ida's lake alone. It was easy to see that the water level was at an all-time low, probably not more than twenty feet. But in all her years of diving, Kate had never violated the "buddy" rule. She knew that only idiots dove without a partner.

As soon as Kate jumped into the water, the cold stung so sharply it took her breath away. Opting for a wet suit rather than the extra protection of a dry suit had been a mistake. But it was too late now. Hopefully, whatever was on the bottom of Ida's lake would be easy to find.

Ida's lake was not large, and even though a shallow dive would allow Kate to stay under for a good hour or so, she still would not be able to stand the cold for more than fifteen or twenty minutes. Kate raised her hose over her head, and slowly let air out of her dive vest, allowing a smooth descent. Then she shone her light on the computer attached to her wrist and watched the numbers increase—ten, fifteen, sixteen, eighteen, twenty feet. At twenty-three feet Kate touched bottom, sending a cloud of silt rising, which momentarily blinded her. When the cloud settled, visibility was no more than five feet.

Despite having an advanced diving certificate, Kate had never mastered the use of an underwater compass. The skill was easy enough for someone who practiced it, but her recreational dives in clear waters, following a dive master never gave Kate a need to develop that skill.

Kate carefully bounced off the bottom, kicked her feet, and swam along three feet above the lake bed. The basics of diving had come back immediately, but the murky water made her nervous. She could hear her heart beating rapidly, which meant she was sucking too much air.

Kate calmed herself by concentrating on the task at hand. Shining her light and swimming straight in one direction until the water became shallow, she then turned and swam in the opposite direction, all the while picturing in her mind a grid along the bottom. Catfish drifted in and out of view. Except for the rocky substrate, there was nothing else to see. She passed in front of the pier and continued to the other side, then reversed her direction and started back. She glanced at her computer. Twelve minutes had elapsed. She kept swimming, kicking harder to generate more body heat and to get this task over with as soon as possible.

On her next pass through, her light caught the object only moments before she swam directly into it. At first it looked like a big piece of farm equipment. An inch or so of thick silt covered its surface. Kate rested her hand on the side and rubbed its surface free of sediment. She waited for the cloudy water to clear. A shiny piece of reddish metal now reflected in her light. She began to slowly swim around it, but before she completed a half-circle, she knew what it was. Now she dreaded what she might find inside.

The vehicle was resting on its side. Kate swam over and shined her light through the open window. Anchored to the steering wheel by a frayed rope was the reason Frank Springfield was murdered.

Kate had been down twenty-five minutes, and was starting to shiver, more, she thought, because of what she had found rather than the coldness of the water. She considered ascending and swimming back on the surface, but her heavy dive equipment would slow her down. Besides, the water was warmer than the cold breeze blowing over the lake. Her heavy breathing had almost emptied her air tank, but she had enough to make it. Kate turned in the direction of the pier. She wanted out, and fast. She kicked hard to put some distance between her and what she had seen. Her right fin caught against the vehicle and slipped off her heel. As she reached around to pull it back on, she dropped her flashlight.

Kate figured the pier to be straight ahead no more than twenty feet. She stretched her arms out in front of her and kicked hard. In seconds, she was under the pier. The bank was not far away. She swam a bit farther to give herself an unobstructed surfacing. But before she cleared the planks overhead, she heard a loud cracking sound. Then something heavy struck her back, knocking her tank across her shoulders and loosening her vest. As she tried to readjust her equipment, she heard a scream, and part of the pier came crashing down around her. Kate felt her legs being pulled under the debris. Then she heard a splash and something heavy fell into the water beside her. Her air-hose was suddenly jerked from her mouth. Someone looped an arm around Kate's throat, but in the tangle of equipment, Kate couldn't fight back. Then it felt as if her hair was being pulled from its roots. She tried to reach back and grab her attacker, but her tank was in the way. The person's knee jammed into Kate's lower back and knocked out her remaining breath. As panic set in, an old memory surfaced. Kate stopped fighting. She realized that whoever had hold of her was trying to bring her to the surface with the standard lifeguard rescue. Within seconds, Kate and the person behind her bobbed to the surface and swam free of the collapsed pier. Someone standing on the bank reached down, grabbed Kate's tank, and pulled her from the water.

Kate flopped down on the muddy bank and pulled her mask off. The first thing she saw was the outline of an eagle, its wings spread in flight. She wiped the water from her eyes and looked again. Now standing ankle deep in mud, wearing only a thin T-shirt and low riding hip-hugger jeans, was a skinny girl with a tattoo across her belly. Although they had never met, Kate instantly recognized her young rescuer. Standing next to her was Clayton Farley.

****

Back in Ida's cabin, Kate told Clayton to put the kettle on the hot plate. She then went to the bathroom, turned on the gas heater, and told Rachel Martin to bathe first. Kate was still wearing the wet suit, but Rachel, in her scanty clothes, was shivering—her anorexic physique showing signs of hypothermia.

Kate fixed a cup of hot tea for Rachel and coffee for herself. She pulled some clothes from Ida's dresser and knocked on the bathroom door.

"Rachel, how are you doing?"

"Okay."

"There's a change of clothes and hot tea right by the door. Just take your time," Kate said.

"You can come in," Rachel said, her voice shaky.

Kate opened the door. Rachel was sitting on the toilet seat. She was wrapped in Ida's bathrobe and combing tangles out of her hair. The teenager gazed at the mirror as tears flowed down her face. Kate had a feeling that she had not been invited in to comfort the girl, but to watch a grand performance.

"So you've been staying at the Nelson place."

"I didn't know what to do," Rachel said. "I've never seen Lucy and Ed fight like that. He was so mad—and he'd been drinking. I couldn't stay there and listen to them. It was horrible. So I ran across the road to Clay's house. He said we should come and find you."

"So you've been staying at the Nelsons' place all along?"

"Lucy is the only person who understands. Nate let me down. But I knew Lucy would help. Lucy's a nurse. She helped me get through a rough time before."

Kate thought about the photo on Lucy Nelson's deacon's bench—Lucy with her arm around a young girl. And later as Kate was leaving the farm, she had seen someone in the window—thinking it was Lucy—but realizing something about the face was not right.

"The tea will make you feel better," Kate said. "When you're finished, we'll talk."

Kate left Rachel to get dressed. She joined Clayton by the fireplace and listened to the rest of the story. When Rachel and Clayton had arrived on the ranch and found an empty house, they wandered around the property and spotted the truck down by the lake. At the water's edge, Rachel had noticed Kate's air bubbles and walked out on the pier for a better look. The rotten structure had given way beneath her just as she saw Kate coming to the surface.

In all the excitement, Kate had not been asked why she was diving in Ida's lake. Just as she was thinking up a convincing story, Rachel emerged from the bathroom.

"We can't just sit here. We have to do something. I've never seen Ed act like that. He was saying awful things to Lucy."

"Rachel, listen to me. I'll see what I can do. But first, you have to go home. Your mother is on the verge of a nervous breakdown. She's thinking the worst."

Rachel flopped on the sofa and folded her arms across her chest. "She hates me. I'm never going home. Lucy is the only one who can help me. I can always talk to her about anything. She's so cool. We have hot tea and talk about all sorts of important stuff."

Rachel defiantly flipped her wet hair over her shoulders. "These clothes are gross. They smell like old, dirty socks." Kate suspected that more tears were about to come, bigger and more dramatic than before. Maybe it was the added misery of having to wear an old woman's clothes and not having a hair dryer, but at any rate, Rachel started bawling again.

Kate's hair smelled like dirty water. The coffee wasn't doing much good at warming her up. And if she had to guess, it would be at least half an hour before Ida's ancient hot-water heater would give up another bath. Instead of feeling sympathetic, Kate wanted to wring Rachel's neck.

"Rachel, Nate is wanted for murder—a murder he did not commit. You're the reason he hasn't come forward and cleared his name. He's been out looking for you. After running from the sheriff for the past five days, he's made his situation so bad I'm afraid Sheriff Phillips will shoot him on sight. And your father is looking for Nate too. While you and Lucy have been playing tea party, your mother's been worried that you'd killed yourself. Lucy Nelson had no business hiding you. If Ida had a phone service, I'd call the sheriff to come get you right now."

Rachel's red, swollen face turned white. Her jaw dropped into her lap.

"Come on, Rachel, I'm taking you home," Clayton said. "Enough is enough."

Chapter Twenty

As they left the cabin, Rachel attempted to negotiate with Kate by reminding her about the lifesaving rescue. Kate reminded Rachel that if she had not stupidly walked out onto a crumbling pier, Kate's life would not have needed saving. No deal was reached—either Rachel would let Clayton take her home, or Kate would deposit the missing teenager at the sheriff's office. Rachel glared at Kate through the windshield as Clayton pulled away.

Despite everything that had happened, at least a ray of hope for Nate had finally appeared, if Kate could just find him first. Kate was on her way back inside to figure out what to do next, when Clayton returned.

"Rachel wants her clothes," he said.

Kate and Clayton went back inside.

"That girl's crazy," Clayton said. "She said that as soon as she gets home, she's going to run away again. She wanted you to help Lucy. She's saying it was a big mistake to even talk to you."

Well, fine, Kate thought. She wanted to tell Clayton that for all she cared the little bitch could run away to China. This high-drama child was not Kate's problem. Lucy Nelson was not Kate's problem, either. If Lucy wanted to have an affair with somebody like Frank Springfield and screw up her marriage, so what? Instead, Kate said, "Just take her home, Clayton, and we'll see what happens. I wish I could get word to Nate that he needs to show up and face this situation and tell him Rachel's been found. There's no reason now for him to be out there alone."

"I really don't know where he is, Ms. Caraway."

"I know, but if he contacts you, please tell him to come to Ida's place. What I've said is true. Sheriff Phillips believes that Nate's dangerous. He needs to be careful."

"Yes, ma'am. Pete's looking for Nate too."

"I know." Kate put Rachel's wet clothes in a plastic bag, thanked Clayton for his help, and wished him luck. As he was backing out, Rachel made one final statement to Kate. As the middle finger of her clenched left hand flew up, Clayton grabbed Rachel's wrist and pulled it down. Then she slapped him on the shoulder as they drove off.

Kate needed some time to think. She showered, made a fresh pot of coffee, and sat down in front of the fireplace. Her deep-down chill was beginning to subside. Now that Rachel had surfaced, Pete might be willing to help Kate find the boy. *It's the least he could do*, Kate thought.

Luisa Miller crept out from Veda's room, and joined Kate on the sofa. Kate hadn't realized the dog was in the cabin. She was also surprised to see it was three o'clock, an hour past the time Kate had told Jack she would call. She needed to get moving. She had one more thing to do on the ranch before she left for town. Kate put on her last pair of clean jeans and a thick sweatshirt. She darted out the door and climbed behind the wheel of Ida's truck. Just as she looked back to make sure she wouldn't back over any dogs, a dark blue Lincoln crept up behind her. She left the truck idling, paused, then walked over to the car as it slowed to a stop.

"Afternoon. I'm looking for Ida Springfield." A man in a gray suit pushed open the car door, hesitating before he placed his shiny wing- tips on Ida's unpaved driveway. The dogs flew around the corner of the barn, and the visitor quickly jumped back in his car and slammed the door.

Kate shooed the dogs away, but it was a couple of minutes before the dust settled and the window of the Lincoln slid down.

"Sorry about that," Kate said. "Ida's not here at the moment. I'm Kate Caraway, a friend of hers. Can I give her a message?"

He scanned the mountains in the distance, a look of uncertainly on his face. "Name's Brian Loger from Billings. Do you know when Mrs. Springfield will return?"

"I'm not sure. She had a family emergency."

"Yes, well, sounds like she's had a difficult time as of late, with her son dying and everything." He opened his console, pulled a business card from a small leather case, and handed it to Kate. "I didn't want to bother Mrs. Springfield, but I just came from Mayor Winford's office, and he wasn't in. And we were wondering if drilling will go ahead as planned."

Kate looked at the card: *Winford/Springfield Land Trusts, Inc.* "Drilling?" she asked.

"For gas on this ranch."

"On *this* ranch?"

"I know it's not the best time now, but the investors in Billings are eager to move forward. We've paid in advance to lease the land. Frank had told us the drilling could start by the end of the month. But if Mrs.

Springfield needs more time because of the recent circumstances, we understand."

Kate stood, staring at the business card, wondering how she could have been so blind.

"Are you okay, ma'am?"

"I'll tell her you came by, Mr. Loger, but I think it's best you leave now."

"Right, well, I'll be staying at the Days Inn tonight. I'd like to talk with her before I leave tomorrow, if possible." The window slid up, and he drove away.

****

Kate missed it on the first pass. It could hardly be called a road—tire tracks now overgrown led off the back road across what seemed like an impossible terrain. Kate stopped the truck and got out. The weeds and grass had recently been mashed down. Someone had driven this route within the last day or so. If Nate left the ranch on Monday, either he had returned like Sheriff Phillips claimed, or someone else had paid this section of the ranch a visit.

Kate climbed back into the truck and started slowly across the rocky road. It was like driving along the spine of a dinosaur. After half a mile, Kate gave up and stopped the truck to walk the rest of the way. The path suddenly rose to a steep incline. When Kate reached the top, she saw Ida's ranch from a new perspective. The mountain where she and Ida had perched on Friday night came into view, and as Kate neared the outcropping, so did the valley of wildflowers and the creek trail she had explored earlier. Without stepping out on the sniper's perch, Kate had no trouble seeing Randy's body in the ravine, as well as the spot where she had been when the sniper had shot at her. Besides Ida, who else would know about this road up the back mountain of her ranch? Maybe Frank, but he was dead. That left Nate. A lot had happened since he had sat in Kate's office. If he had learned about the natural gas reserve from his conversation with Frank on Thursday, Nate might have killed Frank out of desperation. *But shoot at me?* Kate thought. She refused to believe Nate would try to kill her.

Feeling like a fool, Kate turned to leave. And that's when she saw it. Lying on the ground right by her foot, a half-smoked cigarette.

****

Kate street walked into the mayor's office, slamming the door behind her. A distressed secretary jumped, her eyes darted toward the door to the Winford's office. Before Kate could ask, she was informed that the mayor was out. Kate walked over to the copy machine and made a photocopy of Mr. Loger's business card.

"Tell the mayor Kate Caraway came by. Give him this and tell him Mr. Loger will be in town until tomorrow, and that the investors in Billings are getting anxious."

****

Kate used the town phone to called Ida. There was no change in Veda's condition, and no, Ida hadn't heard of a Brian Loger from Billings. Kate believed her. She didn't have to ask if Ida had agreed to allow Winford/Springfield Land Trust, Inc. to drill for natural gas on the ranch. Kate knew the answer.

The sun was slipping behind the mountains as Kate pulled up to the Days Inn. She was going to try her best to convince Loger to come forth with the details.

She didn't have to try that hard. Loger was anxious to find out what was going on. Having heard little, if not conflicting information from the founders of the company since Frank Springfield's murder, the other members of the company had become suspicious.

"Do you have the pertinent maps with you?" Kate asked after reading over the lease giving Loger and his company the right to drill on Ida's ranch.

They were sitting in the bright dining room of the Pryor Mountains Diner adjacent to the motel. Loger pulled several topographical and survey maps from his briefcase, all showing substantial natural gas deposits within the boundaries of the lease agreements. They were all there: the mayor's ranch, Ida's ranch, the Nelson farm, and the hundred and fifty acres bordering the Pryor Mountains Wild Horse Range—the land the National Park Service could have purchased had George Stokes not stalled its acquisition.

The entire area sat on top of a vast reservoir. The deepest and most substantial portion was under Ida's land. According to that lease, drilling was to begin last Thursday, the day Frank Springfield was murdered.

"So this lease was executed just last week?" Kate asked.

"We were told initially that negotiations were ongoing with Mrs. Springfield, and not to expect the lease for her ranch for several more weeks. Then Clyde Winford called last Thursday around noon. He said he'd have everything wrapped up in mere hours and then he'd be on his way to Billings with the lease. This is what we had been waiting for. The other areas were promising, but this prize here—" Loger pointed to the map of Ida's ranch. "—was the deciding factor for me and my partners. We put up a lot of money for that. But we haven't heard a word since last Thursday. I called the survey company, and they told me Winford postponed the seismic survey on this property."

"Was that the survey scheduled with GS&E?"

"How did you know?"

"Never mind. I suggest you talk to Ida in person." Kate shoved the maps across the table. "I'm pretty sure she knows nothing about this."

Brian Loger's eyes widened. Kate heard him stammer as she walked away.

****

Kate drove back to Ida's ranch, fed the dogs, brought in enough firewood, and settled down to try to make the puzzle pieces fit neatly together. If Kate's speculations were correct, when Clyde Winford had discovered mineral reserves on his ranch, he had summoned his old buddy Frank Springfield back to Two Horse to help find investors and cash in. Had greed not gotten the best of them, they could have continued to purchase surrounding leases and tap the underground riches legitimately. Frank must have discovered what was on the bottom of Ida's lake, giving him a perfect opportunity to blackmail Ida into leasing her ranch, the prime area, and speeding up the process. Up until that moment, Frank's plan was to simply let the dam render Ida's land useless, and eventually convince Nate that his money problems could disappear with a mineral lease. But now he did not have to wait. Frank must have called Winford. Too excited to go into details, he just told his partner he'd have Ida's signature that afternoon and to call the Billings investors and let them know. All that was left to do was to call Nate and tell him that if he wanted to keep his great-grandmother out of jail, he'd better cooperate. Frank must have tasted victory.

Karen was right. Frank had been the brains behind the get-rich-quick scheme. But now he was gone, and Mayor Clyde Winford was starting to panic—he was running out of time. He needed Ida's signature on the lease, and with Frank dead, Winford had no idea how to get it. Except, maybe, with a little pressure delivered by the sheriff.

Chapter Twenty-One

Kate arrived at the healthcare center, her thoughts on how to break the news. Ida was in the lounge, staring out the window. Kate sat down beside her and waited. Ida finally spoke.

"She's gone. My little sister's gone. The funeral guy just left. The man gave me the creeps. He shook my hand on the way out. His skin felt like old, dry paper ready to crumble off the bone. I washed my hand in hot soapy water, but it didn't help. Veda will be cremated in the morning. After things settle down, I'll spread her ashes over our mountain. Take me home. This place smells bad."

"I'll meet you out at the truck," Kate said. "I think I left my cell phone here. Have you seen it?"

"Nope. Check over at the front desk."

Ida insisted on driving. Most of the trip was made in silence. Kate had a great deal of information for Ida, but for now, listening to the wind whistle through the windows was all that seemed appropriate.

Finally, Ida spoke, "Find your phone?"

"No, I haven't."

"Sorry. It hasn't exactly been a normal week. Maybe you left it at the cabin." Ida reached up to adjust the rearview mirror.

Kate wasn't ready to deliver all the information she had discovered yesterday at once. Besides, nothing she had learned could help find Nate, and since that task was her top priority, she phrased her words carefully and hoped she could keep the anxiety out of her voice. "I'm still working on that. But first things first. Let's find your great-grandson."

Ida turned and looked at Kate, but said nothing.

"Rachel surfaced," Kate said. "She's been at the Nelsons. Seems Ed and Lucy had a domestic dispute, and Rachel ran across the road to Clayton Farley's house. Clayton brought her to see me. Anyway, I plan to find Pete and convince him to help me search for Nate."

"Make sure he does. Otherwise, I'll kick his ass for taking the note and causing me all this goddamn worry."

They pulled into Two Horse and Ida slowed the truck as she turned toward the phone booth. "Go ahead and call Pete. I'm going across the street to Molin's. Meet you there."

Kate hopped out of the truck. Before she could fish change from her pocket, she was startled out of her skin by the squealing of Ida's tires on the pavement. Ida had missed hitting Karen Gregory by inches. Kate ran over, but Karen was fine.

"Sorry, Ida. It was my fault," Karen said.

"You're too short to be darting across the goddamned road," Ida called out to Karen. Then she parked the truck in front of Molin's.

"What does being short have to do with it?" Karen asked Kate.

"Are you sure you're okay?" Kate said.

"Yes. I'm on my way to the sheriff's office. Lucy Nelson called me. Ed's just been arrested. Lucy's trying to make bail, but I'm afraid that's not going to be easy."

"You mean they're going to deny bail because of a

domestic dispute?" Kate said.

"No, because of attempted murder. Let's get out of the road. I don't know the whole story. Evidently, Winford came to the Nelsons with the deed and other papers for them to look over. Ed found some courage—God knows where—and said he wasn't going to sell. Winford played his trump card, and Ed went for his rifle."

"I can guess what that was."

"Lucy and Frank were having an affair," Karen said. "And the mayor decided to inform Ed at that time, and said he'd do likewise with the rest of the townsfolk if Ed didn't cooperate."

"I just found out about that myself," Kate said.

"How?"

"Well, I've been busy."

Kate followed Karen to the sheriff's office. Lucy was sitting on the bench just inside the front door. What little eye-makeup was left had streaked down her cheeks. She looked up at Karen. "Thanks for coming. Our lawyer is speaking with the judge now. Nothing's been decided, but it looks like Ed will spend the night in jail." Lucy ignored Kate. "There's really nothing more I can do here. Can you drive me home, Karen? I guess it doesn't matter now, but Rachel Martin has been staying with me. She got frightened and left when Ed and I started fighting. Poor girl. I hope she's okay."

"Clayton Farley took her home," Kate said.

Lucy flashed Kate a hateful look, which just as quickly dissolved into one of shame and regret. "I really screwed things up, didn't I?" Lucy cried. "The night before Frank was killed I went to see him to tell him it was over. He pulled his phone out of his pocket. He'd recorded our last time together and let me listen to it. He said he would send it to Ed if I didn't agree to sell the farm to Clyde Winford. That's when I realized those two assholes, Clyde and Frank, were working together. To tell you the truth, when I heard Frank was murdered the next day, I was relieved. Then that afternoon, Clyde called me. Frank had sent Clyde the recording, and it was business as usual. I still thought we could just sell the farm and go back to Mississippi, and Ed would never know about my affair with Frank."

"Let's go," Karen said as she helped Lucy to her feet. "I'll take you home."

Kate's intuition told her it was time to remove Lucy Nelson's name from the suspect list. And with the mayor scratched, the situation became really ugly.

Kate walked back across the street just as Imagene Porter was loading the last of Ida's supplies into the back of her truck.

"Shit's really hit the fan now," Imagene said. "So, old Frank had his fangs in Lucy Nelson. I'd have given my last cent to have seen Ed Nelson holding a rifle on Clyde Winford. Hey, you think it was Ed who killed Frank?"

"I don't think so," Kate said. "Sounds like Ed was in the dark about the affair until today."

"The whole damn town's in the dark," Ida growled. "Let's go. We've got to find Pete."

"Miz Springfield. Miz Caraway." They turned to see Niles running across the street, waving his hands. "Miz Gregory said for me to tell you to wait. She needs to ask Miz Caraway something about a horse before you all leave. Lots of excitement in town, huh? Oh. I'm sorry Miz Springfield. My condolences. I heard Veda passed away."

"Go away, Niles," Ida said. Then she turned to Kate and murmured, "I'm tired of being nice."

Niles scampered back across the street and disappeared inside the sheriff's office. Ida hopped up on the lowered tailgate. "Ed Nelson just rose several notches in my book. Campaigns, town meetings, and all that other crap is worthless. The only way to get what you want done in Two Horse is with a shotgun pointed at someone's head. If I find out who killed my stallion, I'm gonna dispense with questions and shoot first. And no one's moving those mustangs. No one's building that dam. If they try, I'll blow the thing up."

Kate didn't doubt one word of what she heard.

"Sit down. I'm not gonna bite."

"I'm not so sure about that, Ida." Kate said, sounding more serious than she meant to.

"As soon as this is all over, I'm gonna deed the ranch to Nate. I can't wait on the election or that Nature Conservancy to decide if they want my place. It's got to be done now. Nate can find someone to run it until he gets out of college. I guess you know what I mean?"

"I think I do, Ida," Kate said.

"You're one smart cookie."

Just then, Karen pulled up in her park service truck with Lucy riding shotgun. "Kate, I sent Ted and Daniel over to the ranch today to pick up Salty. They just phoned. Salty wasn't in the barn."

"He was when I checked on him early this morning," Kate said.

"Those stupid dogs probably caused a ruckus again and spooked your horse. He can't go far in my canyon," Ida said. "I'm sure he'll come back to the barn once he calms down."

"That's not all," Karen said. "The truck and van are missing too."

"You mean someone stole Salty?" Kate said, not believing her own words. "Why?"

"We'll leave Pete until later," Ida hoped down from the tailgate. "Let's get out to the ranch."

****

No sooner had they arrived at the ranch, Ida insisted on driving around to check on things. Kate wanted to object, but realized that Ida needed something to do to keep occupied. An hour later, Karen arrived. She walked in, not bothering to knock. "Kate, Ida, are you here?"

Kate stepped out of the kitchen. "Ida's out looking around. How's Lucy?"

"Believe it or not, she seems relieved. With everything out in the open, I think she feels she can start moving forward. In fact, Ed's lawyer called while I was there, and he's been doing some fast talking. It looks like the charges will be changed to disorderly conduct. Man, it's nice and warm in here. My tin trailer has zero insulation. I'd do better with a tent and sleeping bag. Is that coffee I smell?"

"Just made some. Sounds like Lucy found a good lawyer."

Karen followed Kate into the kitchen. "I guess. Seems when he mentioned to the mayor that blackmail brought some stiff charges, Winford changed his tune."

Kate set a cup in front of Karen. She noticed for the first time the young ranger's eyes were slightly puffy.

"You okay?"

"Stokes let the hammer drop when he heard about the missing horse and truck and van." Karen took off her cap and massaged her temples.

"You mean he fired you?!"

"It's okay. Now I can focus on my foundation. That's what I've wanted all along. He's really doing me a favor. I don't have to live any longer in that ratty piece of aluminum the park service calls housing."

Before Kate could offer any sympathy, Ida came tearing through the front door and into the kitchen. She flung open a wood cabinet and grabbed her shotgun and a box of shells. "Someone's not only stolen your horse and your truck and van," Ida shouted. "Some goddamn idiot shit-head's taken my whole herd." Ida was in and out of the cabin in a flash. Kate and Karen jumped up to follow. "They can't have gotten far," Ida yelled back. "You two stay here. I don't want you with me. If I have to, I'm gonna splatter blood all over Carbon County."

Kate turned to Karen. "Help me. I'll grab her. You grab the gun."

Kate threw her arms around Ida's waist at the same instant Karen jerked the shotgun from Ida's grasp. Ida kicked and spat like a bobcat, tripping Kate and causing the two of them to tumble to the ground. Kate managed to straddle Ida and pin her arms down. "Listen to me, Ida! You can't go off like this. You'll end up killing somebody."

"That's the idea. Let me go!"

"No. Not until you promise me that you'll come back inside the cabin so we can talk." Kate called over her shoulder to Karen. "Grab the keys to the pickup." Kate stared down at Ida. "You've got no gun, you've got no keys. Understand?"

"That's not gonna stop me. I've got nothing left to lose."

"You have Nate. And without you, Nate doesn't stand a chance."

Ida stopped struggling and looked straight into Kate's eyes. "You're right. I'm a goddamn fool. Now get your ass off me so I can breathe. We're going nowhere, rolling around here in the dirt."

****

Kate, Ida, and Karen sat across from the three surviving members of the Two Horse Social Club. Mayor Winford appeared to have recovered from his brush with death. He refused to look Kate in the eye. At the sight of Karen Gregory, George Stokes's face flushed a deeper red. Sheriff Phillips seemed to have lost some of his cockiness.

"Ida, you've been under a lot of stress lately." Phillips sighed. "Are you absolutely sure the horses are nowhere on your ranch? Where else could they be?"

"Are you calling me a liar?" Ida stood up, walked over to the sheriff's desk, and slammed her hands down squarely in the middle of his purported paperwork.

"No, you stubborn old woman. I'm just saying that, with all the shooting going on around your place, maybe the horses spooked and are holed up somewhere. I doubt even you know all the nooks and crannies of that piece of shit land you call a ranch."

Ida placed her hands on her hips and cocked her head.

"Sorry, sorry," the sheriff said before Ida could spew another round of profane insults. "I'll sent Sam Lucas go over now and have a look around."

"They're gone, I tell you. Gone! Gone! Gone!" Ida kicked a chair sending it across the room.

"Karen, you're a big part of this mess. I'm reporting

you as responsible for the loss of those vehicles and that horse," Stokes said with unabashed hostility. "You women are stirring up your very own hornet's nest."

Karen stepped between Ida and Stokes just as Ida, fists raised, started toward Karen's ex-boss. "You leave this girl alone. I'll pay for your lost property," Ida said through clenched teeth.

"Ida, listen. Maybe Deputy Lucas can help," Kate said. "Another look around is a good idea."

"Right, let's get the hell out of here, before I puke!" Ida turned on her heel and was gone. Karen ran after her. Before Kate could follow, Sheriff Phillips called her back.

"Ms. Caraway, we had a call from Lila Martin early this morning."

"Good, I told her she needed to contact you."

"Your assistance is always appreciated," Phillips said sarcastically. "Her daughter's home. But no Nate."

"Then she must have told you that Nate has been searching for Rachel this entire time."

"I don't care if he was searching for the Pope. Nate's still a fugitive and wanted for Frank Springfield's murder, and your attempted murder."

"I understand that, Sheriff."

"It won't be long before we find him."

"I know Nate needs to be brought in, but despite what you think, he's not dangerous. I'm absolutely sure of that now. You shouldn't act too quickly."

Taken aback by her last comment, Sheriff Phillips covered his uneasiness by hiding behind his authority. "I'll act any way I can to protect the citizens of Two Horse. Be assured of that."

"Then I'd watch where I threw these." Kate placed

the two cigarettes butts on his desk. "As dry as it's been, you could start a pretty bad brush fire, even on Ida's piece of shit ranch."

Just when Kate thought that things in Two Horse could not possibly become more bizarre, she stepped out the front door of the sheriff's office in time to see Pete Bear Walks Slowly lift Ida off the ground and tuck her neatly under his left arm like a bedroll.

"I stopped her from tearing at George, so she thought she'd try her hand at Pete," Karen explained as Kate joined the melee.

"I understand you've been looking for me," Pete said to Kate, Ida flailing away.

"We need your help finding Nate."

"Put me down," Ida hollered, pounding the back of Pete's thigh.

Pete ignored Ida's request. "I talked to Lila. She told me what's been happening. I'm mad as hell at Nate, but we'd better find him. The sooner this crazy bag of bones gets ahold of herself, the sooner we can start. Goddammit!" Pete yelled, dropping Ida to the ground. "The crazy woman bit me."

"That's the second time today I've been thrown in the dirt. Well, what's the plan?" Ida jammed her hat back on. "Are we going to split up, or sweep the county together like a posse?"

Kate gave Ida a hand and pulled her up. "Lila mentioned that Nate was going to Big Horn Canyon last night," Kate said, brushing some of the dirt off of Ida's pants.

Ida slapped Kate's hands away. "Nate's camped there a lot. But I'd put my money on my great-grandson being on my ranch." Ida seemed to have more life in her than was humanly possible.

"I think we should split up," Kate said. "Ida and I will go back to the ranch. Karen can drive over to the Big Horn Canyon area. Pete, try to cover all the back roads around Two Horse."

Before they could get started, Karen's cell phone beeped. Recognizing the number, she instantly returned the call. Everyone watched as Karen's face registered concern. "We'll be right there," she said.

"What's up?" Ida barked.

"That was Lucy. There's something on their farm she wants us to see. Now!"

Ten minutes later the five of them were all standing on Lucy's back patio. "There's another group over there in Clyde Winford's pasture." Lucy pointed to an alfalfa patch on the mayor's land. "They weren't there yesterday."

"Nate's moving the mustangs. And that's what happened to your truck and horse van," Ida said to Karen.

"There's Salty in the middle of this group here," Karen said. "What's going on?"

"Looks like Nate's taking each family group to a different location," Kate said. "Since one stallion has been shot, he's probably afraid more will be killed."

"He's got good reason to believe that," Lucy said. Before she could explain, the phone rang. She went inside.

"The mayor's going to shit when he sees those horses in his prime pasture," Ida said, chuckling.

"Nate should be easy to spot if he's driving a park service van around," Pete said.

Lucy came back. "That was Mr. Farley. Another group of mustangs is over in their pasture across the road. I asked if they were there earlier this morning. They weren't. So Nate must have just dropped them off."

"How many horses does that van hold?" Kate asked.

"Eight," Karen said. "He must have made two trips. I think I know where Nate's headed with the rest of the horses. A few more mustangs wouldn't be noticed among the Pryor Mountain herd, at least not for a while. Let's go."

"Wait," Lucy cried. "There's something else you need to see. Nate just sent this text."

The video Nate texted Lucy left everyone speechless.

"Deputy Lucas needs to see this," Kate said, breaking the silence.

"Send it to me, Lucy, and I'll take care of it," Pete said.

"Ida, listen to me," Kate said with a sternness in her voice. "It would be a good idea if you went with Pete. I need your pickup."

"Where are you going?" Ida shouted.

"Change of plans. Karen and I are going out to the wild horse preserve," Kate said. "Nate's obviously planning to deliver the last load of horses there. Karen, can Nate get to the preserve without driving through Two Horse?"

"There's a road just past the Farley place that skirts the Big Horn Canyon ridge. It winds around to the north entrance of the preserve," Karen said. "It's not paved. If Nate's pulling that van, it will be slow going."

"Let's go," Kate said.

****

Kate and Karen turned off the highway onto the dirt road. Kate drove as fast as she dared over the ruts. The road turned sharply to the left and headed south. Suddenly the flat pasture disappeared. On the horizon, a vast blue sky grew large over an immense chasm—a deep rut formed by the Big Horn River. The road narrowed considerably and wound dangerously close to the edge. Kate sucked in a deep breath and suppressed a shriek.

"Are you okay?" Karen asked, remembering Kate's drive down from Devil's Overlook. "Do you want me to drive?"

"I'm okay. I think."

The truck bounced over a deep hole, slammed down hard, and immediately hit loose gravel. Karen grabbed the dashboard to brace herself. Swerving and skidding, Kate finally gained control. She tried to push the sun visor to her left to block her view of nothingness, but the visor fell off in her lap. Her palms were now slick with sweat.

"I've only been on this road once," Karen confessed. "Four-wheel drive would be nice right now."

"And high clearance even better," Kate said as they bounced over another washout. A mile later, they crossed through an open fence line with the familiar arrowhead symbol of the National Parks Service. Underneath was a sign marking the border of the Pryor Mountains Wild Horse Range. Kate was forced to a slow crawl as the road conditions became worse. Just as she cursed this plan as being a big mistake, she spotted a brown pickup and horse-van over the next rise. "That's him!" Kate shouted.

She stopped the truck and Karen pulled out her binoculars. "He's stopping," Karen said. They watched as Nate walked to the back of the van, opened the door, and stepped inside. Moments later four mustangs backed out and trotted around, inspecting their new home. Nate held out his hand to an old mare. She nuzzled his fingers. Before he could get close enough to stroke her neck, she and the rest of the family bolted. Nate jerked around, hesitated, then ran to the back of the pickup.

"Holy shit!" Karen screamed.

Kate saw flashing lights and the sheriff's vehicle speeding down the main road into the preserve. Nate unhitched the van from the truck, jumped behind the wheel, and tore out across the pasture. Kate knew where he was going. There was only one route leading out of the preserve. With no time to switch places for Karen to drive, Kate threw the pickup into gear and mashed the accelerator to the floor. The old truck spun and fishtailed, gaining traction. Within seconds, Kate was a couple of hundred yards behind Nate—the sheriff a quarter-mile back and closing fast.

"Stokes is driving," Karen shouted.

Kate glanced over her shoulder just as Sheriff Phillips leaned out from the passenger window, aiming a shotgun in their direction. Bullets sprayed the side of the Ida's pickup. Karen pitched forward, slammed against the dash, and fell over. Kate grabbed Karen's arm to keep her from falling to the floorboard. Blood oozed from her right shoulder. Kate started to slow. Karen caught her breath and shouted "No! Keep going. Keep going!"

Kate hit the accelerator again. Up ahead she saw Nate's brake lights flash. Less than fifty yards away, the chain-link fence of Devil's Overlook came into view. Nate executed the first switchback and disappeared down the cliff road. Kate hesitated a moment, but what choice did she have? If she stopped, she knew Phillips would kill them—an easy justification, interfering with the pursuit of a dangerous suspect, or accidental victims in the line of fire.

Suddenly, Phillips and Stokes pulled up alongside the pickup. Kate gripped the wheel and turned to see Phillips smile and wink, as the police car rammed the front fender, sending them careening toward the cliff. The pickup struck the fence—the only thing preventing them from thumping down the mountain. Kate watched as the police car drove ahead and disappeared around the bend after Nate.

Kate didn't hesitate. She righted the truck, jamming the gear into low, and headed straight down. She grabbed for Karen's hand, daring not to look at anything but the road in front.

Karen tried to rise up in the seat. "I'm okay," she gasped. "He just grazed my shoulder."

"No. Stay down," Kate shouted. "Let them think you're dead. Besides, they're after Nate now, intending to take care of him before they come back for me. Slip off your jacket and press it over your shoulder to stop the bleeding."

Karen gripped Kate's hand tighter.

"It's all right," Kate said. "I'm going to need your help soon." But as Kate spoke her head started to spin—vertigo was finding its way into her psyche. She needed to keep talking, say anything to prevent Karen from going into shock, herself as well.

As Kate rounded the first switchback, she saw Phillips lean out the passenger window again and take aim at Nate. The sound of gunfire reverberated in the thin, high-altitude air. Bullets peppered the back of Nate's truck. Nausea arose in Kate's throat. She tried to swallow, but her entire body was paralyzed with terror.

She wanted to pull over to the side and run back to safety. But she couldn't leave Karen. She couldn't let Phillips kill Nate. The thought of those two lives resting on her shoulders gave Kate a momentary spike of courage. She had to keep going.

Kate rounded another switchback. The sheriff and Nate were nowhere in sight. She made another turn and saw nothing but emptiness. Kate glanced at the dash, the needle of the speedometer fluttered at twenty miles an hour. Too slow. Dust rose from the road below. The sound of gravel popping against metal told Kate that Nate and his pursuers were traveling at an unbelievable rate of speed. Then more gunfire.

Kate hugged the mountainside, and for a moment felt safely grounded, only to have that feeling disappear seconds later when she came around the bend skirting the cliff side. After maneuvering three more switchbacks, she caught sight of Phillips and Stokes, and, not too far ahead, Nate. Both vehicles were skidding around corners at deathly speeds. The back window of the park service truck had been completely blown out.

She saw they were approaching the wider spot in the road where days earlier, Lloyd Stenson had driven her past the RV, hanging the edge of his pickup's fender off the road's lip. Then, without any warning, Nate slammed on his brakes and swung the truck around, blocking the road. He jumped out and starting running. Kate saw Ida's pistol in his hand.

Stokes tried to brake to keep from hitting the truck, but he was traveling too fast. The front driver's side of Ida's truck suddenly dropped. The ancient tire had shredded, leaving the rim plowing the dirt. The blowout caused Kate to lose control. As the truck slid to within inches of the road's edge, Kate jerked the wheel in the opposite direction. But there was no way to avoid ramming the sheriff's car. Karen lurched up. Her scream was lost in the din of metal smashing metal.

The last Kate saw of George Stokes was his face frozen in terror as the front wheels of the sheriff's car slid off the road. Phillips scrambled to get out. He clawed at air as the car teetered. Then, as if in slow motion, it tipped forward. Kate watched in horror as it disappeared over the side.

Kate let go of the wheel and clasped her hands over her ears, but she was unable to mute the sound of the two men's screams echoing through the canyon. Seconds later, she heard the explosion of their car hitting the ground a thousand feet below.

Kate opened the door and slid out of the pickup onto the ground. She crawled away from the edge, her legs too shaky to stand. Only after she sat down and pressed her back firmly against the side of the mountain was it possible for her to take a deep breath. The spinning in her head started to ease. She looked up and was elated to see Karen –her arm draped over Nate's shoulders.

"Dr. Caraway, are you okay?" Nate asked, lowering Karen to the ground.

Before Kate could answer, a car slowly nosed around the corner and stopped. Deputy Sam Lucas stepped out, walked away from his car, and peered over the road's edge. He stood for a moment then kicked a rock over the side. "Idle time is over," he muttered then turned, walked over to Karen, and knelt down.

"EMS is on the way," he said. "Hang tight. There's not much we can do about those two down there." He looked up at Nate. "Pete and Ida showed me the video. It proves you didn't fire those shots at Ms. Caraway." Deputy Lucas stood up and held out his hand. Without saying a word, Nate handed over the pistol. Lucas stuck it in the waistband of his pants. "But you're still wanted for the murder of Frank Springfield," he said. Lucas cuffed Nate and read him his rights.

Nate looked at Kate. "I didn't kill my grandfather."

"I know you didn't, Nate," Kate said. "Go with Deputy Lucas. We'll have things cleared up as soon as possible. I can't imagine your great-grandmother will let you go to jail.'

Chapter Twenty-Two

Veda's funeral drew a crowd, but as soon as the service ended most people paid their respects and quickly left the church. It was almost as if saying goodbye to Veda had been easier than finding the right words to comfort her cantankerous sister.

Ida looked twenty years younger. The stress of the past week had been replaced by the serenity that comes after a long-due surrender. She sat down on the steps of the church and Kate joined her. "I reckon I'll need your help with the next project as well. How's that little redhead girl?"

"Considering she has a hole in her shoulder, no place to live, and no job, I'd say she's doing fine," Kate said.

"Spunky little thing. Kind of reminds me of me when I was that age. Reckon I owe her one. I'll see what I can do once this is all over."

"You made the right decision, Ida."

"Of course I did," Ida said with a bit too much conviction. Then her voice softened. "So I suppose you want to come with me when I go talk to Sam Lucas?" Ida sighed.

"Is that an invitation?"

"Yes, yes it is." Ida paused. "I'm not gonna let my great-grandson rot in jail. But would you think bad of me if I delayed this a couple of hours?"

"I don't think that I could ever think bad of you, Ida."

"You say that now. I talked to Nate this morning before the funeral. I told him he'd be out of jail by the end of the day. I just want you to know this story first. But I'm not sure where to start."

"How about starting by telling me why you killed Frank?"

"You're a smart cookie. I need to get my head together. Let's go for a ride." Ida handed her keys to Kate.

"No mountain roads."

"Right. I was thinking of some place more citified, like Red Lodge. I'm too stuck in my old ways. I need to start living a little while I have time. How 'bout Starbutt?"

"'Starbutt it is.'" Kate grinned and helped Ida into the passenger seat. They drove to Red Lodge in silence, taking in the glorious Montana scenery along the way. During the past week, Kate had made this drive back and forth several times. But she had not taken the time to look around. Sharp, jagged mountains rose up on each side of the long, flat highway.

Looking straight ahead gave the illusion of driving on a thin, shiny ribbon through a topless tunnel into a pillow of white clouds. Ida was right. Being stuck in one's ways created personal limits.

Kate wanted to pull off to the side of the road and trek up to the summit that loomed over the landscape to the left. Its giant shadow darkened the narrow highway gauntlet. Instead of feeling vulnerable to this ominous wonder, Kate now felt like part of its majesty. She looked over at her passenger. Ida's eyes were half-closed, a look of peacefulness on her face.

It was late Sunday morning and Starbucks was empty. Despite all the chrome and glass, sitting outside on the patio was almost as nice as the drive over.

After they had walked in, Ida didn't waste any time perusing the menu. She told Kate to get her something sweet and powerful.

"I ordered yours with whipped cream. You can scoop it off if you don't want it," Kate said as she handed Ida her coffee drink. "It's called a Cafe Valencia. It's made with coffee, chocolate, and orange flavoring."

Ida took a sip. "Damn!"

"Like it?"

"Man, oh man. Do you have these coffee shops in Chicago?"

"On every corner. In fact, there's one next to our brownstone. I'm a regular customer."

"No wonder you can't sleep. Honey, it ain't your problems that's keeping you awake nights, it's these drinks. Lay off this stuff, and you'll start sleeping. Trust me."

"Maybe you have a point."

"I'm sure they don't serve these in prison." Ida took another sip. The whipped cream formed a little half-halo over her upper lip. She licked it off. "Okay, here goes. Frank came to see me on Wednesday."

"The day before he died?" Kate said.

"Right. He gave me some cock-and-bull story about wanting to be a real grandfather to Nate. He said he wanted to help Nate run the ranch once the place was his. I didn't believe a word of it and told him so. He flew into a rage, and the truth came out. It was something about a big gas reserve under my ranch. He wanted me to lease the land for drilling. I told him to get the hell off my ranch. I know what drilling does to the land, and I wanted no part of it. And I knew Nate would feel the same way. Then later that day I was on the pier with my bamboo measuring pole. I had this strange feeling I wasn't alone. I was right. Frank was still on my ranch, doing his own surveying, I guess. He must've seen me poking around in the water, and his curiosity must've gotten the best of him because he came back the next day with his scuba gear. I could imagine the shock when he jumped in the water and came eye-to-eye with Colter sitting in his roadster just like he was when I pushed that son of a bitch and his car into the water sixty-five years ago."

"I know the feeling," Kate said.

"Yeah, I guess you do. Anyway, it served Frank right, snooping around. While this was going on, I was out in the pasture behind the cabin fixing the fence. All of a sudden the mustangs came flying by. The only reason they run in such a panic is when people are around to frighten them. So I grabbed my wire cutters and climbed up the mountain. Frank was standing on the pier, stripping off his diving gear. He pulled a sweater over his head and put on hiking boots. But he still had on his swimming trunks. Then he took his gear and started walking toward the canyon. I knew he must've had his truck parked there. I could tell he was madder than a caged badger. I figured after he stashed his things, he'd head for the cabin.

"I hurried off the mountain. I didn't want Veda to get caught in the middle of a row, so I gave her a chore to do in the barn. After about twenty minutes, there was still no Frank. Then I figured he went to get the sheriff instead. So I climbed back up for another look to make sure. There he was, perched on the ledge. Just sitting there. I didn't know he had just used his cell phone to call Nate. I came up behind him and called his name. That startled him, and I guess that's when he dropped the phone.

"I was ready for a big fight, but instead he shot me a cocky look, an ugly twist on his conniving face. I felt like I was looking the devil in the eyes. Then I figured out what was coming. The asshole was gonna blackmail me into deeding him the ranch. I told him he was no better than his worthless father. He lost it and came after me. We fought. He tried to push me off the side of the mountain, then I grabbed hold of the knife in his belt. I stabbed him between the shoulders just like I did his old man sixty-five years ago." Ida paused and sipped her coffee. "You see, I didn't want the dam built because the lake would dry up, and Colter's body and car would become visible. I care about the mustangs, too, and Nate. But I'd just killed Frank, and I saw everything going up in smoke. If I could have hidden his body, I would have. I drug it as far as I could and did my best to cover it. That's why I took you up the mountain the long way the first night you were here. And then you went and stumbled on Frank anyway. I also needed to get rid of Frank's truck, but there wasn't time. So I left it there."

"Frank tried to kill you, Ida. You killed your son in self-defense."

"Self-defense, I reckon. But Frank wasn't my son."

"What?"

"There wasn't a night after I married Colter that he was sober. Seems like the beatings started as soon as I said, 'I do.' I was gonna leave him, but then my parents died and Veda came to live with us. I thought maybe with

Veda there, Colter wouldn't have the chance to terrorize me so much. I thought it was my fault that he beat me. Like I wasn't pretty enough, smart enough, or whatever. Dumb, huh? But I never imagined that he'd start in on Veda. The first time he slapped her, my blood turned to ice. I felt trapped, watching that monster destroy us."

Ida wrapped her arms tight around her body. "I threatened to tell Colter's parents, and that quieted him a while. Then he started staying away most of the day, drinking in town. But as soon as Veda would see his car pull up, she'd start wailing. It all became too much. I even started to get mad at Veda. I couldn't handle it. She'd cling to me, and whenever Colter came in he'd fly into a rage, and she'd panic. One day Colter had gone to Red Lodge for supplies, which meant that he wouldn't be back for the better part of the afternoon. I just needed to be alone for a while."

Ida's hands shook and her throat seemed to close up. Kate could hardly hear what she was saying. She placed her hands over Ida's and squeezed. The old woman took a deep breath and another sip of coffee. She cleared her throat and then continued. "So I saddled my horse. Veda started crying. She wanted to go with me. I told her that she'd be okay. That I was just going for a ride in the back pasture and that Colter wouldn't be back for a long time. Veda started crying louder. The more she cried, the madder I got. I left her there. I told myself it would be good for her. She grabbed my arm like she always did. But I pulled free. I kicked my horse and rode away as fast as I could. I couldn't have been gone for more than an hour. It was the first time I had been alone, at least as far as I could remember. Even when we were little, Veda was always there. And I was always being reminded that she was my responsibility. It was never put into words, but I knew what my mother meant. I was responsible for Veda's problem. She had to wait for me to be born first. It was my fault. I even married Colter, knowing his reputation, just to get away. That day when I left Veda crying on the porch, I thought about riding away for good—away from Colter's beatings, away from Veda's neediness, away where Ida Springfield could discover who she was. I felt so free at that moment—and I wanted the feeling to last forever.

"There I was, sitting on my horse looking out across the property, wondering which route would be the hardest to trace if I got the hell out of Dodge. Then I saw it—a dust cloud coming up from near the road. Back then the paved road stopped a couple of miles from our cabin. That meant one thing. The dust was from Colter's car—he was on his way back. I jerked the reins and headed for the cabin as fast as I could, but I knew he would beat me there." Ida turned white. She put her hands on her head, and tears ran down her face.

"Ida, you don't have to—"

"I've never told a soul. At eighty-two, one tends to think about hell a lot more. Please listen." Ida drew a breath and continued, her voice shaky. "I heard Veda screaming as soon as I got out of the canyon. Bad screams. I still hear them. They still wake me up at night. For the first time in my life, I prayed. I swore to God if he'd let Veda live, I'd never leave her again. When I got to the cabin, they were on the kitchen floor. Colter didn't even hear me come in. I grabbed the knife and stabbed him more times than I could count. I would have kept on, except the knife wedged in his back, and I couldn't get it out. I dragged his filthy body out to the back porch. Veda was in shock. I sat her in a tub of warm water, bathed her, and put her to bed. It was two weeks before she spoke again. Anyway, I put that bastard in the car, drove it to the lake, and pushed him and his fancy roadster in. I told everybody that Colter had abandoned me. No one was surprised, not even his parents.

"Nine months later Frank was born. When I went into town to fill out the birth certificate, I wrote down that I was the mother. That was easy to do since Veda and I hardly ever left the ranch. Veda had blocked out most of what had happened, but every once in a while something would trigger her memory."

"The history channel—the program on automobiles," Kate whispered.

"What?"

"The night I stayed with Veda while you were driving around looking for Nate, she saw some old cars on TV and must have thought of Colter and his roadster. Ida, you acted in self-defense then too, for yourself and for Veda. I'm sure with a good attorney—"

"Never mind that. I'll confess to killing Colter, but no one is ever gonna know that Veda gave birth to Frank. Do you hear me? Swear to it!"

Kate saw no reason why anyone should have to know. Veda and Frank were gone. The truth would only hurt Nate. "Your secret's safe with me," she said.

"Veda never went into the kitchen again. I just made up that story about the fire." Ida sighed. "Let's go get Nate. I'm sure he's getting tired of sitting in that smelly ol' jail."

"A couple more things, Ida. Can I have my cell phone back?"

"Sure. Sorry, I was kind of desperate. I knew you'd

found out about Colter, and I didn't want you to call Nate until I could figure things out."

"That was a good stunt you pulled at the health center."

"Ha! Wasn't it, though? I'd never fainted a day in my life. What's the other thing?"

"Frank's swimming trunks, why did you remove them?"

Ida shrugged. "To confuse things. Seems it worked for a while."

As they were leaving the coffee shop, Ida pulled a small package out of her pocket. "I almost forgot. Lucy gave this to me at the funeral. She told me to give it to you, and to say thanks."

Kate unwrapped the object and smiled. It was Lucy Nelson's prized porcelain elephant that had once stood on her cherry-wood table.

****

Kate heard baseball noises in the background through the cell phone, sounds she had begun to miss. Jack was probably the only pitching coach in major-league history who had his wife explain the details of a murder while sitting in the dugout. "So, what was on the video that Nate sent Lucy Nelson?" he asked.

"When Nate found out that he was a suspect in Frank's murder, he went to Ida's ranch to think things out. He had decided to come forward, but what he saw had changed his mind," Kate said, now hearing a roar in the background. "Are you sure you want to hear this now? Sounds like there's some excitement going on there?"

"Excitement, all right—we just gave up two more runs. Go ahead, your story's more interesting than this game. What did Nate see?"

"Phillips and Stokes shooting at the mustang. Nate thought maybe the sheriff had murdered Frank as well. He needed evidence. He suspected Phillips would return to kill more horses. Nate was right. Phillips and Stokes came back on the day of the gathering. Except they didn't know we were herding the mustangs for testing, and they didn't come to shoot more horses."

"But you told me you heard gunshots during the gathering," Jack said.

"Right. Phillips and Stokes had come looking for Nate, and they didn't plan on taking him alive."

"Wait. How come that BLM guy was with the sheriff and not his deputy?"

"Deputy Lucas wasn't living in Mayor Winford's back pocket. Stokes and Phillips were. Anyway, Clayton Farley heard some rifle and pistol shots. Apparently, the sheriff had shot first, and Nate fired back then disappeared. Phillips and Stokes then split up to look for him. After the dispatcher had called with Karen's report of shooting on Ida's ranch, Phillips had the excuse he needed for coming back. He saw me riding Salty through the back canyon, took a shot at me, and then conveniently came to my rescue, claiming it was Nate who had tried to kill me. Unfortunately for Phillips, Nate had gotten the whole incident on tape."

"But why kill the horses?"

"The mayor was desperate. He didn't stand a chance without Frank getting Ida to agree to lease her ranch for drilling. Nate would never agree to it, either. And if the dam proposal didn't pass, Winford saw the ranch going to TNC. But if there were no mustangs, TNC wouldn't accept the land. They also thought they could get Nate out of the picture by pinning Frank's murder on him or killing him in the attempted capture. And as far as they knew, Nate may have actually been the killer. So with Nate gone and Ida in grief, they thought they could convince her to lease the land."

"Did the mayor confess to all of this?"

"No. Except for what I learned from Nate, most of this is just conjecture on my part."

"I guess you've told your theory to that Deputy Lucas fellow."

"And I also gave him Brian Loger's business card. But for now, we can only piece things together."

"I take it the mayor's not cooperating."

"The mayor's gone—left in the middle of the night. Anyway, I'm helping Karen move into Ida's cabin this afternoon. She'll be staying there for a while, taking care of Ida's dogs and working on establishing the preserve. In fact, there's a TNC representative coming out next week to assess the situation."

"But the dam proposal could still pass."

"There's still that possibility. But with the mayor gone and Phillips and Stokes dead, news of the scandal has already started to spread. I'm sure the voters will begin to question their public servants' true motive surrounding the dam."

"Sounds like things are starting to move there in Two Horse."

"Fast and furious. Nate's spent the entire morning bringing the mustangs back home. With Karen at the ranch, Nate can return to school to finish the semester. Then he'll come back and stick around during Ida's trial. Because of her gun-toting history, she's been denied bail."

"That poor woman's been through plenty."

"I have no doubt that Ida can handle this too. I promised you I'd be home by Monday. My plane leaves at ten tomorrow morning."

"Cancel your flight and book a room at the Days Inn for a couple of nights. Kenya and I will be there tomorrow. I pulled some strings, and the team pilot's flying us into Billings. You can show me that beautiful Montana we missed on our last trip. Then we'll drive back to Chicago. We might even find a cafe along the way that's missing a cook. I could offer my services as a short-order cook."

"But how can you leave the team?"

"They can spare me for a few days. Besides, I'll be there on business as well.

"Let me guess—you have a young pitcher to say farewell to."

"You got it. I would rather have had Mike Chambers on the mound. But with a priest-to-be in our corner, maybe it won't take another one hundred and eight years to win the pennant again. Damn! We just gave up another run!"

"Looks like you need more than a priest, Jack."

A word about the author…

Kathleen Kaska is the author of The Sherlock Holmes Quiz Book, which has been updated and reissued by Rowman & Littlefield Publishing Group. She is the founder of The Dogs in the Nighttime, the Sherlock Holmes Society of Anacortes, Washington, a scion of The Baker Street Irregulars. Kathleen writes two awarding-winning mystery series: the Sydney Lockhart Mystery Series set in the 1950s and the Classic Triviography Mystery Series. She also writes the Kate Caraway animal-rights series. When she is not writing, she spends much of her time with her husband traveling the back roads and byways around the country, looking for new venues for her mysteries and bird watching along the Texas coast and beyond. Her passion for birds led to the publication The Man Who Saved the Whooping Crane: The Robert Porter Allen Story (University Press of Florida). Kathleen was the writer, editor marketing director for Cave Art Press. Her collection of blog posts was released in August 2017 under the title, Do You Have a Catharsis Handy? Five-Minute Writing Tips. Catharsis was the winner of the Chanticleer International Book Award in the non-fiction Instruction and Insights category. Kathleen Kaska is a writing coach who helps new and emerging writers discover their unique voices. With sensitivity and passion, Kathleen guides her clients as they learn the craft of writing and the art of storytelling. You can reach her via her website: https://metaphorwritingcoach.com/

Thank you for purchasing
this publication of The Wild Rose Press, Inc.

For questions or more information
contact us at
info@thewildrosepress.com.

The Wild Rose Press, Inc.
www.thewildrosepress.com

www.ingramcontent.com/pod-product-compliance
Lightning Source LLC
Chambersburg PA
CBHW070048030726

47506CB00002B/404